The stout, square body of the man in the leather jacket stood hidden in the shadows of an armoire—shadows that were as dark as his hair. He'd been there two hours already. He would wait another twelve if he had to. Cleaver in hand, he ignored the dull cramps in his arms and legs.

A board creaked in the hallway. A second one strained under a person's weight. The intruder's ears tensed, perked. Behind the door, he raised the cleaver, and his thick muscles and chest tightened into a solid mass.

Finally the footsteps stopped just outside the door. . . .

BLOOD RUSSIAN

"A blood-chilling surprise . . . Unique and entertaining."
Minneapolis Star & Tribune

"A truly Hitchcockian suspense story . . . highly recommended."
Alfred Hitchcock's Mystery Magazine

BLOOD RUSSIAN

R. D. Zimmerman

BALLANTINE BOOKS • NEW YORK

Library of Congress Catalog Card Number: 87-91485

ISBN 0-345-34463-4

Manufactured in the United States of America

First Edition: November 1987

Люблю тебя,
Петра творенье

I love you, child of Peter,
I love you, calm and stern
The Neva's mighty current
Running in banks of stone.
Your traceries of iron,
Your meditative night,
Clear dusk and moonless glimmer
When in my room I write
And read without a lamp,
And in the empty streets
The huge buildings doze,
The Admiralty spire gleams bright
And day on day runs close . . .

ALEXANDER PUSHKIN *The Bronze Horseman 1833*

Russians are just ordinary people.
They love and they hate . . .
    sometimes enough to kill.

PROLOGUE

Late April, Central Russia

The old babushka was easy to kill because the intruder, the man in the leather jacket, was a good butcher and his cleaver very fresh. Her husband, Iosif, would fall just as easily the moment he returned to the old wooden house nestled at the village's edge.

The leather-jacketed one flicked back his dark hair, set the cleaver down on the table, and studied his hands, which were covered with a fine spray of red dots. The hands were wide and strong, swollen like his peasant's body, from chopping sides of beef. His knuckles, he thought, were like those belonging to the hogs he butchered, coarse and oversized. Yet the hands themselves were bright white. Throughout the workday he scrubbed them, the harsh soap washing away not only the blood and slime, but layer after layer of skin until his hands gleamed. Except for their swollen size, they could have belonged to a doctor.

1

When he heard rustling outside, the intruder resisted the urge to wash away the babushka's blood. He left the stolen roll of rubles on the table, scooped up the cleaver, and cut across the house's wide plank floor. Stepping over the old woman's body, he made his way past the small kitchen and the single bedroom. He parted the red lace curtain and peered out.

The village of Vishnyovka, in the region of Orlovsky, lay covered in the depth of a winter night. Twenty or so one-story houses, resting in the center of square plots along dirt lanes, made up the village. Brightly painted in reds, blues, and yellows, the squat houses were adorned with window frames of wood carved like lace. The only touches of modernity were the towering television aerials stuck into every house. Yes, this was a prosperous village. Even the gray snow on the tin roofs could not disguise it.

The dark-haired man knew that on these small, private plots the peasants grew more food than they could haul to market, cheating the *kolxhoz*—the communal farm—out of thousands of rubles. Tomatoes, potatoes, onions, and cucumbers would grow this summer beneath door stoops, along fences, and over paths, threatening to gobble up the wooden houses themselves.

Even though they didn't look it, Iosif and the dead babushka were among the richest. They appeared a quiet peasant couple; she a tall woman in plain dress, he shorter, unshaven, the stubbles on his chin the color of a dirty brush. But they were great hoarders of money. The man in the leather jacket had seen it. Whenever there was meat for sale, the tall woman and the short man would walk the ten kilometers to the village of Zelonoye and buy as much meat as they could carry from the shop where the dark-haired man worked. Each time, too, he watched as the old woman peeled a skin of rubles from her money roll that was the size of an enormous onion and had just as many layers. The old couple had produced no children, it was known, and so each year their wad of savings grew fatter from their pensions and their vegetables.

The man in the leather jacket was going to change that, though. He needed their money to escape from the countryside. They were twice his age and dying. He was young with a great opportunity before him. It was a simple problem with a logical solution.

The man heard steps slopping through the muddy snow, and his fingers tightened on the cleaver's handle. Outside he saw moonlight reflected off the snow, the metal roofs, and finally off the bald head. Pleased, he watched Iosif stumble and grab hold of the fence. He knew the old man had joined his comrades in a troika—three friends and a litre of vodka—and that meant he'd hardly put up a fight.

From behind the door, the intruder watched the latch jiggle, then jab up. Confident, he glanced down at the steel-white cleaver. In anticipation of this evening, he had honed the tool until it was as fresh as the sharpest Bulgarian razor.

"Raya!" The old man plowed open the door.

The intruder's leather jacket squeaked as he

closed the door and raised the cleaver. For a split second, he stood young and powerful above the drunken old man, studying the wrinkled forehead as if it were a slab of beef. He spotted a perpendicular crease between the white eyebrows and took aim. He was the best butcher at the meat market, powerful and accurate and sure of himself.

The old man's glassy red eyes pulsed about the room, saw his wife's legs on the floor. He gasped, then stared up at the cleaver positioned above him like a guillotine's blade. His body turned to a solid, rigid muscle. Air squeaked from his lungs, over his lips, hissing as if from a leaky tire.

Meeting no resistance, the stranger sunk the fingers of his left hand into Iosif's fatty shoulder and steadied him. Then, like a spring-loaded instrument, the cleaver came slicing downward.

Realizing his life would exist for only another flash of a second, the old man gasped, "Wha—"

But it was too late for an explanation. The heavy force beneath the leather jacket was in motion, and the butcher could not have stopped his blade even if he'd wanted to. As always, too, he never missed his mark. The blade slit through the bald head, cracked the skull in two, cut easily between the eyes, and finally stopped at the bridge of the nose. The white face parted like a chopped beet, then flooded with its own juices.

The intruder shook the cleaver free, and the body sunk down in a heap. Quickly, he dragged the old man across the cabin floor. He rounded the heavy table, passed the wood stove, and dropped Iosif close to his wife. Next, he dabbed some blood on his right thumb, then stamped the eyelids on the man and woman with it. Now, he thought, their deaths are sealed for eternity.

Grinning with pride, the man pumped water from the sink, rinsed off the cleaver, then found some soap and lathered up his white hands. He held his fingers beneath the stream of cool water, then toweled himself dry. Once he'd patted dry the cleaver, too, he unbuttoned his leather jacket. Inside, just as Raskolnikov had done, he had sewn a loop out of old cloth. He slipped the cleaver into the noose, and its cold blade sucked the warmth from his body. Once the jacket was buttoned, the fine leather gave no hint of the cutting instrument.

The stranger grabbed the wad of money from the table, the bills filling his thick grasp. It would be more than enough to start his new life. The money might even last several years. Not to overlook anything, though, he checked the babushka's pockets for any money she had not confessed to. He found none, but did seize twenty rubles from Iosif's pocket.

He gazed momentarily at the couple's gold wedding bands, but then reconsidered. Stolen possessions would have to be hidden, he knew, whereas stolen money could simply be spent. Now was not the time to be greedy, for that would lead to mistakes.

Satisfied, at last, that he possessed all that he had come for, the dark-haired man took a kerosene lamp—used when the electricity failed—from a side

5

table. He lifted off its glass globe, raised its wick, then sparked his West German electronic lighter. The lamp bloomed orange.

The aged bodies were at his feet, their fluids soaking into the floorboards, dripping through to the dirt beneath. He scanned the room one last time, and when he was certain there would be no trace of him, backed toward the rear door. Then he lobed the kerosene lamp as if it were a Molotov cocktail. The glass shattered on the floor and liquid flames poured across the room.

With the old couple's life savings in his pocket, he hurried out the back. He trotted through the potato patch, out the gate, and into the snowy meadow beyond. As the wooden house was swallowed up by the yellow flames, the man's heart surged with excitement. He was free at last. No more peasant life for him. In minutes his past would be nothing more than a pile of cinder, while ahead lay Leningrad, the very center of Russian culture. Soon he'd begin his new life and never again associate with the ignorant likes of this province.

He pressed his hand to his chest and steadied the cleaver beneath his leather jacket. There were a few things left to be done—people to be rid of—but come autumn he was certain Leningrad would be his.

CHAPTER

1

September, the Environs of Leningrad

Boris should never have gotten involved. He knew it now. He knew it as he neared the drop-off point. The *militsiya* could be bad, but this gang was much worse. Not Siberia, but death was their final solution.

The cold mid-September rain beat down on the truck's windshield like handfuls of gravel. The two-lane highway into Leningrad had melted into the black night, and the tenseness burned in his back. This could have been his ordinary run down to Riga and back. The bed of this GAZ truck could have been filled with his normal cargo, portable short-wave radios. He could still be a normal truck driver zipping back and forth across central Russia.

But no. For the sake of rubles he had let his friend, Sergei, also a truck driver, talk him into this. And who knew what lay ahead—extra rubles or extra trouble, the *militsiya* or perhaps the gang?

7

According to Sergei, Boris Arkadievich Volkov was now more normal than ever. It was true. All the drivers were doing this sort of thing, transporting black market goods. Especially those lucky enough to be selected to cross the international border, which Boris and Sergei were not. Those who did, though, visited Finland or West Germany or Switzerland and brought back scads of Western goods to sell at five and even ten times their original price. They built false flooring on the beds of their trucks, then stashed stereos from Holland and digital watches from Bonn. Once Boris had even seen an entire auxiliary gas tank drained and crammed full of Levi's and Wrangler jeans.

Everyone else exploited friends and jobs and Party connections, too. Even his own father, Arkady Yakovich, a Communist bigwig, had taken advantage of his position to procure such items as the almost-impossible-to-get Stolichnaya vodka and canned hams from Yugoslavia. Ai, thought Boris, his father's considerable influence was the only way they had secured one of the largest apartments in the very center of Leningrad. Also, the dacha on the grounds of Zarekino—a deserted palace plundered during both the Revolution and the Great Fatherland war—had come into the family through the use of his father's power and bribes. And what would Boris do without the cabin? He lived for the days he could escape from the city to the rustic tranquility of Zarekino, where he would pick mushrooms, read long novels, and write. Tyotya, the old caretaker there, had long ago become the grand-mother he'd never had.

Boris could go only so far, though, and this was too much. Back there with the carefully packed short-waves were crates of stolen car parts, over twenty thousand rubles' worth. Forward to Communism! That's what Sergei said he and everyone else wanted. But they weren't there yet, Boris' little friend explained, so in the meantime you did what everyone else did. You made up for the inadequacies of the system. You had to—everyone had to—or else there wouldn't be any meat in the stores or fruit on the stands. Or parts to fix cars. It was like Lenin's NEP—the New Economic Policy—a smattering of capitalism tolerated by the government. The reason was simple: it would maintain the Motherland until Communism was achieved. All of this dealing to help the country operate was a lot of work, explained Sergei, which is why the industrious deserved their small profits. This philosophy, Boris knew in his heart, was wrong, a step too great.

He pinched his small lips together and leaned over the steering wheel. Extra rubles. So what. Yes, he probably would need the extra money but . . . He reached up and clenched a fistful of his curly blond hair and pulled until it hurt. He twisted his fist and yanked.

"To hell with it!"

His father had been right. He'd said it hundreds of times. Boris had no spine. Here he was in his mid-thirties still letting himself be pushed around.

Why couldn't he act the way he looked, big and powerful? At a meter and eighty-one centimeters tall and weighing eighty kilos, he stood out in any crowd. But once people came to know him, they realized Boris Volkov would do just about anything for anyone if asked long enough. His inability to refuse people was his particular weakness. His father—so well-known, so important—had always said that he would not go far in the socialist world because of this. His mother, who had died when Boris was not yet ten, always declared he'd simply inherited the artistic nature of one of his great-uncles.

The GAZ truck sped through the deep night and along the narrow highway. By day, this road was full of dark green trucks, passenger busses, and a few cars. This late—almost midnight—the road was empty, especially during rainstorms. Usually he liked his route—down to Riga and back, four nights a week—because there was so little traffic. It worked well with his wife's schedule, too. She was a nurse, and the two of them arrived home about the same time in the morning.

The continual stream of rain across the windshield gave him a painful reminder. He had to take a leak, expel himself of almost as much liquid as the clouds. Two glasses of tea and he was as full as a tsar's samovar. He had to wait, though. The drop-off was just a couple of kilometers up the road, and then he'd be free.

His fingers clenched the wheel. He forced himself to focus not on the burning in his crotch but on how this would be the first and last time. He wasn't going to let himself be shoved around anymore. This wasn't just simple speculation, hoarding something and then reselling it at a profit. This whole operation was wrong because those car parts back there had been stolen from the automobile plant outside Riga. That was robbery. And this wasn't America.

The truck hit a bump and he felt his bladder bulge like a tire ready to explode. Soon the transaction would be over. The meeting place was just up the road. He squinted, trying to discern the heavy shape of the bridge ahead. His vision was instead filled with two blurred white lights that grew and grew on the rain-blackened road. The lights seemed so far away, but were suddenly upon him like a charging wolf. With a bolt of light, a bus shot past, hammering a hard wall of water on his windshield. In an instant, Boris was alone again in the early fall night.

A cool sweat broke on his forehead, and he played Sergei's instructions through his mind.

"You don't have to worry, Borinka. I've arranged it all. That's why I'm receiving a commission," Sergei had said, trying to reach up and put his arm around him. "Just take a smaller load of your radios than you usually do and leave as much space as possible. Then all you do for the rest of the night is drive to the right place at the right time and stop. That's all. First, you go to the factory. Pull up at the dock at eight sharp. They'll load you up. Don't worry, the plant manager is in on the deal. You won't have any problems or be asked any questions.

11

Then head back to Leningrad. At midnight pull off the highway just before the Baltic line train bridge outside of town. There's a dirt road. Go down it a bit and turn off your lights. It's well-protected—lots of trees—and sit there. You'll hear them unloading. Wait fifteen minutes before leaving. Oi, and remember one thing. Don't ever get out. Don't ever try and find out who's back there. You see their faces and . . ."

Sergei had made a sound like a rusty zipper and sliced a finger across his neck.

Finally, there it was. The unlit bridge came into view, and Boris put the truck in neutral and edged over. The wheels dropped off the pavement and onto the gravel. He sighed, lifted his foot from the accelerator, yet hesitated before settling on the brake. He slowed, steered to the right, and nosed the truck down the muddy lane. He winced when he hit a deep hole, heard the cargo fly up and crash down. Oi, the radios. He'd forgotten about them.

Boris pulled to a stop beneath a large oak tree, and the drops of rain fell larger and noisier than ever on the hood and windshield. The sound was like water torture, and he wanted to jam the truck in reverse and escape as quickly as he could. But he knew he couldn't. The gang would come after him and kill him for stealing their stolen goods. There was also no way he could go to the militsiya. Arriving there with a truckload of hot auto parts would be suicide.

So he shut off the engine and the countryside quiet nearly devoured him. On his left was a large berm of earth, on top of which sat the tracks of the Baltic railway. Right up there, only a few meters away, were slender strips of iron that curved around and led all the way back to Leningrad. He wanted to follow the tracks, to be away from all this—to be back in the city. Shivering, he thought of slipping into her bed and of how her skin would burn against his, steaming away the cold, wet night. . . .

He shook. Pushing back his sleeve, he squinted and tried to read the dials of his watch. Faintly, he could make out the luminous hands. 11:50.

"Tfoo."

The black night held him in its grip. Ten minutes before his unknown colleagues arrive, and then another fifteen. He groaned. He was going to have to sit here in the black for a whole twenty-five minutes. He couldn't make it, couldn't hold it. Wasn't there a can or a cup or something—anything—he could pee into?

There wasn't. He just had to exercise self-control. He had to get this rendezvous over with. Then he could shoot back on the highway, piss all over the pavement, and race back to Leningrad. You *durak*—you idiot—he told himself. Why did you ever become involved in the first place? You're just going to have to finish this stupid business. It will be the first and last time. Just think of her, think of her warm embrace and that hot body to melt into.

He clenched his hand over his crotch. What if something went wrong and the *militsiya* showed up instead of the gang? They'd haul him and the stupid radios and auto parts off. Siberia would be his home

13

for ever and ever. Or perhaps he'd only make it as far as a firing squad.

His hands felt his abdomen swell. What was this, a kid's game or something? Why did he feel so dumb? This was just like being a child again: hiding and knowing you were going to make a noise so that they'd find you and you could come out of hiding and go to the bathroom. Well, whatever, but he knew he could never endure a twenty-five minute wait. Checking his watch, he saw in the faint glow that it was five till midnight.

Not giving it another thought, Boris burst his large body out of the cab. He had to urinate worse than ever now, and he dashed around the front of the truck, through a puddle, and across the early fall leaves. To the sound of the pouring rain, he ripped open the buttons of his pants, stood beneath the edge of the bridge, and aimed into the night.

Nothing happened. He'd sucked in his muscles and the liquid so much that he couldn't reverse the flow. He pushed, only to be met by a sharp hot pain. He pushed again, and the burning urine trickled, then flowed in a strong, steamy stream out of him.

There was so much, as if he hadn't done anything all night except drink *kvass*, the ale-like drink made from fermented bread. The liquid pouring out of him seemed endless. Yet he had to hurry. He couldn't take all night. His blue eyes shot over his shoulder. The wet bushes and trees were lighting up, glowing with headlights. They were coming.

They'd be here in seconds and he couldn't stop pissing.

With the whole area lighting up, he broke off the stream, shook himself, and fumbled with the buttons as he ran for the truck. They were coming too fast. It was turning to day all around. The protective darkness was fading away. *Bozhe*, he prayed, if I make it out of this I'll never do anything illegal again. He slid on some leaves, then glanced toward the road. He wasn't going to make it.

A hand grabbed him.

"Ai!"

"Get down!" ordered a deep voice. "Don't move!"

"But . . . but . . ."

The approaching lights came in all around. Alongside Boris stood a shorter man wearing a dark leather jacket over a wrestler's body. Boris glanced down and saw thick dark hair, a mustache, and a silvery blade.

"You idiot, you weren't supposed to get out of the truck!"

The man grabbed Boris and yanked him down behind the front fender. Seconds later a truck whooshed through the rain and beneath the bridge. In the last flash of light Boris turned and saw a handful of men huddled at the rear of the truck. The darkness snapped back just as quickly, and the men disappeared in the black of the night.

"I . . . I didn't hear you come," said Boris. "I had to go to the bathroom. I didn't know you were—"

15

The shadowy figure rose. "Get up."

He braced himself on the truck's wheel and pushed himself up. "Really, I—"

A sharp object pressed against his navel. He lowered his eyes and saw the outline of the knife.

The words spilled out of him. "I . . . I didn't see anything. You don't have to worry."

"Shut up and get in."

Boris' hand shot back and grabbed for the door handle. He ripped the door open, jumped up into the passenger's seat, and slammed down the lock. Breathing as if he'd just run ten kilometers, he hit the lock on the other side, then settled behind the wheel.

"Bozhe moi." My god, he sighed, running his hands through his wet, curly hair.

The truck bounced and swayed as the men heaved the small crates out of the back. Boris heard steps and mumbled voices, followed by a crash and an outcry. Oi, wonderful, thought Boris. They probably tipped over the whole stack of short-waves. He'd really be in trouble if anything was broken. He only hoped the gang didn't help themselves to the radios. Boris had to account for all of them.

Suddenly the truck's bed stopped rocking back and forth. He heard leaves rustling, then nothing, and he sat still. Finally, he jerked to the left and looked out the window at the side mirror. Nothing but black back there. No movement. No noises. Were they going to let him go? Well, he wasn't going to wait for them to tell him.

Boris lunged for the ignition, brought the engine

16

to a roaring charge, and jammed the truck in gear. Spitting wet leaves and muddy rocks, the vehicle jerked backward. The rear of the truck shot across the road, blocking the entire highway. Boris tore the gear out of reverse and crammed it into first so fast that the transmission bucked and clanked, making as much noise as a rack of dropped frying pans. He pressed the accelerator flat to the floor, and the truck sputtered, roared, and lunged toward Leningrad. Boris hit the headlights but couldn't see the road. He swerved to the right, felt the truck tipping into a ditch. He yanked the wheel to the left and the vehicle steadied. But still he couldn't see.

"Gospodi!" Dear lord!

He hit the windshield wipers and the wet road emerged before him. As he shifted to higher and higher gears and the bridge fell behind him, Boris began to relax. Thank god. He'd delivered as he said he would. He'd escaped alive and free, and without a doubt he never wanted to see a stolen auto part again.

Just get me back to Leningrad, he thought. I want to be there now. I just want her to hold me in her arms. . . .

CHAPTER

2

$\mathcal{T}$he mustached man in the leather jacket stepped silently from the trees where the van was hidden. He watched and listened as the GAZ truck, driven by the one with the curly hair, tipped off the edge of the road, pulled back, and flashed on its lights. Then, as if he were escaping with his life, the driver charged back to Leningrad at a speed that was sure to attract attention.

He stood there, the rain pelting his jacket, his eyes focused on the red taillights that were dissolving into dots. This was no good. People like him were of no use in a business that depended on a market that was all black.

Behind him, a tall figure with a thick chest emerged from the woods.

"We're all loaded," announced the man to his superior.

The leather-jacketed one motioned down the highway. "Look at that."

He saw the swerving lights and laughed. "Scared him, did we?"

"To hell and back." The man stroked his dark mustache. "We can't have people like him around. Too dangerous. Find out who he is, where he lives. Find out right away, this morning. Clear?"

"Da, da."

"Good. I'll take care of him after that."

Disgusted by the situation, the man in the leather jacket headed back into the woods toward the hidden van. The man with the curly hair and loose mouth was no good. People like him led execution squads right to one's doorstep, brought death to profitable situations.

There was no doubt about it. The driver of the GAZ truck would have to be dealt with. The sooner the better.

CHAPTER

3

Leningrad

When he entered Leningrad that morning, Boris viewed his native city with renewed appreciation. After the endless kilometers of flat, soggy fields that stretched out on either side of the highway, he felt a surge of pride at the sight of the honeycombed highrises that blossomed on the city's periphery. Just beyond the cabbage patches and hectares of hothouses, the tall, white buildings glistened even though dawn was hours away. The rain had stopped, the night sky cleared, and everything sparkled with cleanliness. He felt so safe, so tranquil here. He was glad to be going home, glad to be away from those thugs and their stolen merchandise.

Boris circled a towering monument to the victory of the Great Fatherland War. The Fascists had come this far, just a streetcar ride from the center, and nearly choked the city to death. At the expense of over a million lives, though, the hero city had held on for 900 days, never surrendering. It seemed hard to imagine that this area, now filled with so much new construction, had been a wasteland of war and death.

As he drove down Moskovsky Prospekt, the buildings grew shorter and older the nearer he came to the city's center. Leontev's hit song, "There in September," trickled over his lips and filled the truck's cab. He sang as he made his deliveries at Gostini Dvor, the city's largest department store just a few blocks down Nevsky from his apartment. He continued on his way, making his usual round of stops, rather glad that he worked while everyone else slept. The city—Peter the Great's city, Lenin's city—belonged only to him and the streetcleaners.

Toward six o'clock he drove his empty truck to the lot on the north side of town. He tapped the steering wheel and sang a tune that he had heard Elton John sing at that packed concert back in 1977. Obtaining a ticket had been another benefit of being the son of a Party boss.

Well, he thought as he neared the lot, thank God all that business with the stolen auto parts was over. Never, never again. He'd call Sergei this morning and tell him to count him out in the future. For a fleeting moment he again thought how disastrous the incident could have been. Suppose the *militsiya* had come? Suppose he had been caught with all of those stolen parts? And what if the gang had decided to kill him? He had to face it—he was lucky he got away from them. After all, he'd had a fairly good look at the stocky, dark-haired man in the leather jacket.

No, thought Boris as he parked his truck in the fenced lot, he didn't need that gang or their rubles. He had as much as anyone should want. It was true, most of what he had he'd inherited from his father—an enormous apartment filled with antiques right on Nevsky Prospekt, a color TV, stereo, a dacha, and a two-door Moskvich—but really he didn't need any of that either. He just needed her. She was the only one who'd ever understood him. Everything seemed at peace when they were together.

Boris bid good night to his dispatcher, then made his way to Kirovsky Prospekt. He boarded a nearly empty tram and let the electric motors whirl away and carry him back toward the center of Leningrad. The dense apartment buildings lining the street finally gave way to the yellowing fall leaves of a park. The river lay just ahead. Realizing he was near Revolution Square, Boris rose and climbed out at the last stop before the Neva. He needed to walk, digest what had taken place that night before returning home. The moist air off the river embraced him like an eager lover, and he walked right over the water onto the Kirovsky Bridge.

How he loved Leningrad! Walking along its granite embankments, running his hand along its kilometers of patterned iron railings, was like a stroll along the beach or a hike in the forest. He could lose himself here in time and history, amid the turrets and stone sphinxes and parapets. Beauty overwhelmed him, always soothed his soul. Peter the

Great had started it all, forcibly moving the capital from Moscow to what was then a mass of marshy islands cut into hundreds of pieces by a muddy river and its splintering tributaries. Only a tsar—an autocrat that decreed tariffs in terms of rocks needed to build his dream—could defy nature and build this northern port.

Boris paused beneath one of the ornate lamps on the bridge and gazed off to his left. Against the first of the morning's light, the gold cupolas of the Smolny Institute stood outlined like great upside-down onions. He turned to the right, and the river's vast expanse filled his vision. On one embankment rose the golden spires of the Peter and Paul Fortress where Peter the Great and Catherine the Great were buried. On the opposite side, the colonnaded Winter Palace glided on block after endless block. And in the far distance, the massive golden dome of St. Isaac's Cathedral was coming to life with light. He sighed, staring out again at the broad Neva River that spread out before him like a black prairie swirling devilishly in the wind. Hadn't he stood right at this very point and fished with his father?

Boris wished he'd understood his father, Arkady Yakovich, as well as he understood and loved this city. Neither father nor son, however, had been so planned by a single tsar, and hence neither one of them read like a clear map of straight boulevards and striking monuments. Ever since the start, they kept wandering, hoping to find each other in a jumble of confusing streets and houses. Sometimes they came close, hearing the other just around the corner or catching a faint glimpse across the broad river. But they never met up. Boris had always assumed it was he alone who had failed. He had always sensed that Arkady Yakovich had been waiting for him the entire time, his disappointment and dissatisfaction growing each year because Boris would not follow the same path.

His forehead a mass of wrinkled regrets, Boris stumbled on. How he wished he could have his father back just for a minute. There was so much to say, to explain, to beg. How awful this was, this burden of being left with a stomach churning in anger and a mind packed with hopes unfulfilled. What was he to do with it all? When they could have talked, they didn't. Now his father was dead, the silence as permanent as the granite Soviet star above his grave.

The Marble Palace, the open Field of Mars, the Summer Garden. Boris clicked past all of them. Soon he found himself walking along the Fontanka. He paused, bent over the iron railing, and peered into the slow waters. By the light of a street lamp, he saw his curly hair and hopeful face floating on the surface. He still looked boyish; it was the blue eyes, he'd been told, that never stopped moving. There was no doubt, though. He was getting older. Those tense wrinkles were turning into permanent grooves. Such was life. *Shto delat*? What could be done?

Life and death were both beyond his control.

CHAPTER

4

*T*he stout, square body of the man in the leather jacket stood hidden in the shadows of an armoire—shadows that were as dark as his hair. He'd been there two hours already, having slipped unnoticed into the building long before the sun would greet the day. He'd had no trouble entering the flat, finding it empty as he'd expected. Now it was just a matter of waiting for him to return. And even though these last moments seemed to drag by, the intruder would wait another twelve hours if he had to. After so many years of waiting to establish himself in Leningrad, he wasn't about to let one man ruin his chances. Cleaver in hand, he ignored the dull cramps in his arms and legs. He'd leaned against the wall behind the door only once or twice. Otherwise, he was as still as a Yakut stalking a sable.

The room was flooded by moonlight the color of

the man's pale skin. Before the Revolution this had been a mere corner of a nobleman's expansive, fashionably located apartment. Nevsky Prospekt—the Champs Élysées of Imperial Russia and still the city's most famous avenue—crossed the Fontanka Canal just a few floors below. The former palaces of princes and grand dukes lined Nevsky and the Fontanka in every direction. Even the bridge across the canal—the Anichkov Bridge with a rearing, bronze horse at each of its four corners—was among the most celebrated of the hundreds that crossed the city's sixty rivers and canals.

Still this remained one of the best addresses in the country, even sixty-five years after the Great October Revolution. The city—St. Petersburg-Petrograd-Leningrad—had passed through revolution, civil war, and international wars, but its people always valued its heart. Great ideas as well as merchandise and *farsovchiki*—black marketeers—always flowed along Nevsky, and the closer to it one lived the better.

The man's small, dark eyes passed over the room. What had once been a nobleman's home had long ago been divided into more than fifteen residences. This apartment with its corner view, airy living room, two bedrooms, and private kitchen and toilet, was by far the largest in the building. It had never been given over to the masses, he had learned. Instead, it had been handed down through a line of government officials like a noble title assigned to generation after generation. When the last *sheeshka*—important one—had died, however, this apartment had not been reassigned by the housing authorities. Instead, it had been inherited by a mere truck driver. Tonight, however, the man in the leather jacket was going to change all that.

He wondered what it would be like to live here among the antique armoire and sofa and large, carved dinner table. He imagined himself lounging about, reading Tolstoy, and enjoying the meats and cheeses of Leningrad which were so difficult to obtain elsewhere. He saw himself strolling over to the corner windows and throwing them open. He'd stand on the balcony, gaze over the Fontanka, and watch the busy shoppers and tourists on Nevsky. . . .

A board creaked in the hallway. A second one strained under a person's weight. Was it an early riser? The first on his or her way to work? No, the steps were heading directly for this door. It was him, returning at last from a long night of work. The intruder's little ears tensed, perked, and heard the slow, heavy movement. Good, he thought. He's tired, worn out, unsuspecting. And alone. Behind the door, the intruder raised the cleaver, and his thick muscles and chest tightened into a solid mass. Staring at the door of the dark apartment, his small eyes—eyes that carried a trace of Asian ancestry—dissolved into black dots. His face—broad and hard like his body—was stone-still.

The footsteps trod slower and slower. Finally they stopped just outside the door. The man's eyes drifted shut as his ears sucked in every noise. Clothes rustled. There was deep, odd breathing, and finally the jangling of keys. Suddenly a burst of coughing shook the air. Good. He was sick, which would only make the deed all the easier.

He heard the key slide into the lock, saw the door knob twist. But silence followed. The person on the other side of the door stood frozen. The intruder felt the cleaver's handle become damp with sweat. Did his victim know what awaited? Had something tipped him off?

A bolt of light sliced into the apartment. But the shadow thrown from the hall lamp wasn't that of a tall, curly-haired man. Rather, it was short, round. Suddenly it shook. A spray of saliva shot inside as the person was overcome by another spasm of coughing. And the intruder understood.

It was the old woman he'd been told about. The tenant who the housing authority had assigned to the spare bedroom because the apartment exceeded in size the space allotted for two. Everyone knew the minimum standards: six square meters per person. And this place was big enough for five. Only the previous inhabitant's high standing in the Communist Party had kept it a single-family dwelling.

To the devil's mother, he thought. The old lady wasn't scheduled to be back until tomorrow. She was supposed to be in the country picking mushrooms for at least another day. But now she stood there, a small suitcase hanging from each hand. She was going to ruin everything. His real target would be back any minute. He had to act immediately.

The man kicked the door shut, and the light was sucked out of the room. Raising his cleaver, he saw a scarf-covered head and neck that were thick with age. Full of distrust, the round, wrinkled face stared up at him. She stood firm in her tightly buttoned wool coat, the whites of her eyes swelling in the dark.

"Boris?" she croaked, her voice loud and scratchy.

He shook his head.

"Who is it then?"

He thought a moment, found it amusing that she might know his real name only an instant before her own death.

The man in the leather jacket said: "Kyril."

"Who?"

He should have killed her by now, but he realized he couldn't risk blood. Not here, not by the door. That would give it away the next time the door was opened. Slowly, the man known as Kyril brought down his arm, then loosened his fingers. The cleaver landed on the hardwood floor with a thump, and then his two clamp-like hands floated like white ghosts up to their target. She, however, did not move, anchored to the floor by the suitcases hanging from her hands.

"Nyet."

Hers was an order, a command that was to be obeyed. Kyril grinned, and was upon her that instant. He lunged for her throat, his thick, white fingers sinking into the fat of her neck. But there was so much skin, so many folds, protecting her throat. He squeezed and her double chin squirmed like congealed fat in his hands.

"Nyet . . . nyet!" she gasped.

At last the two suitcases dropped from her hands and crashed to the floor. One of the worn bags burst open, and hundreds of mushrooms scattered across the herringbone parquet. Though her hands were now free, the old woman didn't reach up and try to wrestle Kyril away. Instead she jabbed up her chunky leg, and the one bony part of her body—her knee cap—stabbed into Kyril's crotch. He cried out. A burning shot of pain screamed through his body, the air exploded from his lungs, and his muscular arms turned flaccid. He buckled over, grabbing himself, and saw the old woman throw her body down to the cleaver.

Gathering all his strength, Kyril kicked the weapon out of her reach. He took a deep breath, stuffed the pain in the back of his mind, and lunged. He caught the woman by her arm, but she twisted away.

"Nyet," she squealed like a stuck pig.

She scrambled out of his hands and charged toward the kitchen. Kyril was surprised by the strength of her will to live. He ran across the living room after her, each of his strides covering two of hers. He chased around an end table, jumped over the sofa, and clawed after her. He caught her, clamped his fingers through the woolen folds of her coat, spun her to the side. The faint, first light of the day glowed through the far window and washed over her jowly face as again his hands encircled her throat.

But she wouldn't die easily.

Locked in a deathly embrace, Kyril stared down

at her and watched the air bubble over her lips. He squeezed with all his concentration, his muscles turning to knotty lumps. Her large body, though, was filled with air, and she refused to die.

"N . . . ye . . . nye . . . t . . . t . . . t."

She scratched out, and Kyril sensed her jagged nails scrape down his fancy leather coat. He bent up his thumbs, caught her chin, and pressed upward. He leaned into her, and under his weight and muscle, her head bent back. Sensing the resistance of bone, he nudged himself further. Then with a sudden dry snap, her neck broke and her body fell into him as if she were a drunken lover.

Kyril didn't move. With the old woman dead in his arms, he gazed out the arched windows and into the chilly morning. But he was confident. No one could have seen him, nor were there any sounds from the apartment hallway.

Her lifeless body hung heavy as he dragged her back across the living room. Later, he'd seal her death with a thumbprint of blood. Later, too, he'd dispose of the body, perhaps dump it in the Neva. There wasn't time, though, not now. He just had to get her out of the way, scoop up all the mushrooms, then return to his position by the side of the door. He had to be quick about it, too. There was little time because Boris would be home any minute and he, by all means, was much stronger than the old woman.

This time, though, Kyril would be able to use the cleaver without fear of making a mess.

CHAPTER

5

Boris continued along the canal almost until he reached Nevsky. Just before the drugstore on the corner, he turned into the small entrance of his building and started up the marble steps, passing from the ground floor to the first. On the second floor landing a door opened and an old man—a tall, proud soldier now defeated by time—stepped out in his bathrobe. A hero of the Great Fatherland War, his once robust health had failed, and he wore his war medals pinned to his robe. In his bony hand was a mound of garbage wrapped in yesterday's *Pravda*.

"Morning, Yuri Gennadiovich."

"Boris," gasped the old man. "I thought you were already home." He raised his cloudy eyes up to Boris's apartment, which was directly above his. "Heard a little tumbling a little while ago. Thought maybe you and your wife were going to it."

Boris glanced at his watch. His stroll across the bridge and along the canal had taken longer than he realized. Musya, who usually came home just about now, must have left work early.

"No, I'm just getting home now." He smiled to make light of the night's events. "I had a long night—must have been my wife you heard."

"Yes, and she'll have a bowl of hot kasha waiting for you." Yuri Gennadiovich squinted and studied Boris. As if his knowledge were absolute, he said, "You look exhausted, young man, but I can still see it on your face. You can't fool me. You're in love. It's true, isn't it?"

"Well . . ."

"See, I could tell. My body's giving away, but it's all still here," he said, patting his chest. "It's good to see young people with a commitment to each other. All this divorce. People moving, switching partners as if life were a simple dance. It's a disgrace to the Motherland. But you and that lovely Musya, you're something different. How many years have you been married?"

"Seven."

"Seven! And still so in love. You should be thinking about children, though. Don't make the mistake of thinking just of yourselves and possessions. Family, that's what counts in the end. A big family, too. The more the merrier. And the better for us Russians. Just look at how the population in our Asian republics is growing!" he said with a wink. "Life goes faster than you think. Now go up and have fun. Go to it." He bent toward Boris, and

33

the war medals on his chest tinkled. "Do some great things for me."

Boris waved him off. "*Da, da, da*. But you can be certain we'll be more quiet from now on. I didn't know how much you could hear."

Yuri Gennadiovich wheezed a fit of laughter, then headed downward one slow step at a time with his garbage.

As Boris continued up the broad marble stairs, he thought of Musya, his wife. Things must have been slow at the hospital and she left early, as she sometimes did. Or perhaps she was sick herself. A terrible flu was spreading around Leningrad, aided by the early fall chill in the air.

On the top-floor landing he stopped just outside his door. There was no noise, no movement from within the apartment. Good, he thought. Musya was probably already in bed asleep.

He slipped his long key into the lock and twisted the knob. Easing open the door, he was surprised to see that the light next to the sofa wasn't on. Musya prided herself on being a good wife. Whenever she arrived home before him, she always made things look warm and cheery. If she went to bed early, she at least turned on the lamp and set out a plate of black bread and cheese for him. Now, though, everything was dark. Only the windows glowed with the first of the morning's light.

Bozhe, thought Boris. They hadn't been robbed, had they? He edged open the door and peered into the darkened apartment.

"Musya?"

The apartment was as still as a morgue. In the dim light from the windows, all he could make out was the heavy outline of the furniture. He hesitated, felt silly for doing so—he'd seen too many foreign films lately—then stepped in and reached for the lamp alongside the sofa. He pulled the chain, but nothing happened. Hadn't he just changed the bulb?

His eyes drifted toward their bedroom. "Musinka, are you here? It's me, Boris."

As he moved around the sofa, something squished beneath his right foot. He raised his leg and stared at the bottom of his shoe. His weight had flattened the brownish-gray object, spread it out as if it were nothing but a pressed leaf. Touching it, he sensed moisture. He rubbed his fingers beneath his nose and smelled little. What was this? A mushroom?

He knew what that meant and shook his head. Lila Nikolaevna, their tenant, must have come back early from the country. All this rain must have slowed the start of the mushroom season. Yes, the rain was good to get the fungus started, but you needed sunshine and warmth to have an explosion of growth. Boris had known it was too early, but he was so glad to have Lila Nikolaevna gone for a few days that he had said nothing to stop her. He shook his head. Wherever she went she was carting mushrooms, talking mushrooms, or picking mushrooms. In a few weeks, at the height of the fall season, her room would be strung like a spiderweb with hundreds of strands of drying ones.

He disliked her and her mushrooms because he

disliked having a tenant in his apartment. She repelled him all the more because she was smelly and hadn't bathed since she moved in. Lila Nikolaevna resented the situation too. She had been removed from her apartment of twenty years because her husband had just died and the space was too big for one alone. And so a silent war had developed between them—he hated having her, she hated being there—mushrooms often serving as ammunition. If only she'd disappear, he mused.

He scraped the object from his shoe and started toward her room. They were going to have to have words about this. Just because she'd been assigned to the spare bedroom didn't mean she could go littering about.

On his way to her bedroom he noticed a swatch of black clothing sticking out of the armoire. Lila Nikolaevna wasn't supposed to use this, either. The bathroom and kitchen, yes. But not their personal things, which certainly included this cabinet.

Shaking his head, Boris reached for the handle of the armoire. He twisted the key. Without even pulling, the mirrored door burst loose. He braced it with both hands, and glanced up. In the reflecting glass he spotted a figure just behind him, a huge knife raised high.

"Ai!" cried Boris.

He ducked to the side and a cleaver swooped past him and bit deeply into the side of the armoire. At the same time a dark mass tumbled out of the wardrobe and onto the floor. Then he fell back and saw a heavy-set man in a leather jacket.

Gospodi, thought Boris. This wasn't a robber. That leather coat. He recognized it instantly. It was the man from the gang. Boris had thought he'd escaped. But he hadn't. Oi! If only he hadn't emerged from the truck, if only he hadn't smashed right into this man from the gang. They'd let him go earlier, but now this man was going to kill him so that Boris could never identify him. Sergei was right after all.

Boris leapt over the divan as the man charged. He grabbed a lamp, ripped off its shade. He slammed the tip of a bulb against the table, then pointed the lamp with its broken glass against his assailant.

"Honestly," pleaded Boris, "I won't tell anyone. You don't have to kill me. I won't tell. You can trust me."

The man paused for a moment as if thrown off guard. Then he raised the blade again. Boris jumped to the side and ran around the back of a chair. Desperately he swung the jagged tip of the lamp. But all he could think of was writing about this morning's sunrise. Write. That's what he really wanted to do with his life.

The assailant jumped out, the cleaver whizzing through the air. Boris blocked the massive knife with the lamp. But it was useless. In a single slice, the lamp was cut in two.

"Oi, *mamichka*," muttered Boris. Oi, my little mother.

He heaved the remainder of the lamp at the man and spun. If only he could make it to the door, if only he could make it to the landing. He could cry out for help. The entire building would come to his rescue.

He tore into a run, and the carpet shot out from under him. Boris feet slid back. He tumbled to the floor. He landed on his chest and rolled over. The man in the leather coat was above him, cleaver poised to chop. Then the assailant dove and landed on Boris like a boulder. Boris was certain his ribs and lungs had collapsed.

Gasping, he forced the words out. "Really, I won't tell . . . anyone."

Again the man hesitated, but only for an instant. The next moment the cleaver came flying downward, and Boris twisted to the side. The cleaver skinned his ear, bit into the wood floor. Boris took advantage of the moment and jabbed out his fist. He caught the other on the chin, stunning him.

The assailant was slowed only momentarily, though. He shook his head, grabbed the cleaver with both hands. He jumped up and came crashing down on Boris a second time.

Struggling for air again, Boris closed his eyes for a moment. When he opened them, he looked up and saw the cleaver ready to chop into his chest. This was it. The end of his life. He'd never expected so violent a death. And who'd ever thought it would be because of some stolen auto parts?

Suddenly the apartment door was thrown open directly behind him. Boris glanced back over his head. Musya stood frozen in disbelief, her wide figure filling the doorway.

"Nyet!" shouted Musya, dropping her packages. *"Nyet, nyet!"*

Resigned to his fate, Boris managed a weak grin. At least she tried, he thought as he watched her run to his rescue. But he knew she was too late. Within seconds his heart would be carved out of his chest.

He called out his final word. "Musya—"

And then the world disappeared so quickly that he felt no pain.

Kyril ran out of the apartment and slipped his cleaver into the noose beneath his leather jacket. Not pursued, he ran down the marble stairs. He crossed no one's path on the way down until he reached the bottom. There, blocking the entrance, was a babushka draped in black. Her back to him, she was bent over the stubby handle of her broom. Kyril slowed as he came upon her, then sunk into the shadows beneath the staircase.

For a full five minutes he watched as the old woman swept slowly toward the front door. Rather surprised that she had not noticed him when he'd come down, he found a broken chunk of marble in the corner. He tossed it just behind her and it crashed and split apart. She did not, however, move. So she was deaf, just as he had guessed. That would make it all the easier.

He could wait no more. He could not risk being

seen by a single person in this building. Not yet, anyway. Reaching into his leather jacket for the cleaver, Kyril knew he had to be quick. His fingers tightened around the smooth wooden handle and lifted. This would be simple. He could carve anything with his cleaver.

Kyril slipped partway out and saw the babushka—half as wide as she was tall—step backward. She stared down, amazed to see the bits of broken marble. Shaking her head, she bent over and brushed at it, her black garb dancing from side to side as she moved.

Kyril glanced at the stairs, discerned no one, and edged over to the deaf woman, who was entirely focused on her sweeping. Raising the cleaver, Kyril eyed the white curls that poked out beneath her scarf. A strike at that point would mean instant death.

Within three large strides, he was behind her. He pulled his arm back, ready to swing. Just then, though, she spotted a dry crumb of mud off to the side. The air heaving in and out of her, the babushka turned and started at once for it. Kyril took a step after her when suddenly he heard a door open and close. He glanced upward. Someone was coming down.

The woman turned again, leaving the way open to the door. Certain at least that the woman hadn't seen him, Kyril carefully slipped the cleaver back into his jacket and reached for the door. He pushed it open and slipped out.

He was struck at once by the faint morning light

and the dampness of the cool air. He glanced across the still waters of the Fontanka and turned right toward the Anichkov Bridge. When he reached Nevsky, he turned right again, and within seconds was engulfed by an early morning crowd bundled in wool clothes.

Kyril continued on Nevsky until he came to Tolmachov Street. He turned, stopped at a bread store, bought a roll and returned to the small room he was renting unofficially. Breakfast and a little rest would follow, he decided. Then he'd return to the apartment at the corner of Nevsky Prospekt and the Fontanka Canal.

Kyril, after all, was determined that Boris Arkadievich Volkov would not live to see tomorrow's light.

CHAPTER

7

Boris was floating in a luxurious pool of black water. Warm, soothing black water. And she was showering him with kisses. On his forehead, his cheeks, his chest. He felt her soft lips touching him everywhere. God, he wanted to wake up just to be with her. She was the only person he really loved. She was so beautiful, so wonderful. He reached out into the blackness and his hand descended on a large thigh.

His eyes popped open and his smile disappeared. "Musya . . ."

"Boris, darling, I was so worried!" said his wife. "I love you so much and . . . and . . ."

She sat next to him on the edge of the sofa, her big face filling his vision. With a thin, pointed nose and high, meaty cheekbones that pushed her eyes into slightly almond shapes, she looked very much a woman born on the steppes between Asia and Europe. However, something was quite wrong—one cheek was all bruised and puffy. Yet before he could say anything, her thick lips puckered in a hard kiss and dove into him. Boris lay there as cold as an empty vodka bottle as her mouth dragged across his forehead.

"What happened?" he asked.

Lying on the sofa, he gazed about. The morning sun streamed through the windows, filling the large living room with vibrant light. So he wasn't dead. Just knocked out. But for how long?

"Are you serious?" she said.

He sensed something under his arm and realized that his shirt was open. Reaching over, he felt a large flat thermometer stuck neatly in his armpit. Musya, ever the domineering nurse, pushed his hand aside and slipped out the glass gauge. Her eyebrows pinched together as she studied it.

"Thirty-six-point-six. Absolutely normal!" She laughed, scooped him in her arms, and squeezed him until her bones hit his. *"Slava bogu."* Thank god. "I'm so glad you're all right."

Though much shorter and a few years younger, Musya was almost as heavy as Boris, and her presence on top of him was crushing. The springs of the couch beneath dug into his back. Boris squirmed, tried to protect himself. At the same time, her thin, mousy brown hair dragged across his face and his nose twitched.

"Musya," he said, pushing her off him, "what . . . what happened?"

Her almond eyes grew large and she brushed back

a wisp of thin hair. With her fingers barely touching her black and blue right cheek, she didn't know what to say.

"You . . . you really don't remember?"

"No."

Incredulous, her eyes skipped from the dining room table to the carpet to the front door. She simply didn't know where to begin. Her shoulders rose and her cheeks puffed up even more.

"There . . . there was a burglar, Boris. Oi, love, it was awful. Just look at my cheek. Do you see how swollen it is?" He nodded, and she clasped his right hand and raised it to his own temple. "Well, feel this."

Boris felt a foreign lump of soft material on his head. In the center of it was a dot of warm moisture. Blood? So something really had happened.

"The burglar hit you, Boris, and knocked you out. He . . . he almost killed you, and then . . . he came after me!"

Boris turned his head to the side, resting his cheek on the sofa's cushion. He gazed at the pattern of the carpet, at the white light caught by the crystal bowl on the dinner table. Out the window was a velvety blue sky.

"What time is it?" he asked.

"A little after ten."

It was dawn when he'd come home; he knew that much. He'd walked part of the way. Over a bridge, along the Fontanka. It had been so tranquil. Then he recalled coming into the building, up the stairs. He'd talked to someone, hadn't he? When he reached the apartment, he'd found it dark. But not empty. Someone was there. Someone he didn't know.

"Yes . . . yes, I remember."

"Boris, I love you so much."

She started kissing him again and her full body melted over him like butter over hot potatoes. He lay there motionless as her wet lips ran up his cheeks and her subtle moans filled his ears. He struggled to push her away.

"Yes, I was attacked," he said, his arms held defensively over his chest. As his eyes fixed on the ceiling, he began to remember. "I came in and someone jumped out at me. A big man. He came at me and then he pinned me down."

"Right, that's when I came in," murmured Musya between kisses.

"Sure." He saw the clear image of his wife in the doorway. "I was held down and I looked over my forehead and you seemed upside down." He frowned, took Musya by the shoulders, and pushed her up. "The burglar had a knife or something, didn't he?"

Musya wiped her lips and nodded. A child's sad, frightened look gripped her wide face. She quivered as she relived the scene.

"Boris, it was terrible. He was about to chop you in two. I saw that cleaver and I screamed. I was certain you were a dead man."

The memory of her words screeched through his ears. *"Nyet!"* He stared up at her. "That's what you screamed, wasn't it?"

"Da, da!" Her head bobbed up and down. "I saw that horrible cleaver and I was so afraid. I screamed out and I grabbed the letter opener by the front door and charged him."

Boris studied the sofa and the table nearby as he tried to recall the entire incident. He stared down at the little pieces of parquet, then looked up at Musya's pointy nose. His mind was as empty as the expression on her face.

"I don't remember anything after that."

"Of course you don't."

She sat back, licked her lips. Her dark eyes bounced from side to side as she struggled to recount the episode. Then it came to her with a gasp, she tugged her blouse over her breasts, and began.

"The burglar saw me coming and he knocked you in the side of the head with his fist. Then he jumped up. I was crazy, you know. I was so worried about you. He had that cleaver, but I didn't care. I slashed out at him with the letter opener and screamed. He just caught my wrist with one hand and with the other he . . . he hit me." She touched her cheek where it was a dark gray. "He hit me right here and then I fell down and passed out. When I woke up, the burglar was gone."

"A burglar?" But the door had been locked, hadn't it? "How did he get in?"

"I don't know. But I suppose we're lucky he didn't kill both of us. I woke up about a half hour ago and he was gone and you were just lying there. I rolled over and touched you but you didn't move. Boris, at first I thought you were dead and I was so

47

afraid. But you were breathing and so I just hugged you and rocked you. Then I carried you up on the couch and nursed you. Lucky for us I had my medical kit with these bandages. Oi, Boris, I love you so much!''

He stared up at her, touched her cheek as lightly as he could. What would have happened had she not come home that instant?''

"You saved my life."

Her eyes bulged with happiness. "Did I? Did I really?'' She laughed, entirely pleased with herself. "Then what a wonderful thing I've done.''

She dropped onto him again, her chest squishing into him. As she planted kiss after kiss on his forehead and face, Boris brought his arms around her and tried to return her affection. But he could hardly move. Drunk on love, Musya was smothering him.

"Musya . . . Musya," he managed to say beneath her. "You're so good to me. I'd be dead if it weren't for you. I . . . I love you.''

She raised herself up so that her nose was only a few centimeters from his. "Of course you do, Boris. I do a lot for you, don't I? I'm a good wife, aren't I?''

There was only one answer he could give, the one she wanted. "The . . . best.''

"Thank you, *golubchik moi*.'' My little pigeon. She sat back and smoothed the wrinkles across his forehead. "Just relax. Relax because I'm here. And without me you wouldn't be as happy. I make you happy, don't I? I cook for you. And clean. I take good care of you.''

He gently touched her on the cheek where she'd been bruised. "You're the best wife anyone could want. Are you sure you're all right?"

"*Da, da.* Like I always told you: 'Marry me,' I said that night you proposed to me. 'Marry me and you'll be happy for the rest of your life.' "

He nodded. That's exactly how she'd expressed it after hinting at marriage for over a month. She promised, too, that she'd always be fun, that their lives would be awash with the best that life could offer. Yes, she swore. She had a lot of ambition—*jeanzi, kosmetiki*, furs, restaurants. Ambition that would rub off on him and help him abandon truck driving and pursue another more profitable career. Boris had drunk it all in, too, and flown high on her fast pace and her insatiable sexual desires. Boris came to believe it as well. Yes. She would lead him on to bigger and brighter things.

From the start, however, Boris' father had seen in Musya something quite different than his son's salvation. An opportunist, that's what he called her when he tried to forbid the romance. Musya was uncommitted, he had shouted. The worst of a spoiled generation that had gone soft, that wanted everything and wanted it this moment. He'd disliked Musya from the start and had barely even spoken to her after the wedding when she moved in. He didn't care that she might be able to improve his son's lot. He simply never trusted her.

Boris pushed away the memory of his father's rage—rage that had never dissipated but only gone

49

unspoken. But what would the old man say about Musya's selfless actions today?

"Thank you, Musya. Thank you for saving my life." He kissed her on the cheek. "Now let's see what damage was done."

Musya scooted out of the way, and Boris edged himself up. He grabbed the edge of the sofa with one hand and with the other held his head. His vision was a rolling sea, gray and wavy.

"That guy really hit me, didn't he?" He felt like he was waking up after a long binge, still drunk and unable to stop his head from spinning.

"Yes, my love." She stood, rubbed her pointy noise, and started for the kitchen. "Should I make some tea? How about some nice hot borscht?"

"In a minute. Was anything stolen?"

"I don't think so. I looked around but couldn't think of anything missing. Maybe I frightened him away."

A tidal wave of pain flooded through his head as he swung his feet to the floor and sat up. His eyes shut; he gripped his head. If only everything would stop floating around in there.

"Oi yoi yoi."

"Are you all right?"

He opened his eyes, blinked. The room seemed fairly stable. He pulled the bandage from his head and studied the dark brown blot of dried blood. Remembering the size of the cleaver, he was thankful the wound was so small.

"I guess so." He tried to shake his head in disgust but couldn't. "What's the world coming to,

Musya? What if you'd arrived first? Maybe that burglar would have raped you.''

"Boris!"

"Well, I'm sorry, but I mean it. This city used to be so safe. It still should be. That's what a government's for, isn't it, protecting us, taking care of us? We both work at night. And we should be able to come home anytime along safe streets to a safe home. And here we could have been killed! We have a right to better protection. Control is growing slack in Leningrad. Musya, did you say you called the *militsiya* yet?''

"No . . . no I was so—''

"Well, we have to!" he said in an authoritative voice that was quite similar to his father's. "They must catch that criminal, put a stop to this sort of thing." He tried to stand. "I'm going to call them right now." He teetered, then felt her reassuring hand on his shoulder.

"Boris . . . you . . . you shouldn't get up yet. We'll call the *militsiya* after you've rested.''

"No, now, Musya." Looking across the room, he ordered, "Bring me the phone. It'll reach here.''

His eyes, however, rested only for a second on the black phone. Off to the side was the armoire. He stared at it and a flash of memory burst in his head. Something else had happened.

"Boris . . . are you all right?''

"The armoire . . ." No, that wasn't it. "The mirror. Yes. I saw him in the mirror first." He cursed as he pictured the man in his mind. "Tfoo!''

He leaned back in the couch, unable to believe

51

his dilemma. This was all much worse than he'd imagined. What was he supposed to do? Where could he go?

"What, Boris, what?"

"We can't call the *militsiya*."

"Why?"

"He . . . he was wearing a brown leather jacket."

"Who?"

"The burglar."

"He was?"

"And I recognized him. The brown leather jacket. It was the jacket."

"Oi." Musya could barely speak.

Boris leaned back in the sofa. He was sure of it, though. It was a fine leather coat, the leather sleek and shiny as if every square centimeter had been hand-polished. How many coats were there like that in Leningrad? A half-dozen at most. You had to be important or rich to have one of those. Rich like a *farsovchik*. A black marketeer. Someone who dealt in *jeanzi* or foreign records or stolen car parts.

So he was that guy from the gang. Boris rubbed his hands together. Yes, it was the same coat. He had touched it twice last night. The leather was so soft, too, its squeaking hide so deep and rich. He had felt it once colliding with the guy near the railroad bridge, then again here in the apartment.

"Musya, that wasn't a burglar. That man wasn't trying to steal any money. He was waiting for me. Waiting to kill me."

Musya's face went from red to sour white. She stood as still and frail as a china doll.

Boris looked up. "Musya? Musya, are you all right?"

"I . . . I . . ."

"You look terrible. Sit down."

She stumbled back a few feet and sunk into a chair. Boris felt her eyes staring at him in fear.

"Hey, don't worry, Musya." He reached out and patted her knee. "I'm all right. He didn't get me. Everything's okay."

Still she said nothing.

"I'm so stupid," he said.

He bowed his head into his hands. His skin was rough, his beard prickly. Under his fingertips he sensed the distinct ridges across his forehead left from worry as much as anything else. A little higher he felt a few more centimeters of scalp—a little more each year—then his thick blond hair.

Bozhe, he was getting old, and he still wasn't doing what he wanted with his life. And tonight he'd almost been killed because of that. If only he'd made that decision years ago then he would never have become involved with black marketeers. Ink and paper. Those were the materials of his dream. He'd have been a writer by now. He could have been very successful. He was resolved not to follow the course his father had set for him. At the same time, though, for fear of hurting his father, he hadn't the courage to follow his own ideas. So his life had fallen somewhere in between the two, landing in a truck.

Boris raised his head. Musya was as still as the waters of the Fontanka Canal. He had to tell her everything that happened last night. Would she be furious at him?

"I'm such a louse," said Boris. "I was asked to do something—and I agreed." He paused in his confession. How was he to explain all this? "It's all such a long song I don't even know where to begin. Musya, I got involved with a group of black marketeers. A very nasty gang. The meanest. I . . . I . . . well, Sergei told me about them and he's getting a cut of it, too, for setting everything up. He went on and on about what quick and easy money it would be. They smuggle stolen auto parts up from Riga. I only did it once. Last night. You see, they loaded the parts on the back of my truck and I brought them up here. I wasn't supposed to see any of them. But I did. That guy in the brown leather coat."

Musya awoke from her stupor. "What?"

"Musya, haven't you been listening? That guy in the brown leather coat—he's from a gang of black marketeers I got involved with. I wasn't supposed to see any of them, but I screwed up and ran right into him. I think that's why he tried to kill me. I mumbled something about wanting out. And I looked right at him."

Her voice almost a whisper, Musya said, "I can't believe it."

Boris hung his head. "I know. Of all the stupid things I've done, this is the worst. Now I'm involved, I guess, with a gang that's selling stolen merchandise on the black market. There's a big crackdown. That's why we can't report this to the militsiya. I'm already involved.''

Musya's eyes blinked. "You're right. It would be suicide to go to them. We have to keep this quiet.''

"*Da, da, da*. And tell no one. Absolutely no one. Can you do that, Musya?''

She eagerly nodded her head. "I'll do anything for you, Boris. You know that.''

She pushed herself out of the chair and came stumbling forward. Falling to her knees, she dropped her head in Boris' lap.

"I'm scared, Boris, so scared.''

His hands in her thin hair, he said, "Ts-s-s, don't worry. I'll go see Sergei—he's the one in contact with those hooligans—and get this whole affair straightened out. Somehow I'll find the gang and set matters right. I'll let them know I'm not an informant. Then they'll leave us alone.''

"But it might be dangerous talking to them directly. Oi, Boris, you'll be careful, won't you?''

"Of course.''

He rubbed the back of her neck. He felt where bone melted into muscle, where muscle lined up into spine. This was what marriage was all about, knowing certain parts of your spouse's body better than your own. That was the definition. But what was the meaning?

"I'm going to be thirty-six next week, Musya.''

"I'll get you a wonderful present. *Jeanzi* or a record of American jazz. Or maybe a nice new fur hat. Something spectacular, something—''

He turned away from her, certain she didn't un-

55

derstand what he was trying to say. "I've been thinking a lot about all I haven't done. It sounds so old—thirty-six. I'll be forty in a few years. My life might be half over."

She kissed his hand. "But thirty-six is young, Boris. You have so much ahead. You're so young, so strong."

He shrugged. "Don't you understand? Musya, I'm frightened."

He dared not bring up the subject of children. Yes, he wanted a son or daughter, a child to take care of. But how many abortions had Musya had? Five? Six? At least that many. Yet no matter how hard he tried, Musya would not change her mind. She claimed to carry some illness in her genes and swore she would therefore never be a mother.

"It scares me, you know, this birthday," he said. "Almost half my life is over and I've never really gotten down to living. I've always been so afraid of disappointing people, of hurting others."

"Boris, your father's been dead almost two years. It's time you broke free."

"*Da, da.* You know what I really want to do?" he said, recalling the only place he'd been truly happy. "I want to write. I want to go out to the dacha at Zarekino and think and write. Start a novel. A war novel set at the palace itself."

Within eyesight of the burned-out palace of Zarekino, his father's cabin was nestled between a silvery river and an almost endless birch forest. Boris would start his story there at the outbreak of the Great Fatherland War. He'd write how the Fascists captured the palace on their march to take Leningrad, then settled in for the 900-day blockade, using one wing as a barracks, the other as a stable.

"There's so much to be inspired by—the palace, Tyotya, her hounds. You know how she almost single-handedly drove the Fascists out of the palace."

He'd heard so many stories about Tyotya and her family, all members of a circus, and how they had been forced to perform for the Nazis. Then the others had been killed. Only she, a knife thrower, escaped, later returning to use her talents for a bloody revenge.

"Now she lives alone out there, no electricity, no plumbing. Just her and the hounds she raises." He shook his head in frustration. "I can no longer worry so much about hurting others. There's only so much—"

Boris was cut short by Musya's fingers settling on his crotch. She didn't hear a thing, he thought. Sex. Whenever things got serious, Musya turned to sex.

"Musya, please . . ."

He tried to press her head away from his lap, but she was locked in place. She sunk her nails into his thighs, dragging them upward. Boris shook his head. There was no escaping. There never was. What could he do? Whenever he tried to hold back, she taunted him by telling him what a real man would want to do to her.

He flinched, then sat stock-still as her fingers pressed hard into his genitals. She grabbed at his belt, wrenched it open, and one by one unfastened the buttons of his pants. Finally, she yanked his shirt out, then dove against his abdomen.

"You have such a cute tummy," she gasped, kissing his navel. "And all your furry hair here drives me crazy."

With a free hand, she shoved him back so that he was spread-eagled with his legs draped over the couch. Boris lay there looking at the ceiling as she tugged at his pants.

"Bozhe moi," she moaned.

A tense knot formed in his throat. He couldn't do this anymore. He couldn't pretend any longer. Things had to start changing, changing now.

"Musya," he said, and sat up.

He reached down, surrounded her head with his hands and nudged her back. She wouldn't budge and instead clawed out at his belly.

"Ai!" he cried. "What are you trying to do, take a blood sample?"

She sat back, her large lower lip puffed out.

"But Boris," she muttered in a girlish pitch, "I love you so much and . . . ."

He looked at her, hair a mess, one cheek purplish where the burglar had struck her. He simply couldn't perform this charade anymore. For at least the past two years he'd acquiesced to her desires because he didn't want to hurt her. But no more. He had to start considering himself. He would take care of this business with the black marketeers, then tell her the truth.

"Not now, Musya. Please, not now." He touched

his head. That's how he'd evade her. "My head is killing me."

Yes, it was true. He was wonderfully, deeply in love. But not with her, not with Musya, his wife.

CHAPTER

8

Several hours later Boris made his way into the water closet and turned on the faucet. As he waited for the water to run hot, he stared at himself in the mirror. Gravity was winning. The bottom eyelids were just a tiny bit droopy. So were his cheeks. It wasn't too bad—the little pockets of extra flesh didn't really sag yet—but for the first time Boris had a clear vision of what he'd look like as an old man. He could see how his face would melt with age. The curly, blond hair would slip back and his forehead would slope further back, and one day that hair would turn a dull gray. Those worry lines above his eyebrows would become permanent creases. And when his full cheeks fell, his face would become jowly.

He didn't like the vision. As a child, adults had always pinched his cheek and commented on his bright visage. Such a happy face, they always said.

But as an adult his face was growing sadder and sadder. Unless he redirected his life, he would grow into an old man with the face of a melancholy clown.

Funny, he thought. No one had ever promised him anything specifically, but he'd always assumed that adulthood would be better than this. Next year, his parents had told him as a boy, you'll be taller and able to see over the counter. Next year, when you're a little older, you'll be able to do that. Next year . . . next year . . . next year . . .

Everything was an entreaty that life itself would yearly become easier and better. It hadn't, though, and he was almost angry with his parents for misleading him. He'd waited all these years, tried to do all the right things. But life kept getting worse around him. He hadn't done anything to make it so bad, of that he was sure. He'd just waited patiently and, for the most part, honestly.

To try to increase his opportunities at happiness, he'd tried only one strategy: to *look* happy. Act carefree and everything will be fine, he'd always assumed. Look happy and people won't cross or question you.

To maintain the happy exterior, though, he'd sacrificed a bit of himself at each step along the way. Over time he'd chiseled away his own wishes, his own dreams, and sacrificed them for the sake of others. He saw how as a boy he always tried to please his parents. Now, as an adult his every action was determined by what his father would think. And everything that went sour, he'd always assumed, had

61

been his fault. With an upbringing like his—the best schools, the best summer camps, the best contacts—he could have been a great Communist leader by now. Yet here he was today, his life half over, an ordinary truck driver.

There was so much to mourn, he thought. The dreams he'd let slip through his fingers, the parents he'd lost. Why, he always wondered, had his mother's heart failed when he was just ten? They said it was because of the war, because she'd nearly died of starvation during the Blockade. But what was the real reason? And why had he never found his father before he was lost forever just two years ago? He loved them both desperately; he saw that now. Yet all that was left of them were memories.

For the first time he understood why his face was growing not just old, but unhappy. Time was wearing his mask thin. Gradually, he sensed his inner feelings—the bundle of conflicting regrets—showing up on the outside. If he didn't do something— if he didn't stop worrying about hurting others—he would become a sad old man who'd forgone his happiness.

Boris flashed his best smile in the mirror, raised his arms, and flexed his muscles he-man style. Gravity wasn't going to win; happiness wouldn't lose. He would take control of his destiny.

He wondered if he hadn't already made some decisions along the way, at least partial ones. His father had pushed him to become a young, loyal Pioneer, then later a Komsomol. But Boris never shone, never became a brigade leader or a real activist. Nor had he joined the Party as an adult. In his own silent way he had resisted, had recognized that his personal dreams lay elsewhere. It wasn't that he didn't believe in the socialist doctrine— hadn't the government always taken care of him, hadn't it always provided free medicine and education, then guaranteed work?—it was simply that he knew a life of politics was not for him. So he had to follow his heart. Nothing would come of searching for yesterday.

"Boris! Boris, darling!"

He cringed. All this meant, of course, he must reveal the truth to Musya. Not eventually. Soon. He'd been so afraid how Musya would take the news that he'd put off telling her for over two years. She'd scream and cry, he was sure; he feared she might even throw herself into the Fontanka. It would be so easy if only she didn't love him so much.

"Your tea's nice and hot!"

"I'll be right out, Musya, my—" He cut himself off. He had to start being honest right now.

Reaching down, Boris felt the water run pure yet just as cold as ever. He shook his head. No hot water. They must be doing repair work down at the city's central heating plant, perhaps cleaning the boilers for winter. He took a deep breath and bent over. In doing so, his rear end bumped against the opposite wall. He twisted to the side, leaned over the sink, and splashed his face with the chilly water. Everything about the apartment was great except the tiny water closet. As his father always joked, there wasn't even enough room for toilet paper.

Hence the torn sheets of Pravda. Hence the communal shower outside the apartment and down the hall.

Minutes later, wearing a fresh shirt and sweater, he stood outside on the balcony. From this corner perch he watched the bundled pedestrians below hurry down Nevsky and across the Anichkov Bridge. With his wife right behind him, he held his glass of tea.

"Careful, it's hot," chided Musya, her breath spewing out like smoke. "Spill some into the saucer and sip at it. That's right. Do you taste the strawberry jam in it? That's from the wild berries you picked out at the dacha."

He tasted the sweetened black Georgian tea. "It's good."

"It'll make you strong, too. In a bit I'll go out and get you fresh black bread, some sweet Leningrad cheese, and if I can find it, some *Doktorskaya* sausage." She wrapped her arms around him from behind. "How's your head?"

"Fine. Just a little scratch."

"That bandit hit you so hard! I'm so glad you're all right." She hugged him for warmth. "You have to come back in. There's a fall chill in the air."

Gazing beyond Nevsky over the waters of Fontanka, he said, "In a minute."

A fine mist hovered over the silvery river. Someday he'd write about this intersection of street and water where tsar and revolutionary had crossed. Someday, too, the three-arched Anichkov Bridge and its four statues, each depicting a youth taming a wild horse, would be his in fiction.

"I'm going to get everything straightened out," said Boris.

"Good."

"There's no city more beautiful than Leningrad—its rivers, canals, bridges, palaces."

"Of course not. We're the Venice of the north."

"*Nyet*. Venice is the Leningrad of the south," he countered. "Just look at what beauty and history we have around us."

He swept his hand toward the rich red palace diagonally opposite and across the river. A prime example of Russian Baroque architecture, it had tall columns, figurines, and deep-set, elaborately decorated windows.

"That's the Beloselsky-Belosersky Palace. Alexander III's brother lived there, the Grand Duke Sergei Alexandrovich." He nodded toward a large colonnaded palace directly across the street. "That's the Anichkov Palace. Nicholas and Alexandra lived there for a while. Then the Dowager Empress called it home until the Revolution."

Musya laughed. "I thought your father taught you to be a good Communist." She looked toward the red building. "That's the Party headquarters." Indicating Nicholas II's former residence, she said, "And that belongs to the Leningrad Young Pioneers."

"I know that. And you know that Papa was a great Communist. He loved Leningrad. He understood its history, where we came from. That's why all this was restored after the Blockade—to help us understand how we arrived here.'' Boris shrugged. She'd never understood him or his dreams. ''Anyway, I'm going to tell that gang that I won't have anything to do with them. Don't worry, I'll fix it. Then I'm going to write.'' An electric trolley bus passed below, its wires snapping with blue electricity. ''First I want to go the dacha. Zarekino's where I grew up—in my heart, that is—so I'll start there. I'm thinking about quitting my job.''

''Boris!''

''I really might.'' But he didn't want to discuss the future with Musya. They had none together. ''Listen, I have to go. I want to find Sergei and get this ugly business straightened out.''

Without letting her say a word, he turned back through the French doors and into the apartment. It was approaching noon and he had to get moving.

''Can't we talk?'' called Musya, trotting after him. ''Let me get you something to eat. You're as thin as a matchstick.''

''Later.''

He didn't stop. He didn't want to. If they started now, the words would come shooting out like steam from a kettle. Just grab your coat, he told himself, and get out of here. He scanned the sofa.

''But Boris!''

''Musya, where's my jacket? I was wearing it when I—''

''Boris!''

He stopped and slowly turned to her. She came

to him but he held out an arm and halted her before she could embrace him.

"We have a great deal to talk about, Musya. So much." He angrily shook his head. "A lot of things have to change . . . are going to change."

She nodded like an eager schoolgirl. "Yes, yes, my love."

"You don't understand!" He couldn't look at her. "Where's my jacket?"

She pointed across the room. "Probably in the armoire."

Boris held his breath. Suddenly, his head began to pound, and he touched the bandage above his ear.

"Boris, what's the matter?"

Staring at the armoire, he couldn't speak. Then he was moving forward slowly, drawn to the tall piece of furniture. He wove around the overstuffed couch, pushed aside the end chair. Something happened here, something he couldn't remember.

"I . . . I . . ."

He rushed up to the cabinet and placed both hands on it. His palms moved over the wood as if he were a craftsman rubbing in oil. There was a secret here that he wanted to extract from the piece of furniture. No matter how hard he tried, though, he still couldn't make sense of what had happened.

Musya's voice broke right behind him. "What's the problem?"

He spun around. Her tiny eyes riveted him with a questioning, yet innocent look.

"I don't know," mumbled Boris. "Maybe it was a dream."

His left hand rose to a splintery gash in the wood. In his mind he saw the intruder rush up behind him, hurl the cleaver at the back of his head. Boris had ducked, but the chopper had bit here, into the armoire.

"I had this dream," he began. "It must have been after that fellow knocked me out. I dreamt that Lila Nikolaevna was in here dead. I . . . I saw a bit of her coat hanging out." He touched a spot where he imagined the material to have been. "And then I opened the door. She was inside. Dead."

She threw her hand to her mouth. "I know you can't stand her, Boris, but what an awful wish." Then she reached out and tried to pull him to the sofa. "Boris, you shouldn't go out. You're not well. You've had a big shock. Now come here and let me give you a massage. That'll calm you. Everything's fine."

"But . . . but . . ." he said, one hand still on the armoire. Hadn't he seen something else?"

"Boris, that was just a dream. A very odd dream. Besides, it's impossible. Lila Nikolaevna's out of town. You know that."

He gazed at her dark eyes set in the pearly white skin.

"Boris, come here. Now."

She grabbed him and pulled him away from the armoire. He withdrew his hand, backed away from her.

"Boris, stop it."

She shook her head, then cut right in front of him, blocking his access to the cabinet. She screwed up her eyes, stared at him as if he were deranged.

"Foo! What's the matter with you?"

"I want—"

"Boris, there's nothing in here," she said, interrupting.

In an impulsive movement, she grabbed the armoire's door and twisted the key. Expecting a body to tumble out, Boris flinched as she swung open the door. But it was empty. He pushed Musya aside and touched the inside walls of the cabinet. There wasn't even any blood. Only coats and boots.

"See?" said Musya, "Nothing."

He shook his head, touched the cut. "What a strange dream I had."

She reached over his shoulder and lifted his jacket from a hook inside. "Go if you must, but are you sure you're all right?"

He stepped away and took his jacket from her. But that dream. It was so real.

"I'm . . . fine."

He started for the door, walking as if he were in a deep trance.

"Are you sure?" Musya hurried her large body after him.

"What? *M-m-da*," he said hesitantly.

"At least promise that you'll come back soon. Promise, please?"

He stared past his wife at the empty armoire. None of this made any sense.

"Yes, Musya. I promise. I'll be home in a couple of hours." He rubbed his wrinkled forehead. "We . . . I . . . have some things to . . . to tell you. Just wait for me. I'll be back as soon as I can."

He walked out of the apartment and pulled the door tight behind him. He hadn't even reached the stairs, though, when he spotted several small objects on the floor. He reached down, took them in his hand.

They were mushrooms. Fresh ones.

CHAPTER
9

S ergei made a sound like a rusty zipper as he drew his finger across his throat.

"Don't do that!" pleaded Boris. "You're always fooling around."

Early afternoon sun streamed into the living room of Sergei's highrise apartment. Boris watched as his friend turned back to the convertible couch and pulled up a wad of sheets, tossed them aside, then flipped back the bed on which he and his wife slept. In seconds a couch appeared and Boris dropped himself onto it. No sooner had his little friend sat next to him than he slit his finger across his throat a second time.

"You're a dead man, Boris. A very soon-to-be one. I told you to stay in the truck. I told you to keep away from them."

"Tfoo!" Boris' blue eyes gazed out the window of the ninth floor apartment. "I had to take a leak."

"Well, you should've peed in the truck. You shouldn't have jumped out. Who do you think these thugs are, a bunch of Pioneers out working for Uncle Lenin?"

"I . . . I . . ."

He turned to his friend, a small-framed, balding man with frizzy hair. Why, thought Boris, had he let Sergei outtalk him? Why did he always allow Sergei to push him into things? It had been so for all the twenty-some years they'd been friends. Boris was always the one who suffered, too.

"This is serious business, man." Sergei rubbed his narrow, pale face. "About as serious as you can get. Those guys are a bunch of crazy Georgians. Who knows, they might even be cousins of Stalin. They're rich, too, and they have every intention of staying that way."

In a daze, Boris shook his head. "I didn't even hear them coming. So I got out—but just for a minute. Then I saw this car and I ran back. That's when I smashed into him, that man in the leather jacket."

"They probably didn't kill you then because you still had the truck." Sergei jumped to his feet and crossed to the hall that lead to the kitchen. "Mama, bring us a cold bottle!"

Boris watched as his friend took two tall glasses from a shiny sideboard. The next moment, a hand holding a bottle extended into the living room. Sergei took the chilled vodka from the unseen woman and returned to Boris.

Once he was certain his mother couldn't overhear, Sergei lowered his voice and continued.

"They probably didn't finish you off because if you were found dead near the truck the *militsiya* would have connected it with smuggling. So they let you go, figuring they could take care of you later. Less danger for them."

Boris stared out the window at a phalanx of dwellings identical to the one he sat in. The white nights were long gone, those safe summer days when the sun never surrendered its power. The northern light was growing more and more frail every day, and this was just the beginning of fall. The damp, dark winter—the sun rising at ten and setting before three—would be upon them in a matter of weeks. Would he even live until the first snowfall?

"It all makes sense. *Bozhe*, how could I be so stupid?" said Boris, rubbing the ridges of his forehead. "You know what I told him? I told him I wanted out."

"You've really done it this time, you fool."

"So there he was, waiting for me when I got home. All set to kill me. If Musya hadn't come home just then . . ."

Sergei twisted open the vodka bottle. "He must've wanted to keep it quiet."

Boris raised his head. "So what do I do?"

Sergei poured almost a full glass of vodka for each of them. "Well, you can't go to the militsiya or we'll all wind up in Siberia—or dead."

"It's hopeless."

"Maybe." He handed Boris a glass. "Here. It's

samaogon.'' Home brew. ''My uncle in the country makes it from sugar beets.''

Boris lifted the drink and studied the cloudy liquid. This was a libation that made you want to give up vodka.

''Go on,'' said Sergei. ''Drink it. All of it. It doesn't taste the greatest, but it's as full as a cossack with life.''

Boris exhaled, then tipped the glass into his wide-open mouth. The liquid seemed harmless at first, then started burning until it finally exploded in his stomach. His eyes became like a rabbit's, red and teary.

''Ai!'' gasped Boris. ''This isn't vodka. It's turpentine.''

''Shut up and drink. It works the same as the finest wheat vodka.'' He poured more. ''Drink!''

Boris took the second glass and downed it with one quick toss of the wrist. He tried to speak, but a rush of air hissed out instead.

''What?'' asked Sergei, his face a puzzled frown.

Still unable to speak, Boris tapped his chest, then his friend's wrist. ''What . . . what are we going to do?''

''We?'' Sergei screwed his eyes up and pulled away.

''You're the one who talked me into this in the first place. Besides, you're the contact person and you're in for some money, too.''

''Well, I would have jumped at the chance to do it alone if they'd wanted something on my route. And I wouldn't have messed things up like you, either.'' His face puckered up and he turned away. ''I just don't know what we can do, how to get you out of this. Boris, don't you see what kind of people we're dealing with? If we go sniffing around, we'll have our heads chopped off!''

''Well, that's better than doing nothing and having my heart axed out of my chest!''

Sergei sighed and leaned back. His eyes drifted shut and he rubbed his balding forehead with the heels of his palms. Then he sat forward, and poured them each another glass of vodka. The short man nodded and looked at Boris as if he wished he'd never met him.

''You know, people like you are the most dangerous friends to have. You don't know what it takes to get through life. I shouldn't help you, but I will.''

''Oi, Seryozha, you are a friend.'' He bent over and kissed him on both cheeks. ''The best of friends. I'll never forget you.''

''Don't talk like that. We're not dead—yet.''

Boris sat back, raised his glass. ''A toast.'' He clinked his glass against Sergei's. ''But a toast to what? How about to my new life? All these years I've been struggling, beating against the ice like a fish. But tonight I'm going to straighten everything out.''

''Congratulations,'' said Sergei reluctantly. With one hand he scratched his frizzy hair, with the other he raised his glass. ''Your mother would be very proud.''

They clinked glasses. With a professional toss, they downed their vodka, the coarse home brew careening down their throats and crashing in their stomachs.

Boris gasped. "So what's the plan?"

Sergei set down his glass. "I'll call this friend of yours, the one in the leather jacket. He's the leader. I'll ask him to meet us tonight. How's that?"

"The sooner the better."

"Good. Then we can clear the whole thing. You know, maybe you really should go to your dacha for a while."

"*Da, da*. I'd be out of everyone's way at Zareki-no. And what harm could I do there? I just want to write."

"Well, then that's how we'll explain it—you're leaving town. We won't tell them where, but I'll promise them everything will be all right." He looked toward the hallway, and shouted, "Mama! Mama!"

In the distance Boris heard the sizzling of frying meats and the continuous striking of a knife against wood. There was, however, no break in the work.

Sergei pushed himself to his feet, stumbled, and said, "We need some food. A little lunch."

Boris slapped his forehead. "Oi. I have to call Musya. I told her I'd be right back."

While his friend went to the kitchen for food, Boris stretched to a side table and grabbed the phone. He set it in his lap and dialed home. She answered on the first ring.

"Hello, Musya. It's me, Boris."

"Of course it's you, *golubchik moi*." My little pigeon. "Are you cleaning up your great mess?"

"Yes, and everything's wonderful. Sergei's going to set matters right. We're going to meet with those men tonight. But you and I need to talk."

Musya voice hushed on the line. "Is . . . is something bothering you?"

He cleared his throat, tried to lie. He couldn't, though. Smiling, he knew things had already begun to change. There was no holding it back now.

"Yes. Actually something's very wrong." He caught himself, reined himself in. With the vodka swelling his head, he wanted to explain right now. But he stopped. He at least had to tell her face to face. "I've been doing a lot of thinking. And I've finally figured out something. Will you be there? Can we talk?"

Her voice was weak and cautious. "*M-m-da*. Boris, *dusha moya*." My soul. "Yes . . . yes, I'll be here. I'll always be here for you. But—"

"Good. I'll be home in a few hours."

Not letting her say another word, he hung up. He stared at the cradled phone, a wide grin across his face. He was going to do it, really going to do it.

"A little *zakooski*!" proclaimed Sergei, carrying several plates of appetizers. "There'll be borscht in a few minutes."

On a table he set a loaf of black bread and a plate of cheese, pickles, and *vobla*, dried fish.

Boris reached for a shriveled fish, and with a smile smeared across his face, said, "Things just haven't been right between Musya and me. She loves me so much. But . . . but . . ."

"Tsk, tsk. Always the martyr, Boris. Still playing along with her?"

"Well, not for much longer. I'm going to level with her."

He stood, but Sergei caught his hand.

"What are you doing? Where are you going?"

Boris said, "I have to leave. There's something I must do before tonight."

"But the bottle's open and just look at all this food! You can't leave before we finish it all."

"Sergei, I've got to. You sure our friend in the leather jacket will meet us?"

His eyelids heavy, Sergei blinked. "Haven't I always fixed things for you? Don't worry, I'll call him and try to set something up for six or seven. Call me later and I'll tell you where."

"*Da, da.* And my thanks to you. Listen, I have somewhere to go, then I'll be back at the apartment. Sergei, my friend, I haven't felt this good . . . ever!" He took a deep breath. "At last I'm going to straighten out my life!"

He turned and grabbed his coat. He rushed out, eager to check on Lara. And to tell her the splendid news.

CHAPTER

10

Even though a chilling mist began to fall by late afternoon, people were packed on Nevsky like herring in a barrel. A meat store sunk in a basement had a long line wiggling out of it, the customers huddled together for warmth and covered by a bubbling canopy of bright umbrellas. Farther down, past the Aurora Theater, Kyril noted men and women of every age being sucked into Gastronom No. 1, the Yeliseyev, for some new shipment.

As the early darkness settled upon the crowded street, Kyril—his cleaver hanging in the cotton loop beneath his jacket—made his way across town. His head bowed, he crossed Nevsky, hurried past the Pushkin Theater, wove in and out of bundled shoppers, and turned left on Sadovaya Street. He passed block after block of five and six story apartment houses and crossed through Peace Square, the old

Hay Market Square where Raskolnikov was often found. He hurried on, not even bothering to stop at a line of some hundred people leading up to a parked truck; a young man and woman in white robes were selling bottled chicken. And even though it was a favorite of his and he hadn't seen it in years, there just wasn't time. He had to obtain the gun before this evening's meeting with Boris Volkov.

He wasn't pleased with what he had to do, but time left him no alternative. Knife or cleaver would be of no use tonight in the dark. Only a gun would do, would kill quickly and surely at such a distance. Not long ago he'd received word that Boris Anka-dievich had requested a meeting for tonight, and because there was so little time until the rendez-vous, Kyril couldn't leave town, obtain a pistol from one of his sources out in the country. So he was forced to follow up on a name given to him, that of an old war veteran, who was reputed to have many artifacts left from the days of Nazis and Fascists. Still, Kyril would take every precaution. Over the phone he hadn't told the old man what he really wanted. And Kyril had decided, too, that he would leave no possible trail for the *militsiya* to follow.

Several blocks later he came to one of the granite embankments of the Griboyodov Canal, a narrow strip of water famous for the frivolous cast iron bridges over it. He slowed and gazed across the channel of water that lay as still as black pavement. There before him rose a dark four-story building, plaster peeling from its face. The structure hung flat and plain as if it had been cut out, then pasted back into the city.

This was where Pavel Semyonovich lived and had lived ever since the Blockade when his family had died there. Kyril had also been told the old man lived all alone in the building, which was now mostly used for storage. That would make it much easier for Kyril to slip in and out.

In silence, he crossed the canal on a narrow pedestrian bridge, hugged the shadows, then headed through the building's low, arched passage. He swerved around stacks of crates, a handful of steel drums, and penetrated the building's heart, a tiny courtyard. Slowing, he studied the building for any sign of life and found none.

The courtyard had been heavily damaged during the war and was still not fully repaired. Where the cobblestones were loose, weeds sprang forth. A heap of wooden wheels filled an entire corner. Crumbling over the entire area were great scabs of plaster peeled from the surrounding walls. There were only two sources of light—one from the circle of dim sky way above, the other from a small window. Pavel Semyonovich's window.

Quickly, a torn cotton curtain was pulled aside and a whiskery face appeared. His short, ruffled crop of white hair and his sunken face were a beeswax yellow in the light of his single lamp. His small eyes pierced the night like a partisan scouting a forest.

Good, he's alone, thought Kyril. Slipping on a pair of gloves, though, he knew he had to be careful. Stories were told of the thousands of fascists Pavel Semyonovich had killed with his bare hands.

Being quite obvious, Kyril headed directly to the door. He knocked and waited patiently. Several minutes passed before he rapped again.

Pavel Semyonovich appeared, four rows of hero's medals freshly pinned to his undershirt.

Peering through the door's glass pane, he squinted and said, "Who's there?"

"It's me, Kyril Aleksandrovich."

The old man's face puffed then sank in a mass of wrinkles.

"I spoke to you in regard to my father," Kyril reminded him.

The weathered face before him remained blank.

"My father, the partisan."

Instantly Pavel Semyonovich lifted the hook and pushed open the door.

"Your father—he was a good partisan? A good Communist, too?"

"Yes, he was a great blessing to the Fatherland. He helped fight off the Hitlerites."

Pavel Semyonovich's eyes settled on Kyril. He studied the face, the shape of the body. The war had taught him that truths were to be seen, not spoken, and his eyes, though cloudy, were as sharp as if the war had ended only yesterday.

Pavel Semyonovich stared at him. "So what is it you want from an old man like me?"

"My father is very sick now and I'd like to give him a present. A souvenir."

Before the other man could say anything, Kyril

reached into his pocket and pulled out a roll of rubles. He held it upright between his thumb and forefingers, and Pavel Semyonovich stared at it in silence. Finally, he pulled open the door and allowed him entry. Still without a word, he started up a half-flight of stairs. After disappearing for a moment into his apartment, Pavel Semyonovich reappeared with an oil lamp, then continued upward.

With the old man in the lead, Kyril headed up the steep wooden steps. He twisted around and around, floor after floor, until finally there were no more stairs.

Without looking back, the older man said, "Follow me exactly."

Steadying the cleaver beneath his leather coat, Kyril carefully passed over a series of planks lying on the rafters.

"Ten times more people were killed in Leningrad than in Hiroshima," said Pavel Semyonovich up ahead. "More people died in our hero city than in any other in modern times."

" 'Let no one forget and no one be forgotten,' " quoted Kyril. "I lost three uncles, four aunts, and nine cousins in the war."

"A few of our twenty million killed." The old man's voice cracked in the dark. "My mother and father were killed by a rocket. My wife and son starved to death right downstairs that first winter of the Blockade. I was with the partisans. Didn't come back into the city until that spring. That's when I found them, two piles of thawing flesh and bones."

Kyril tapped his foot along the plank. "What a nightmare!"

"The Fascists almost got us all, but they didn't," grunted the old man. "And neither will the war-mongering capitalists in America."

With his deep voice, Kyril said, "Of course not."

Pavel Semyonovich stopped, set the oil lamp down on the edge of a brick chimney, and turned to Kyril. As if he had just stepped out of a hidden trench, the old man's face appeared tired and without hope.

"Now what is it you want?"

"My father is dying," began Kyril, brushing back a lock of his raven-dark hair. "I want to take him a present—a souvenir—that will remind him of his stronger days."

The war veteran crossed his arms. "These items are expensive. Relics from the war belong in a museum."

His words firm and without doubt, Kyril said, "Nothing is too much for a hero of the Great Fatherland War."

Pavel Semyonovich appeared satisfied, thought for only a moment. "A deposit will be necessary."

From his roll of money, Kyril peeled two fresh ten-ruble notes. Pavel Semyonovich inspected them in the light of the oil lamp and nodded his approval.

The white-haired man continued down the single plank, then stepped to another board. He disappeared behind the brick chimney, then reappeared dragging a large suitcase of torn leather. Kyril guessed that it had once been used by a merchant for international travel.

Kyril's right hand slipped into his jacket. He'd have the gun and be out of here within minutes.

"My prices are firm. No bargaining."

Kyril said, "My mother always told me not to dicker with a war hero."

With Kyril's help, Pavel Semyonovich pulled the case onto two beams. The older man blew a cloud of dust from it and flipped two latches.

Raising the lid, in a low voice he said, "I hid this up here during Stalin's time. Still aren't supposed to have some of these things."

Peering downward in the faint light, Kyril said, "I'm very discreet."

"Well, I'm not selling you anything a civilian shouldn't have."

"Of course not," said Kyril.

Pavel Semyonovich laid back the lid and exposed a thick suitcase crammed with trinkets from the Great Fatherland War. He extracted a helmet, a layer of neatly folded, dingy-green uniforms, and a dagger embossed with a swastika.

Pausing at the knife, Pavel Semyonovich said, "This belonged to a Nazi captain I killed."

Kyril spotted the bullets first. Then he saw the black butt of a pistol sticking out from beneath a yellowed newspaper.

Kyril unbuttoned his jacket. "That newspaper there from Victory Day—I think Papa might like that. How much?"

As the old man rubbed the back of his neck, Kyril

lifted the cleaver from the loop in his jacket. Just then his attention was caught by the flickering flame of the oil lamp and he had an idea.

"Newspapers like these are very rare, you know, and—"

He swung open his jacket, and the silvery cleaver streaked out of the black. Using both hands, Kyril slammed the flat side of it against Pavel Semyonovich's head. There was a loud slap as the metal smacked his cheek and temple. The air burst from him like a pained burp and he crumpled to the side.

Kyril stepped back, looked down at the body, and was pleased how simple his plan was so far. Quickly, he then stepped over Pavel Semyonovich, dug into the suitcase, and pulled out the dark pistol. Pushing aside the paper, a uniform, and other objects, he recovered over a dozen bullets. He understood, too, why Pavel had not only the gun but everything else hidden away. Had the wrong people seen this paraphernalia, they might have thought he was a revolutionary instead of a dedicated Communist.

Suddenly Kyril felt something creep up the toe of his shoe and move higher. He gasped and jumped up. At once, he realized that he'd forgotten to seal Pavel Semyonovich's eyelids with blood. Now the old man was reviving and his shriveled right hand was wrapping itself around Kyril's ankle. Kyril tried to lift his foot and kick, but the thick, gnarled fingers were wrapping tighter and tighter. He jerked his foot again, and again was not able to free himself. With a will to live that had carried him through the war and far beyond, Pavel Semyonovich was refusing to let go of life.

Kyril's body tensed in repulsion. He dropped the gun and grabbed his cleaver. As the old man's fingers dug deeper into his ankle, Kyril raised the blade. He spent a moment taking aim, then hurled the knife down and into the wrist. Like a razor slicing through cloth, the finely honed edge of the cleaver separated wrist from hand. With a final spasm, the fingers of Pavel Semyonovich clutched into Kyril's ankle, then loosened and dropped into a puddle of shiny liquid that pumped from the quivering body.

Wasting not a moment, Kyril plunged his thumb into the blood, then stamped his finger over each of the old man's eyes. Back. Back into death, which is now forever yours, he chanted in his mind.

That done—the only way Kyril knew to keep the murdered from haunting their killers—Kyril grabbed up the gun and bullets. His heart beating fast, he gazed down at the handless arm. When the body was discovered in the cinders, he hadn't wanted any sign of a struggle to exist, any oddity that would spark an investigation.

But even though it was too late for that now, he continued his original plan. He wiped the cleaver on the cuff of Pavel Semyonovich's pants, dropped the instrument back in its noose. Then wasting not a second more, he placed the gun and bullets in his pocket, and finally raised the oil lamp and lobbed it against the wooden rafters. For a moment he stared at the fire as it devoured all, and he was reminded of the house in that village, the one that had belonged to the elderly couple. That cozy little house, too, had crumbled into black cinders.

When the bright flames rolled over the not-quite-dead body of Pavel Semyonovich, Kyril hurried off and down the steep stairs. There was little time left if he were to intercept Boris Ankadievich Volkov before the meeting and extinguish his life as well.

CHAPTER

11

Boris left the towering, inhabited walls surrounding the southern part of the city and returned to the historical center. He took the metro; his car, rarely used except to go to the dacha or for a drive in the country, was parked and covered near his apartment. Then he switched to a tram, which he rode to the Strelka, the tip of Vasilevsky Island. It was here, at this easternmost spit of land, that the river was divided in two—the Bolshay Neva and the Malaya Neva—on its way into the Bay of Finland.

Boris stepped down from the yellow streetcar and was hit by a blustering wind from the north. Putting up his collar, he peered at the graying sky. The sun was setting earlier each day, it seemed, and soon the wooden landing stages would be towed upstream for the winter. It was only a matter of time, too, before the statues in the Summer Garden were

89

boarded up and the open air dance floors removed. Another season was upon them, its raw winds beating down upon the stone metropolis.

It was all exhilarating to Boris, this death of one season, the birth of another. Perhaps, he mused, it was because this matched his own situation—his decision to end a phase of his life and start anew. He was filled with hope for the future and, standing on the spit across from the old Exchange Building, he reveled in the beauty of Leningrad. One couldn't escape it.

He gazed across the river and past the apple-green walls of the Winter Palace. The cityscape was low and solid, pierced only by church domes and spires. What had his father always called Leningrad? A glorious paradox. A city modeled after Amsterdam, designed by Italian architects, then over-boiled in severe classicism. There really wasn't anything Russian about it except for a few golden domes. Yet at the same time it was all Russian. A place of imagination and beauty that had been brutally forced upon its people by their greatest revolutionary, Peter the Great.

Papa, Papa, thought Boris. You always call me back just when I'm about to break free. Boris knew he could stay here forever, staring at the colorful palatial façades with their columns and deep-set windows. Filled with regrets, he could gaze a lifetime from the heavy granite embankments over the dark waters of the Neva. But a blast of wind burst across the flat waters, chilling his bones. He had to move on. Lara was waiting.

He jogged across the street and cut around the side of the Exchange. As he headed toward the center of the island, he passed alongside the university. The streets were empty, free of the bustle of students. That meant the harvest was still going on. It couldn't be much longer, though. In a week or two the weather would be too wet to harvest potatoes. Then the students would return from their required duty and fall would begin in earnest.

Soon Boris was in the middle of Vasilevsky Island, passing down Sredny Prospekt. Within minutes, he raised his eyes and saw her butter-yellow building, a five-story structure reconstructed after the war. Lara had lived here for three years, ever since her widowed mother had moved to Novgorod to help her son, a top official in the militsiya, and his wife with their newborn twins.

He passed through a gate, into a courtyard, and entered a single door. The narrow staircase turned and turned upon itself, growing ever darker the higher he climbed. He passed the communal kitchen and bathroom she shared with three other families and finally came to her room, a garret perched under the eaves. It was alone up there on the top floor, a tiny hideaway in Leningrad.

"Lara, it's me!" he called, huffing and knocking at the same time.

From inside came a rustling of clothing, the sound of a book dropping to the floor. Always books. She worked at *Dom Knigi*, the House of Books, on Nevsky, and she was always reading. Poetry, fiction, travelogues—her mind feasted on the printed word. He loved that about her. Loved that their dreams meshed, that she held high his desire to write. Then a bolt was loosened and the door to the one-room apartment pulled open. A smallish woman stood there, a faint smile on her face. The last doubt left his mind forever.

"I love you, Lara." It made him happy, too, to see the familiar brown and white sweater that hung like a bag from her shoulders. "You're wearing my sweater."

"I always wear it, you know that. It's warm and it reminds me of you." She grinned and rolled her green catlike eyes. "You've been out with Sergei again. I can tell. How much have you had to drink this time? Do you have a headache yet? Need some drops? Come on in."

"Honest. I'm as sober as a priest. Now, anyway." He stared at her. "Stand back. I want to look at you."

A puzzled expression came over her face. She was still before taking a hesitant step back.

He admired her unashamedly. The thick light brown hair. The green eyes so delicately shaped. The pale complexion—a creamy English complexion, he called it—that lit up all rosy at the first chill.

"I've loved you ever since Sergei introduced us."

That was over two years ago, and their souls had touched right at the start. She sensed his pain, he her loneliness. He admired her intellect; she wished she had his imagination. At twenty-nine, she was six years younger than him. Inside, though, in a place where skin and bone faded into nothingness, they had the same curiosity, the same eagerness, the same spark.

"But just today I realized how much I love you . . . how much you mean to me."

Lara was so alive, so much more than Musya. An ideal day to his wife would be to sleep late, loll about the apartment, shop for nylons or Bulgarian *kosmetiki* or search out her black market connections for another *jeanzi* skirt, then drink cognac or brandy late into the night. Lara would pass the same day by rising early and reading, visiting the art collection at the Hermitage, searching out a rare book, strolling in the woods, then visiting friends.

Confusion and fear plain on her face, Lara cleared her throat. "Is everything all right?"

His head bobbed up and down. *"Da, da, da."*

A long stream of air poured over his lips in a sigh that left him at peace. It was as if he had just exhaled the last confusion of his life, the last tension.

He moved forward like a ballet dancer, his steps strong and sure. He raised his arms, and Lara leapt out at him.

"Ya tebya lubloo." I love you, he said, as he caught her and spun her around. She slid downward in his arms, her feet easing onto the floor. But he still held her firmly. Grasping her waist, he kissed the top of her head, bent down, and kissed her ear through her thick brown hair. He sensed her lips on his neck.

"Are you all right?" he asked in a whisper. "How do you feel?"

"I'm fine now."

His eyes ran from the cabinet with its hot plate, to the table, to the iron bed by the single window. The only other furniture was a bookcase and three chairs around the table. Books were stacked everywhere, filling the case, covering the table. But there was no food.

"Have you been eating?" he asked.

She shrugged. "Some cheese and bread and tea. I'm not hungry."

He brushed aside her hair and ran his fingertips over her smooth cheeks. "Just take care of yourself."

She backed away and voiced her fear. "Boris . . . is this goodbye?"

The shock of her words threw him back. He saw her pale face, the quivering lips, the glassy eyes.

"Wh-what?" His brow shot up in confusion. "What are you talking about?"

Her green eyes dropped to a button on his shirt and she picked at it. "This feels like a farewell. Is everything over between us? Is that what you came to say?"

"Oh, not goodbye, Lara." His broad shoulders bounced up and down with gentle laughter. "It's a hello." The warmth of his proposal brought chills to his spine. "Would you like a roommate?"

Stunned, her face was still and white. Then she blinked.

"Well, would you? I mean, a roommate for the rest of your life?"

Speechless, she broke into an incredulous grin. She shook her head, brushed back her brown hair.

This is what she'd wanted all along. Now that it was here, though, she couldn't believe it.

"I . . . I . . ."

"Lara," he blurted, wanting to tell her everything immediately, "someone broke into my apartment and tried to kill me this morning."

Her delight vanished. "No!" She searched his face for an explanation, grabbed at his arms. "What are—"

"Ts-s-s." Quiet, he said, a gentle finger on her lips. He patted his chest. "See, I'm all right. Not hurt at all. Though I would have been if Musya hadn't come home." He shook, took a deep breath. Closing his eyes briefly, he forced himself back on track. "When I thought I only had seconds to live, I realized I was about to die without doing what was right in my heart. Lara, I need you. I want you." Grinning, he added, "I've decided to leave Musya."

Lara gasped. "No!"

He saw the joy burst back on her face and they both started laughing. He opened his arms and they flew together again. Boris shook with laughter and closed his eyes as she kissed him on his forehead, the bridge of his nose, his eyelids.

"You don't seem sick!"

"I'm not . . . I'm not anymore!"

He tried to hold her, but she was too excited. And he knew it then. He knew as she clambered all over him that he'd never made a better decision in his life. He caught a glimpse of her face.

"Lara, you're crying!"

Her head bobbed up and down. "I'm so happy!"

"I feel like I've had a headache all my life," he said, "and suddenly . . . suddenly it's gone."

He wanted her to understand and to know everything. No more secrets. No more denials. No more games. He took her hand and started across the small room. He wove around the table and a chair stacked with books, then pulled her toward the iron bed.

"Come here. Let's talk."

He flopped back on the bed, his body sinking in the soft mattress. She lay next to him.

"Lara, I got mixed up in something . . ."

The same long explanation came pouring out of him for the second time that day. He told her about Sergei's involvement with the gang, the stolen auto parts, and his involvement in transporting them.

"It was awful," he admitted. "I don't know why I let myself get talked into it in the first place. The extra money, I guess. I kept thinking that as soon as I had money saved up, I'd leave Musya. Maybe it was an excuse. Maybe it was just a way of putting off making a decision. I've been so afraid of hurting Musya. You know how much she loves me."

"Not half as much as I do."

"And not half as much as I dislike her." He groaned at the thought of his soon-to-be ex-wife. "So when I was coming home from work this morning, all I could think about was honesty. And you."

She squeezed his hand. "Boris, you're a wonderful writer. You must make time for your dream."

He was lost in the memory now, the fright overtaking him, and he seemed not to hear her. "And then I was attacked by this maniac with a cleaver, and . . . I knew. I knew everything had to be changed around." He took a deep breath. "I phoned Musya earlier. Now I'm going to tell her that I'm leaving her. Tonight. Do you have room for me?"

She bent over and kissed him on the nose. "Welcome home."

He looked directly at Lara. "I'm going to give her the apartment. That'll be her settlement. Will you still love me even if I lose the nicest apartment in Leningrad?"

She patted the bed. "This is the nicest place in all of Russia. No place has seen so much fun."

"Seriously, Lara. You know we'll never get another apartment even half as nice as that again."

"I don't care. I don't care about anything but you. All I need is you—and a few books."

He clasped her hand to his chest. "What a couple we'll make. You and your books, me and my writing." He shook his head. "You know, I don't care about the apartment either. I've lived my whole life there, but it's not important to me. I might have to give her Papa's car. But I don't care about that either. The only thing I really want is the dacha. That's what's special to me, that funny little log cabin. That'll be ours together." He thought of the wonderful experiences he had had there. Now there'd be many more. "Maybe we could even go out to Zarekino next week. I want to start on my novel. The birches are beautiful this time of year and . . .''

''It sounds perfect.''

He laughed. ''Now that it's come time to tell Musya, I'm not even dreading it. In fact, I'm excited. I can't wait.''

All too easily he could picture Musya collapsing on the floor. She'd kick, scream, plead. He knew how much she loved him—he could never satisfy her lust for him—and he knew how much she'd beg him not to go. But he would.

Boris shook his head. ''I hope it's not too bad. I really don't want to hurt her.''

''Boris, stop it.'' Lara sat up. ''Honestly, you spend eighty percent of your time anticipating other people's feelings—really, how *you're* going to make them feel—and eighty percent of the time you're wrong.''

He nodded. ''Maybe that's why I'm so tired.''

She took his hand and pulled him. ''Sit up.''

''What?''

''Sit up. I have something important to tell you.''

Boris' muscles became knot-hard. He shot up. Maybe she didn't like his plan. Maybe . . .

''Boris, relax. I have very good news for both of us. I don't have the flu.''

''Good. You look fine.''

She ran her hand through her thick hair. ''Boris, I'm not sick at all . . . I'm pregnant.''

He stared at her. ''Wh-what?''

''I'm pregnant.'' Lara clasped Boris's hand and

placed it gently on her stomach. "We're going to have a baby."

He blinked, pointed to himself.

"Of course you're the father!" she said. "There's never been anyone else."

"Oi!"

Boris plopped back on the bed. He couldn't believe it. Him, a father. He shot back up, looked at Lara, touched her stomach.

"Oi!" He fell back down.

"Boris, I'm going to have this baby. I won't have an abortion. Just tell me the truth. Do you still want me?" She touched her stomach. "I mean, do you still want us?"

He sat back up and his eyes were teary. "Lara . . . Lara! I love you. I want you!" He burrowed both hands into his curly hair, tugged, then reached out and embraced her. "A baby!"

"You're happy?" she asked in disbelief.

"What? Of course I am!"

He jumped up and started walking around the room. His whole life was going to change. He was about to leave so much behind. Soon he'd be free of Musya. No longer would he have to pretend he loved her. Within hours he'd be out of his parents' apartment, the only place except Zarekino he'd ever called home.

Thank God, he thought. This was all he'd ever hoped for. A woman he loved. The opportunity to pursue writing. A child. Yes, a family. That's what he wanted. He hadn't really known how much until now. There'd never been even a chance before. Musya had aborted all of his hopes.

Boris stopped pacing and leaned against the bookcase. He couldn't remember ever feeling this good.

"Lara, you know what?" he said, staring at his hands, examining his own body. "For the first time in years I . . . I feel like I'm not dying." A tear rolled down his cheek. "We're going to have a child. Part of you . . . and part of me is going to keep on living after we're gone."

"It feels good, doesn't it?" she said, delighted at his swell of emotion.

He nodded and wiped away that tear and another. Laughing, he said, "Can't you see us—the three of us—out at the dacha on a summer day?"

Her eyes drifted shut and she inhaled as if she were breathing the aroma of an entire forest.

"The meadows, the birch forest . . . I can see it all, smell it all. Is there anything more beautiful than our countryside? Anything better for health and happiness?" She gazed over at him and reached out for his hand. "Once I dreamed of being this happy and it made me depressed for weeks. I never thought life could be so good."

"From now on our lives will always be wonderful. You and I—we're berries from the same field."

He crossed to her and, standing above her, held her close to his stomach. He massaged her head, winding her hair around his fingers.

"Just a few things to do," he said, "and we'll be free. From here I'll go tell Musya that I'm leaving her. Then I'll go directly to the gang and tell them I'm out.''

She looked up at him. "Boris, if someone tried to kill you before, shouldn't you go to the militsiya? Oi, Borinka, I . . .''

"I can't go to the militsiya, Lara, or I'll get arrested. Don't worry. It'll be fine. Wait and see.''

She grabbed him around the waist and held him tight. "Just be careful, all right? Be very careful.''

"Of course I will. I've never been so close to happiness before—and I don't want to lose it.''

He eased himself down on the bed and their mouths drifted together. He felt her soft skin press against his parched lips and something stirred deep within him. Lara did that to him, aroused him so much more than Musya.

"Can we toast to our child?'' he asked.

"Vodka? Now?''

He bent her back, lying on top of her. "That's not quite the toast I had in mind.''

She understood and worked her hand to the top button of her blouse. "A toast of love. Oi, Boris.'' She kissed him on the nose. "Promise me you'll always stay young in your heart.''

He shrugged. "You're the one who makes me so. You give me hope.''

As was their fashion in their afternoon meetings, Lara pulled the curtain over the window and they shed the outer world. A shirt, her cotton blouse, his socks dropped to the floor. When all of their clothing was removed, Lara lifted aside the covers. Boris slipped into the sandwich of soft sheets and reached out. In the muted, yellow light seeping through the curtain he watched the pointed tips of her breasts swing over him, then felt her skin burn into his. He kissed her and his hands glided down her back to the tip of her spine and beyond.

Holding her firmly, he tipped her to the side, then rolled her on her back. All at once he knelt, then disappeared beneath the covers. He rested his head in the valley between her breasts, then kissed her long and slow. He slipped down further and laid his cheek on her stomach that was so full of life. How he loved the creaminess of her skin.

"Hello, you little peanut in there," he whispered, and kissed her belly.

She laughed, and said, "I love being hidden away up here, but someday can we go far away and make love outside? Just you and me and nature."

"Sure."

"Naked under the stars . . . it sounds so delicious."

He kissed her more, heard her sighs, and felt her hands grasp his curly hair. Then she pulled him up, ran her lips over his ears. Chills filled his body as she rubbed him, and all at once a great stone fell from his heart never to return.

"Ya tebya lubloo." I love you, he said.

And they held each other so closely that not even water could split them apart.

CHAPTER

12

When Musya looked at the clock in the corner of the living room, she realized she had to leave. Time was running out, and everything would be ruined if she didn't hurry.

Quickly, she pushed herself out of the squishy couch and bustled into the bathroom. In front of the mirror, she dabbed on fresh lipstick, brushed her hair, and studied her face. Like a fashion model, she cocked her head sideways, batted her eyes, and stuck out her breasts. She was beautiful and this was a glorious night.

Gospodi, dear lord, she was excited. With a little laugh, she practically flew out of the bathroom. She stopped briefly at the dining room table, took a pen and paper and wrote in large letters:

Borinka, darling!
Tanya called from work. The boots are in

and they're putting them on the shelves tonight. I'm so excited—I've been waiting
months for these! Sorry to rush off, but she's
sure there'll still be a pair if I can get there
within the hour. We'll talk later. Hope there's
no line! Back soon!

> Love and kisses,
> Your Musinka

She laid the note on the table where he couldn't
miss it, then dashed for her raincoat. Boris wouldn't
be happy that she'd be gone by the time he returned.
But that didn't matter. This was far more important.

As she fastened the buttons of her coat over her
large body, though, she couldn't help but reflect on
Boris' anxiety. He was always blabbering about
something without really saying anything. Still . . .

"Oi," she said, shaking her head and banishing
the thoughts.

She flicked off the living room lamp and hurried
to the door. From an antique trunk—which now
served as a table for mail—she scooped up her keys.
Her hand on the lightswitch, she gazed back into
the apartment. It was so beautiful and she was so
lucky to have it all—the furniture, the color TV,
and, best of all, the location right in the heart of
Leningrad. Oi, life was being good to her at last.

Except that smell—a heavy, rotten odor emanat-
ing from near the front door. Later. She'd take care
of it later. For now she just had to go, be on her
way, because . . .

She froze. Just outside the door she heard faint steps. Could Boris have returned already? No. Now she heard nothing. But . . .

She flicked off the light, opened the door, and stepped into the hall.

''Boris?''

And suddenly the thick arm of a leather jacket was thrown over her mouth.

CHAPTER
13

Boris called Sergei before he left Lara's. Everything was arranged, his friend assured him. The man in the leather jacket, the gang leader, had agreed to a meeting at six-thirty that evening. Boris was simply to proceed to the end of Nevsky Prospekt and look for a red Zhiguli parked near the walls of the monastery. Sergei would lead the way from there.

Leaving Lara's bed wasn't easy. He lingered longer than he should have, in the end allowing as little time as possible to break the news to Musya. Just the mention of a divorce would make her fall apart, of that he was sure, and while he was eager to tell her, he also wanted a solid excuse to leave. The ruffian in the leather jacket was as good as he'd ever have.

Shortly after five, Boris paused outside his apartment door. He took a deep breath. He couldn't back down now. He had to tell Musya that he didn't love her, that he wanted a divorce as soon as possible. He had to tell her for Lara's sake. For the baby's sake. He smiled. He was going to be a father.

He pulled at his curly hair, then knocked. When he realized what he had done, he laughed out loud. There, he told himself, you see. You've already moved out. In your mind you no longer live here. He knocked louder. Perhaps that's how the conversation would start. Musya would open up and ask what in the world was he doing knocking at his own front door. He'd hand her his keys and say it wasn't his door. It was hers. He was giving the apartment to her. All he wanted were his clothes and a divorce.

There was, however, no movement from inside. No hello, no heavy footsteps. His brow began to tighten as he reached for the door handle. When he twisted it, nothing happened.

"Musya?"

From his pocket he took a long thin key, twisted the lock, and opened the door. The apartment was as dark as the late afternoon sky. Not a single lamp burned. Only the lights of Nevsky filtered in through the large windows, bringing the shadows to life. Could Musya be asleep? That was it. She'd worked all night last night and now she was just trying to catch up.

Sleep, he thought. He'd forgotten all about that and just the idea made his body ache. He leaned against the wall, unable to recall when he'd last closed his eyes. Ach, how wonderful life would

107

be when this unhappy episode was over. The excitement alone had carried him this far, but . . .

Boris froze, then threw himself up against the wall. He must be more tired than he realized. The last time he'd entered this darkened room someone had been waiting to kill him. Could the man in the leather jacket have returned? Could he have harmed Musya? Was he now waiting for Boris in the shadows of the apartment?

His eyes scanned the low, puffy shape of the sofa. Up there on the right was the tall armoire. Were those feet protruding from beneath it? No. Nothing by the windows, either. Only framed night lights of the city.

"Musya?" he whispered. "Musya, are you here?"

He heard traffic outside, but nothing from within. Could she be dead? No. Please no, he thought, and lunged to the wall by the armoire. He hit a switch. A naked bulb illuminated the middle of the living room.

"Musya!"

Terror bubbled in his stomach and he ran to the bedroom, his heart racing ahead of his feet.

"Musya!" he cried.

He flung open the door and hit the switch with his fist. The overhead light exploded with life in a deadly still room. But Musya wasn't there. The wide bed lay flat and smooth, not even the white bedspread was wrinkled.

He heard something behind him, spun around.

Bozhe. The closet. This time he wasn't going to wait for anyone to leap out at him. He flung open the door ready to attack. A broom fell, striking him on the shoulder. He kicked it aside. Then he heard the rattling again. Someone was in there, charging out. Whoosh! Something streaked out toward him.

"Ai!"

He ducked as it flew past, a dark shot out of nowhere. With radar-like precision, it skimmed past but didn't try to hurt him. He turned. A small brown bat whizzed back and forth across the room. Not waiting a second, Boris grabbed the broom from the floor and charged. He swung once and missed. He brought the broom back and waited for the creature to charge. Then he swung again. He hit the bat, flung it across the room, and on the same stroke smashed the bulb. Shards of glass along with the tiny body dropped onto the wood floor. Boris stared for just a moment at the sparkling glass and at the redness of the bat seeping into the cracks of the oak. Then broom in hand, he ran out.

"Musya!"

He scrambled into the living room and into the second bedroom. He kicked open the door and ripped open the closets. Lila Nikolaevna's clothes and belongings were, however, in complete order. He turned, tripped over something. A shoe went flying out of the room before him and he charged out after it. He paused by the armoire, glanced down at the shoe. The bathroom! His mind flooded with visions of finding her bloody body stuffed in a cor-

ner. God! He should never have left her. What a
fool he was. He should have warned her not to open
the door for anyone. He should have hustled her
out, hidden her in a friend's apartment.

Holding the broom up in defense, he yanked open
the door to the small water closet. There before him
stood a sink, a toilet, and torn newspaper tacked to
the wall for toilet paper. But no wife. He stepped
back into the living room. A car outside honked.
He spun around. The large room was empty.

The balcony!

He jumped over the couch and tore open the
doors. A cold breeze flew over him. The white lights
of Nevsky struck his eyes, the bustle of traffic filled
his ears. He glanced down at the crowds swarming
past the statues of the Anichkov Bridge.

Knives! The kitchen. How could he be so stupid.
He spun around, broom still in hand, and ran toward the kitchen. He pushed a dining room chair
out of his way. In his frenzy he almost missed the
note laid carefully on the dinner table. The large,
florid writing was recognizable in an instant, and
he dropped the broom. As he read, rage like a sudden fever overtook him and the paper shook in his
hand until it rattled. Then bit by bit he slowly crumpled the note in a single fist, wadded it into a ball,
and threw it on the parquet floor.

"Boots!" he cried out.

Dresses and jean skirts and nylons and, yes,
boots. Cosmetics, too. Those were all she thought
of, all she wanted out of life. How had their marriage lasted this long? Had he been crazy, too? What

a fool he'd been to marry her, what a bastard to tolerate her foolishness this long.

Cursing himself, he lumbered over to the sofa and dropped himself onto it. The thick cushions bounced up, then hissed as they softened. He should have left her years ago. Actually he never should have married her. His father was right. The old man, the conservative Communist, had recognized Musya's worth from the start, found her taste for Western fashion and personal consumption appalling. She won't spur you on to greater things, Arkady Yakovich had said. She won't make your life rich and satisfying. She'll suck the life from you, waste the precious sands of time. He constantly reiterated that she was only after what Boris possessed—by virtue of being the son of Arkady Yakovich: the car, the dacha, the apartment on Nevsky. Yet the more Arkady Yakovich persisted, the more determined Boris became. He was certain that Musya, with her sweet kisses and smothering embraces, truly loved him. She wanted sex until Boris ached, till he could hardly stand in the morning. Musya was fun, vivacious, exciting. And Boris was determined to make up his own mind. That, in truth, was how he'd resolved to marry her: to do something his meddlesome father was entirely opposed to.

With his head slumped back against the sofa, Boris stared up at the naked bulb. How depressing, he thought. The one and only time he'd openly defied his father and used his own judgment was a complete mistake. His feelings for Musya had never, not even then, had anything to do with love. There had been too many issues—primarily, how a Party official's son was wasting his life—to see the circumstances simply. Now at least he knew what to do.

He sat up. There was no use stewing in his own juices. With Musya away, well, he'd have to straighten things out with the gang first, then return to face her.

With fresh determination, he pushed himself to his feet. He turned toward the armoire, crossed around the end of the sofa, and then tripped again over the same black shoe. Pausing, he picked it up and turned it over. It was a woman's shoe, the leather cracked and muddy, and the short heel ground to almost nothing. Fat, too, the shoe obviously belonged to Lila Nikolaevna. How odd for it to be loose.

In a quick impulse, he went to the armoire and twisted its key. He hesitated, thought of the bizarre dream he'd had of Lila Nikolaevna—it had been so real—then swung open the door. Nothing unusual—the armoire was filled with a few coats and scarves. As if it were a scar on his memory, however, he was unable to rid himself of that vision of the body.

Boris tossed the old shoe on the sofa and, rubbing his brow, walked around the apartment shutting off lights. The blow to his head that morning and his lack of sleep were all too much. But the sooner he finished with Sergei's group, the sooner he could join Lara. Yet . . .

He neared the front door and stopped. Something was nagging at him, pulling him back, and he shoved aside a few bills and sat on the edge of the trunk next to the door. What a vivid dream! He had seen the old woman's body so clearly, heard his own gasp. The memory made him cringe and he nervously began to flip the latches on the trunk. This was going to drive him crazy.

Suddenly his nose twitched. The air around him stank like overripe cheese. He shifted uncomfortably, recognizing the smell right away. Something had died, and whatever it was lay very close.

Boris wrinkled his nose. Another mouse or rat had died—judging by the sharp stench, probably right in the wall behind him. It would be weeks before the creature decomposed thoroughly. The smell would linger for months. Why didn't the building superintendent use traps that exterminated the rats outright instead of a slow-killing poison?

He laughed. Well, that putrid smell was Musya's problem. This was her place now.

With a quick flick of his wrist, he extinguished the light and headed out into the darkness of Leningrad.

CHAPTER

14

As Kyril's leather arms wrapped tighter and tighter around her in the chilly night air, Musya thrashed like a wild animal.

"Oi," she whimpered, "I want to fuck you right here, right now. I want you to lift me up and nail me to this tree."

He pressed the hardness of his body against her clothing. "Promise you'll never leave me."

"Oi, never, Kyrozhinka! Never!"

The two lovers, locked in a fluid embrace alongside the Fontanka Canal, waited for Boris to leave the apartment once again. Earlier, when Musya was preparing to depart, they'd almost bumped into him on the stairs. Kyril had prevented the encounter, though, by throwing his hand over her mouth, then pulling her up the next set of stairs and out of sight.

Now, he leaned back, studied her bruised cheek in the pale night light. "I'm sorry, my love. If only that fool hadn't been an hour late this morning, if only he hadn't run into the old man downstairs. Will you forgive me for striking you so hard?''

"Of course I will."

She realized that Kyril hadn't risked killing Boris earlier because he'd already been seen in the building. She knew, also, that Kyril had been obliged to make it appear as if she'd been attacked as well.

She said, "There was no other way to keep Boris from suspecting me. And it worked. Funny, isn't it? I abhor him and he doesn't even know." She reached down to Kyril's pants and stroked him. "Actually, I'll only forgive you if tonight you do exactly as I say."

"Anything . . ."

Sinking into his embrace, Musya squeezed the thickness of his body made so strong from his butchering.

She ran her lips over his neck. "You have to kill him tonight before he—"

"That feels wonderful."

"Before he realizes it's not a gang that's trying to kill him, but us." She looked down the river toward the Anichkov Bridge and the four bronze horses. "All this stuff about this gang of his makes me nervous, but what a lucky break for us."

She bit his chin, glanced up at the apartment. With lights blazing, it was obvious Boris was still there.

"I just can't stand the sight of him another minute."

"Patience, my love," he moaned, sliding his cold hand up under her blouse.

"I've been patient for the last four years, but now . . . oi, Kyril . . ." She delighted in his large, soft hand on the tip of her breast. "I would have been a great actress. That's what I wanted. I wanted to be an actress instead of a nurse. Oi, Kyril . . . I should have divorced him years ago," she added, pressing him with kiss after kiss.

"I'm glad you didn't."

"I know, I would have lost the apartment. Oi . . . don't stop."

"I won't . . . until that pig comes down."

Had she divorced Boris while his father was still alive, she would have been forced to leave. Even a more recent divorce might have robbed her of her true desire: the apartment. It had belonged to the Volkov family for so many years that the courts might have ruled in favor of Boris. But since he had fully inherited the right to the apartment, she too could claim it—as his widow.

"Oi, Kyrozhinka, you're so wonderful!" she said as his thick hands rubbed her.

"Musya . . ."

They had planned everything scrupulously. Six months or so after Boris' death they would start dating publicly. A few months later she, the lonely widow, would invite him to move in. And then they would marry. That, of course, would mean Kyril would receive a legal permit to live in Leningrad and neither of them would ever have to return to their native village.

She glanced up again, and again saw burning lights up in the apartment. "I just hope he doesn't find Elizaveta Nikolaevna." While Boris was still unconscious, Kyril and she had crammed the old woman into the trunk by the door. "She's really beginning to smell."

"Don't worry. I locked it and still have the key." He pressed his waist firmly against her skirt. "This is like old times, eh? Just like out in the barn."

Yes, she thought. Quick, daring. Together they had helped each other survive those painful years of youth stranded in the countryside. From the start Musya had delighted in finding someone who finally needed her, had delighted in the anger that he so easily transferred to her sexually. In Musya, Kyril had found escape and a kind of comfort.

"Oi," she said, trying to squirm away. "The lights are going off. He'll be down any minute."

Like teenagers caught necking, they sprang apart and adjusted their clothes and hair. Kyril slipped off his leather jacket and handed it to Musya. She tucked it under her arm, then handed him a bag that held the gun. She touched Kyril's dark wool sweater.

"He won't recognize you without the jacket, but aren't you going to be cold?"

Always stoic, Kyril shook his head.

She kissed him one last time. "Don't fret about Boris. That husband of mine is as dumb as a fish and he won't suspect a thing. It's this gang he keeps talking about that perplexes me. You'll be careful, won't you?"

"Of course, soul of mine." He felt the hard metal

in the bag. "Don't worry. He won't know what hit him. Now get out of sight before he comes down."

She pecked him one last time on the cheek, then started north along the embankment away from Nevsky. At a bend in the river she stopped and stared back. In the distance Boris was emerging from the building and turning toward Nevsky. Then she saw Kyril—not much larger than Boris but stockier and beefier—as he shifted in the shadows and started after him.

That, she thought rapturously, would be the last she'd ever see of Boris. Kyril was following him to this silly meeting with the gang. Then Kyril would stir up some trouble and shoot Boris. The militsiya without a doubt would blame his death on a gang war and those wild Georgians. So simple, so clean. There'd be absolutely no reason to suspect Kyril or her. After that, the apartment would be hers and within a few months she and Kyril would finally be married and settled in Leningrad, the heart of Russian culture.

A moment later she saw Kyril slip onto Nevsky and disappear from sight. He was so wonderful, so strong, so assured. Who, she thought, could ask for a better cousin?

CHAPTER
15

Boris stepped around the corner and ordered a glass of tea and a meat-filled *pirozhok* at a little café. He quickly ate the pastry and was out the door in five minutes. All he had to do was catch a blue trolley bus to the end of Nevsky, meet Sergei and the gang, hop another bus home, and then be off to Lara's. And some much-needed sleep.

The misty rain having subsided, he jogged across Nevsky and headed toward the Pushkin Theatre. Boarding a trolley from the rear, he dug into his pocket and took out two two-kopeck pieces; the bus was already in motion before he and the other passengers had collected their thin paper tickets. He found a seat and settled in for the four-kilometer ride to the end of the avenue.

The electric trolley hummed along until it reached Insurrection Square—the center of the uprising against the tsarist government—and slowed to an island of greenery in front of the Moscow Station. Then the broad street shot off at an angle, becoming Old Nevsky and shrinking in size. The bus sped down this last part toward Alexander Nevsky Square, bordered on one side by the modern, curving Moscow Hotel and on the other by an ancient monastery.

At this last stop before the Neva River, Boris and a handful of other riders clambered out into the early night. He glanced to his right at the classical domed archway of the monastery, the blackness of centuries of death lurking beyond. Not much was to be seen, but Boris was well aware of the massive overgrowth of gnarled cottonwood trees, the roots of which had slowly twisted gravestones and caskets. Nature had provided a violent finale for the best of Imperial Russia who slumbered here in neglect.

Across the broad square, Boris eyed the large Moscow Hotel, its square windows ablaze with life, the sidewalk in front glutted with pedestrians. Sergei was supposed to be around here somewhere, and then they'd be off to the meeting. Just let it be quick and easy, he thought, as he followed the beige and white stone wall of the monastery.

As he neared the Neva—here strong and straight before it bent east toward the center of the city—he saw a fire-orange dot glow in a parked car. Squinting, Boris recognized the small red Zhiguli. He walked over and climbed in on the passenger's side.

"Okay, let's go," said Boris, rubbing his brow.

The little man took a long puff on his Marlboro.

120

His narrow face swelled and then, with a sigh, a slender stream of smoke filtered over his lips.

"Not so fast," Sergei insisted. "These cigarettes are almost as expensive as hashish from Afghanistan."

Boris twisted in his seat. "Come on, just start it up. Do you want me to drive?" He motioned toward the ignition.

"Drive where?" Sergei took another long drag. "We're here. We don't have to go anywhere."

The lines in Boris' forehead deepened. "What?"

"We're meeting them in there."

He let a trickle of smoke seep over his lips, then nodded past Boris. Across the sidewalk rose the wall; behind the wall spread the cemetery of the monastery. What lay inside had long ago sunk deep into death and rot.

"*Nyet!*"

"*Da, da,*" said Sergei calmly. "Where else could we meet in the middle of Leningrad and not be noticed? Everyone in there will be dead except for you and me and the gang."

"Yes, but . . . but . . ."

"But what?" Sergei shook his head in disgust. "Listen, you're the only reason we're here. You don't want to back out, do you?"

"Ah . . ." The thought of Lara catapulted forward and overrode the images of the ancient burial ground. "No. I'm ready. Let's go."

Sergei took a final drag, then reached beneath the seat, and pulled out a flashlight. He opened his door and tossed out his cigarette.

"Ready?" His hand looped back and stuffed the light in his companion's lap. "Take this. Just don't turn it on until we're deep inside."

Electric torch in hand, Boris sighed and climbed out of the car. They followed the wall toward the river, cut around the corner, off the sidewalk, and onto a grassy knoll. As they passed deeper into the deserted nook, the hotel, the busy street, and the life of Leningrad fell behind. Off to their left the waters of the Neva swirled on to the Bay of Finland. On the bank across the river, the residential towers of a new district rose out of the flatlands like artificial mountains dusted with lights.

Boris spun around and stopped still in the wet grass.

"Sergei!" he whispered.

At once his friend pressed himself against the wall. "What?"

Boris stared into the night behind them. Hadn't he heard footsteps rushing through the grass? Hadn't he seen the tip of a black shadow?

"I thought I saw someone."

The two of them melted into the shadows and peered back toward the sidewalk. A few cars and busses sped down the road and across the bridge, but the space between them and the street seemed a vacuum.

Sergei nudged Boris. "Come on. We can't stand out here."

They continued along the knoll for another twenty meters until they reached a crumbling section of the stone wall. Sergei glanced back one more time then nodded toward a small pile of stone.

"Go on. Step on that and climb over."

"Wait!"

His eyes adjusting to the faint light, Boris looked back and struggled to see gray moving across black. Only the distant lights of the city, however, greeted him.

"Come on," insisted Sergei. "No one's back there."

Hoping his friend was right, Boris caught his breath, stepped on the rocks, and dug one foot into a hole. He spread his broad shoulders wide and without too much effort pulled himself up and over. Once inside the cemetery, he pressed himself into a bush and made room for Sergei. With a huff, his friend came hurling over the top, and then they plunged into absolute darkness; the bushes and trees were like canopies that blocked out everything that lay beyond the ancient walls.

Boris had gone only a few steps when his shin cut into stone.

"Oi!"

"Tss!" said Sergei. "Careful. There are headstones all over the place."

"Where are we supposed to meet them?"

"By Dostoevsky's grave."

"Where's that?" asked Boris, pushing aside a branch.

"Somewhere up there in the Tikhvin Cemetery. This is the Lazarus. Keep the flashlight off until we're further inside."

All around them the cottonwood trees swayed in the dark wind and showered their shriveled fall leaves upon them. Boris and Sergei wove stealthily among headstones and around short iron fences marking the hundreds of graves. All around them, crumbling mausoleums spewed their stone walls into the paths and worn boards propped up fractured statues and headless angels.

After winding their way in and out of the graves for a few minutes, Boris flicked on the light.

"Do you know where we are?"

"No," sighed Sergei.

Boris lifted the lamp's beam to one of the markers. Worn letters, as if drawn in soft sand, came to life.

"Look."

There lay Natalya Alekseyevna, Peter the Great's sister. Boris stared at the tomb, transfixed by history. He glided the beam to the next gravesite, which was in a ruined pile. Spires and wreaths and figurines had been smashed from the granite edifice; sunk in the mud around it were chunks of stone hands and wings. Such, thought Boris, was the pent-up fury of the Revolution.

The wind died for a moment, and from one side they heard steps rustling through the leaves.

"They're up there," whispered Boris, pointing to the left. "Beyond the path."

"Just remember. Let me do the talking," said Sergei. "Here, give me the light."

Boris handed it over, and the two of them made their way across a path that led from the entrance to the old cathedral. They climbed into the Tikhvin Cemetery, skirted a puddle and reached a clump of trees that sat on the edge of an opening. Sergei put his fingers to his lips, motioned for Boris to stay behind a tree, then started forward. With the light pointing just ahead on the dirt path, the short man moved cautiously into the clearing.

A sharp light burst on his face.

"Ai!" cried Sergei, lifting his hands to his eyes.

Boris, behind the tree and unseen, saw the vague outlines of several men on the other edge of the opening. He couldn't distinguish any faces, but one thing he was able to recognize. Behind the light and seeping out of the dark was the bottom of a jacket. A rich, dark leather one.

"Why do you want to meet tonight?" asked the man, his Georgian accent deep and throaty. He held the beam of light steady on Sergei's face.

"It's about my friend, Boris. The truck driver."

The man laughed. "A real coward."

Automatically, Sergei said, "Yes. Absolutely."

Some friend, thought Boris, shifting behind the tree. He strained to see how many others there were but couldn't tell.

The gang leader said, "What's the problem?"

"You see, he decided . . . ah . . . he decided he really . . ."

Boris stepped from behind the tree and into the edge of the clearing.

"What he's trying to say is—"

Four men burst out of nowhere and a second electric torch seared Boris' eyes. Squinting, he made out several steel-gray pieces of metal trained on him. His heart bulged in his chest and his hands shot upward.

"—is . . . is that I don't have the stomach for this."

"Da, da, da." Sergei's voice shook. "That's right. He's a very good man, *tovarischi*." Comrades. "There's no need to worry. He just wants . . . out."

"And I wish you well with your business. Really, you can trust—"

Suddenly a branch snapped behind Boris. As he turned, he saw a gray figure dive behind a tree. Then a gun emerged, the black hole of its barrel aimed right at his head.

One of the gang members shouted, "He's not one of ours!"

The unknown man behind Boris shouted, "*Militsiya*! Stop!"

"Sergei, look out!" cried Boris.

Boris dropped to his knees just as the man behind him fired his gun. The bullet whizzed to his side, past Sergei, and slammed into the man in the leather jacket. In automatic response, three of his men leveled their weapons at the stranger near the tree. Sergei, shocked and confused, stood in the middle of it all waving his arms.

"No, no!" he cried. "There's a mistake! You—"

Without hesitation, three guns exploded with fire and bullets. Almost instantly Sergei grabbed at his chest and his throat. He cried out and splotches of red gushed from his body as he twisted and stumbled to the ground. The electric torch dropped from his hand, hit a stone, and shattered. Then the other lights were flicked off, and the cemetery fell again into blackness.

"Sergei!" shouted Boris at the empty space before him.

Hugging the muddy earth, Boris dug his fingers into the dirt and crawled to his friend. Two more shots streaked over his head as he pushed through the deep grass and around a log. Up ahead, the murky figures of the gang members dropped behind gravestones and returned gunfire.

"Get them all!" shouted the wounded leader.

Scraping his chin over rocks and fallen branches, Boris slithered across the ground. If only he could reach Sergei. He ducked behind a log, raised his head. Up ahead lay the crumpled figure of his friend.

"Sergei! Sergei!"

Several shots blazed in his direction. Then Boris heard a faint moan. A desperate gasp for air hissed and bubbled somewhere out there, followed by complete silence.

"Sergei!"

Boris leapt to his feet and ran to his friend. A shot was fired, another one. Boris dove and hit the ground, burning his cheek along the grass. He dragged himself over to his friend, wrapped his arms around him.

"Come on, Sergei, we can make it!"

Sergei, his body like ten wet blankets wrapped in a knot, didn't answer.

"Please," prayed Boris. "Sergei, please!"

Boris' shaking hand passed from a cold cheek to a splotch of hot liquid oozing from Sergei's chest. Lower, more blood bubbled as if from an artesian well. Boris grabbed at his friend's neck, pressed his hand into the muscle and found no sign of a pulsing heart.

"*Nyet!*" cried Boris.

He raised his head and scanned for an escape. With eyes as beady as a cat's, he saw the men of the gang shifting slowly to the side. He spun around, listening intently. The unknown man, the one who had fired first, was stalking along the other side, his feet pushing through the brush.

Boris reached into Sergei's pocket and pulled out the car keys. Then he wrapped his arms around his friend and scooped him up. He focused on a clump of cottonwood trees, burst to his feet, and ran, cradling Sergei. At once a bullet streaked out of the night, rushing past him and richocheting off a gravestone ahead. Another gun fired and a bullet slammed into a tree. Boris ducked to the right, the left, then back again, the body bouncing in his arms.

Then suddenly a figure leapt out from the right. Boris ducked, slipped in the mud. He tumbled to the ground with the body. Footsteps converged all around, charging in for the final kill. One last time, Boris bent over, felt for a pulse, found none. He pressed his cheek to Sergei's lips and sensed no breathing either.

Boris kissed his friend on both cheeks, then ran. Hunkered over, he tore for the trees, then dodged between the thick trunks. He smashed into a marble statue, toppled a stone woman to the ground, and ducked behind a gravestone. He started to move, but felt something like a burning poker touch his left arm. He shot forward. Running steps and heavy breathing were all around him, reverberating off tombs and markers. He tripped over a crib-like fence around a grave, tore to the right, and vaulted across the path and into the Lazarus Cemetery. Footsteps closed in on him from behind. He dove into a thick clump of bushes, their thorny branches pricking his skin and clothing.

He saw it, a crack in the night just a few meters away: the broken section of a wall. He darted toward it, lunged to the top, and threw himself over. Hitting the ground, he tumbled down the grassy knoll, rolled to his feet, and shot for Sergei's car. As he ran, he ripped off his bloodied jacket and threw it back over the cemetery wall.

By the time he reached the edge of the monastery there were pulsing sirens and flashing yellow lights erupting in the dark. The *militsiya*. A whole herd of their yellow jeeps were zooming in from every direction. If the man who had fired at him, wondered Boris, had been one of them, why wasn't the place already surrounded?

A bus pulled up, its shocked riders staring out the back window at the assemblage of *militsiya*. Boris stepped from the edge of the wall to the front bumper of the bus. Then, as if he had just disembarked, he walked from the front of the bus and calmly up the street. Every bit of his willpower rallied to prevent him from running the rest of the way to Sergei's car.

Someone slithered right up behind him on the sidewalk, and Boris jumped.

"What's going on?" asked a young man.

Boris reached for the door handle. "I . . . I don't know. Leningrad hasn't seen such activity since the war."

He glanced back toward the monastery and saw someone running along the edge of the wall. A gang member. Boris jumped in the car and brought its little engine to a roaring start. No. Calm down, he told himself. Don't give yourself away so foolishly. With both hands he released the parking brake, then sat perfectly still for a moment. He took a deep breath, and pushed down on the gas. The small red car rolled forward, leaving the running man in the dark.

His blue eyes glanced in the mirror. The way back up Nevsky was flooding with yellow jeeps, so he drove straight toward the Neva. That's what he'd do. Cross the Alexander Nevsky Bridge up ahead, circle around the city, back down Lirovsky Prospekt, then to Lara's on Vasilevsky Island. As he neared Obukhovskoy Avenue that ran along the embankment, however, he saw a sedan racing up behind him. He caught his breath. No. It couldn't be, he prayed as he passed through a green light, then onto the large bridge. Still, he couldn't help but check his mirror.

"Gospodi!"

A beige Volga sedan whipped behind him. Boris stared in the mirror, unable to believe his eyes. Yet with each moment the faces in the car grew clearer. So did the gun held out the window. His pursuers were like wolves chasing a hare.

Abruptly, metal screamed and sparked right in front of him. The car heaved, groaned, slowed. Boris twisted the wheel to the left. He'd been so busy looking back that he'd scraped the car along the bridge railing. With the lights of the Volga barreling in on him, Boris steered back into the lane, then slammed the gas to the floor.

Little by little he gained on a bus in front of him. He swerved the wheel to the left and overtook the large vehicle. He waited, letting the Volga pass behind the bus and almost reach him. Then, just as he came to the other end of the bridge, he dashed around the front of the bus. The driver leaned on his horn, but Boris was already out of the way. Just as quickly, he jabbed the wheel to the right, shot over a curb, and swerved down a circular ramp that curled around to the river's edge. Pressed against the door, Boris hung on as his Zhiguli whipped down and around. Holding the wheel steady, he checked behind and saw no sign of the Volga.

Like an amusement ride, the little car was hurled out of the ramp and onto the slick road that ran along the embankment. Just as he was about to pass beneath the bridge, though, a car came speeding the wrong way down the opposite ramp. It was the Volga sedan, and the driver bore down on the Zhiguli. Boris trod on the brakes, twisted the wheel,

131

and screeched a hundred-and-eighty degree turn. A cloud of black smoking rubber engulfed him.

"Go!" he screamed, the gas pedal flat on the floor.

Within seconds, though, the lights from the sedan embraced him. He tried to speed away, but the Zhiguli wasn't fast enough. The larger Volga sped at him, streaking from behind and up on his left side. He leaned on the steering wheel and rocked himself, trying to make the car accelerate. He glanced over. The three men in the sedan were bent in laughter. Then the one in the backseat cranked down his window and leveled his gun on Boris' temple. He was on the brink of firing when the one in the front seat grabbed him, shook his head, and pulled him back in. He shouted something and their laughter grew loud enough to reach Boris' ears.

At once, the Volga careened over, slammed into the side of the Zhiguli. The car's frame seemed to explode in pain and Boris' door crumpled inward. The automobile was hurled to the right, hit the curb and jumped up on the embankment. Boris sensed the car tilt, saw the dark waters right below, and knew the car was ready to launch itself into the Neva. With all his strength, he wrapped his arms on the steering wheel and pulled to the left. There was a thud and the car dropped off the curb and back on the road.

He glanced over at his pursuers. Laughing, they pulled away, then swooped down on him like an eagle. There was a loud crash and instantaneously the side windows disintegrated. Metal crumpled like wadded paper, and the Zhiguli was thrown off toward the river again. Racing along at seventy-five kilometers per hour, the small car teetered on the edge of the embankment as Boris wrestled with the steering wheel.

No sooner was the car back on the road than a large truck came bombing around the corner. The driver of the transport vehicle spotted the two side-by-side cars, sent his horn blaring, swerved right, and shot up and over the concrete curb. Boris' heart practically burst from his chest, and he swerved toward the river. This left the Volga in the center of the road, making it an easy target for the second, equally huge truck that next came barreling around the curve. The driver of the sedan tried to brake, but that only caused the car to swing sideways, and in the next instant the truck soared from the night and broadsided the Volga. The three gang members trapped inside shrieked like a chorus of young boys.

In horror, Boris watched from the side of the road as metal was crumpled like tissue paper. Sparks flew and bodies were crushed like rotten tomatoes. And still the force of the huge truck continued forward, hurling the Volga like a battered soccer ball upon the embankment behind Boris. For an instant, the sedan teetered on the edge, then with a loud whoosh, it dropped into the Neva and sank out of sight.

CHAPTER
16

Boris was greeted by Lara's scream.

"*Gospodi*, what happened?"

But before he could answer, before the neighbors downstairs could hear, she grabbed him and pulled him into her room. He stumbled in, his clothes damp from sweat and blood, not knowing quite how he got there. A dark fog was seeping into his skull, toying with his senses. Something quite terrible had happened and he needed sleep.

Lara began peeling away his shirt. "Boris, you're hurt and—"

He brought her hands together between his and kissed her soft fist. "They killed Sergei."

She exclaimed, "No!" recoiling in disbelief.

Ready to collapse, he turned away from her and made his way to the wooden table. He leaned on it with both hands and closed his eyes. Immediately, he saw the hailstorm of bullets and his friend crumpling to the muddy earth.

He shook away the burning memories. "Don't ask me why, but this gang told Sergei and me to meet them inside the Alexander Nevsky Monastery. In one of the old cemeteries. They were there right in front of us." A flash of the bottom of that leather coat seared his mind. "But then someone sneaked up from behind." He heard the snap of the branch. "He shouted something and . . . and all these guns fired on . . . Sergei."

"How awful!" Her eyes wet, Lara dropped onto a wooden chair. Her head fell in her hands and a mass of her light brown hair tumbled over. "Who, Boris? And why?"

Only gray against black, that's all that came to him. "I don't know."

Could there be some sort of gang war? There'd recently been an American movie on television about two rival Mafia families, each trying to eliminate the other. Perhaps that was the answer.

"I'm sure that the surprise attacker wasn't *militsiya*. He wouldn't have been alone. There would have been a bunch of them waiting outside." He gazed at the floor, his vision weak and hazy. "For some reason he was trying to cause trouble."

"Poor Sergei. . . ."

His face red with guilt, he spun to her. "I . . . I tried to help him, but there was so much confusion! He just didn't move. He couldn't believe what was happening. I went to him, but it was too late. The *militsiya* must have found him by now." Was his

135

best friend really dead? "It was as if that stranger was out for only one reason—to kill someone."

"To kill Sergei? Or you?" Her unblemished complexion was now tortured with a mass of wrinkles. She simply couldn't believe it. "But why? Boris, that just doesn't make any sense."

"I don't know," he said, drifting into a daze. "He couldn't have been after me. Maybe he wanted Sergei out of the picture so he could take over his dealings with the gang." Hadn't that been part of the American movie? Hadn't the lust for financial gain been the spark behind the bullets? "Perhaps Sergei was more deeply into the black market than I thought. Who knows? Maybe he was even dealing drugs. I hear there's a lot of *narkotiki* coming back from Afghanistan."

"No, he wouldn't," she gasped in disbelief. "Sergei did a lot of things he shouldn't have, but he wouldn't get involved in something like that."

His back to her, he heard the legs of her chair scrape the floor, then her quick, light steps. Like a warm blanket, Lara reached up and encircled his shoulders with her arms. She kissed him on the back, long and forcefully. One of her breasts pressed into him, molding itself over his arm. How he wished this had been just a wonderful night, the two of them alone. Then he could sleep this nightmare away.

"Boris, now you must go to the *militsiya*. You have to tell them everything even if . . ."

He held onto one of her hands as if it were a life rope. His mass of curly blond hair bobbed up and down. She was right, even though it meant he might be locked up, sent away. Whatever. He had to confess for Sergei's sake. His friend deserved that.

"I'll explain everything. Maybe they'll be generous." He leaned over and burrowed his cheek against hers. "But first I have to take care of Musya—make sure she's all right."

Her body suddenly tense, Lara stepped back. Pieces of the night flooded her mind, and her green eyes bounced from side to side. A terrifying realization washed over her and her fingers dug into Boris' arms.

"*Bozhe*. That man in the leather jacket—he knows where you live, doesn't he?"

"Of course. He's the head of the gang. The one who attacked me this morning. Lara, what are you getting at?"

Biting her lower lip, she looked directly up at him. "Doesn't that mean they could be on the way there now?"

His eyes widened in terror. If only he weren't so tired he would have thought of that, gone there first.

"The telephone—quick!" he shouted.

Lara rushed to her apartment door and threw it open. Boris hurried behind her, then stopped at the top of the narrow, steep stairs as Lara continued to the landing below. She mounted the stairs a second later, clutching the phone. He met her halfway, the telephone cord stretched to its limit.

"I hope it's not too late," she said from the steps beneath him. "What if—"

"She has to be all right!" he raged.

The telephone system was so slow, but finally there was a connection. Agonizing eons passed between the first ring and the second, the second and the third . . .

"Tfoo, there's no—" The receiver was picked up and he tensed. "Musya? Musya? Are you all right?"

The woman's voice sounded incredulous. "B-Boris?"

"Yes." He clutched the phone with two fists and slumped down on the stair. "It's me. Don't worry. I'm all right. But what about you?"

"Me? Me?" she asked in disbelief. "I'm . . . I'm fine. Of course I'm fine."

Her stunned voice, however, was prime evidence that she knew something was wrong. He just had to keep her calm and get her away from the apartment as quickly as possible. What if the gang leader caught her outside? That madman with the cleaver . . .

"Listen carefully and do exactly as I say." He forced himself to stay calm. "Get the car keys from my dresser, take your coat and your purse, and leave the house at once. Immediately, Musya. That gang's following me and they may be on their way to the apartment."

There was silence on the other end. Boris, clutching the phone, glanced up at Lara, who was focused on his every word. Then he looked beyond her, checking the hall downstairs to make sure no one was eavesdropping.

He rubbed a forefinger up and down the ridges of his brow. "Musya?"

The voice was faint. "I . . . I . . ."

"Listen, it's all very complicated, but you'll be fine if you leave right away. Please do that." He wouldn't be able to live with himself if he were responsible for her death too. "There's a gang war going on with a bunch of crazy Georgians. Sergei—"

"Sergei?"

"Yes, Sergei. For once would you just listen to me?" he shouted into the receiver. "Someone might have wanted him out of the way. He . . ."

Boris caught himself. No, he couldn't go into it now. She might panic or freeze or call the *militsiya*. He'd explain later when he could comfort her.

"Musya," he said in a tortured voice, "you simply must leave the apartment. Just grab your coat. Take the car. You know where it is around the corner?"

"But, Boris—"

"Go, Musya! Now," he said, with a pained look at Lara. "Watch out, though, for any strangers in the hall or downstairs."

"I understand." Her voice sounded stronger. "But Borinka, are you all right, my love?"

"I'm fine."

His mind flew over Leningrad, searching its canals and streets for a safe place. He thought of a small wooded park far from Nevsky Prospekt and the monastery.

"Meet me at Revolution Square in half an hour. Pull the car up on the north side. I'll be there."

"All right. Revolution Square."

"And you'll leave this very minute?"

"*Da, da.* This very moment." Musya's voice melted softly. "And Boris .. I love you."

The receiver pressed to the side of his face, he opened his mouth but he was unable to echo her affection. At a total loss, he slammed down the receiver, slumped against the wall, and sighed in relief. Lara squeezed onto the step next to him and started rubbing his neck.

"She'll be all right, Boris."

His voice was thin. "I'm sure of it. But I just want to be done with her."

"Believe me, I do too. You did just fine, though. Don't worry."

Lara's thin fingers lovingly kneaded his muscles, his worries. She was so adept at that, calming him, making life livable. Wasn't that, he thought, one of the reasons he loved her? Yes. The world slowed when they were together. Slowed to a speed that didn't leave him dizzy.

He opened his eyes. Mud and blood were smeared across his clothing as if he'd just come from some hedonistic ritual.

"I can't go out like this."

"No, you can't."

Lara rose, lifted the phone from his lap, and scurried down the stairs. So calm, he thought. So smooth. She moved as if she had complete control of the situation. He took solace in that. When she started back up the stairs, he found her eyes like rich magnets, drawing him toward her. He rose, caught her in his arms, and kissed her.

"Come on, silly," she said, withdrawing from him.

Boris followed to her room, where he sat on the edge of her table. His eyes on her hands, he watched her fingers grab at a curtain and throw it open. A closet emerged, and she started digging. A pile of sweaters was tossed aside first, then some white underclothes. At the bottom she reached a plastic bag.

"Here," she said. "This was supposed to be your New Year's present."

He tried to catch her but caught the bag instead. The plastic crumpled loudly in his grip, and when he opened it he found a brand new pair of deep-blue pants. Pulling them out, he held them to his waist. The length was perfect.

"*Jeanzi!*" The tags were still attached, with words other than Russian proclaiming the product's beauty and strength. His smile was quick and for an instant the horror of the night was gone. "Lara, they must have cost a fortune. Where'd you get them?"

"From a Danish woman. She was studying at the University and wanted some copies of Dostoevsky and Akhmatova. There weren't any in the stores so I traded her mine." They'd come from Lara's huge collection, built from the access she had to books at *Dom Knigi*. "You know, books for *jeanzi*. They're West German. Sorry I couldn't get American. Now hurry up and change. I don't have a shirt that'll fit, but you can take your sweater."

The periphery of his vision suddenly throbbed light and dark like some sort of power failure. He grabbed at the edge of the table, felt himself sway.

"Boris?"

He blinked once, twice, rubbed his whiskery chin. "I'm . . . I'm fine."

Motionless, he watched as she grabbed at the bottom of the large sweater—his sweater—that she always wore. From beneath the thick wool emerged her stomach, the prized Polish bra that he'd given her and that so nicely cupped her breasts, then a mass of tangled hair. Boris reached to take her in his arms, but Lara instead tossed the piece of clothing in his face. Then she slipped on a plain blouse and crossed to the hot plate, where she put on a kettle of water.

Dropping the sweater onto the edge of the bed, Boris fumbled with his belt and the buttons of his pants. With his soiled clothing dropped to the floor, he pulled on the stiff pair of jeanzi.

"They're perfect," he said, and then slipped off his shirt.

From a cold teapot Laura poured a bit of tea concentrate in a tall thin glass. She flicked her hair over shoulder and turned around with her gentle smile. Then her face went blank.

"Boris, you're bleeding."

He sat on the bed and touched his left arm. Just above the elbow his skin was sticky and warm. He retracted his hand, then rubbed his bloody fingertips together as if to verify the substance. His vision pulsed light and dark again.

A weak laugh bubbled out of his throat. "I thought I was just tired."

His eyes settled shut and he leaned against the iron headboard. She was at his side at once.

"Oi!" he cried when she pressed the raw skin.

"Sit still." She studied the wound. "It's a deep graze. The skin's split, but there's nothing inside."

His eyes popped open. There was no time to sit here. He pulled his arm from her.

"I have to get to Musya, make sure no one hurts her."

Her lips touched his cheek and she held him down. "Always worried about others, aren't you? Just give me a minute to wash and bandage you."

For strength, she also insisted that he drink first one glass, then two, of black Georgian tea, each with four spoonfuls of sugar. Glad to be pampered, he sipped at the steaming beverage, the liquid resuscitating him, as she cleansed his arm. By the time she strapped on a bandage, his vision had improved and his muscles were eager to make haste. He pulled on the large sweater. As he swallowed the last of the tea, she dabbed at his face with a clean damp towel.

"I have to go." He started to rise but she caught him by the hand.

"Wait."

She hurried to the closet, where she dropped to her knees. Shoes and socks came flying out as she clawed her way down to the floor. A moment later, she grabbed at a floorboard and threw aside a piece of wood. She reached into a hole, then kneeled back, her hands cradling a wad of material.

"Lara?"

She glanced at him, reached back into the hole and took out a small box. "Mama gave me this before she moved down to Novgorod. She was worried about my living alone in the city." Her lips puckered in a frown. "It's so ancient I'm not sure it works. My grandfather carried it during the Revolution."

Boris tried to imagine what value something from the Revolution would be to Lara—and to him tonight. Only one thing from those violent times came to mind.

"Lara, you don't mean that's a . . ."

On her knees, she scooted to the table and unfolded an old shirt. First the silvery barrel, then the trigger of a gun emerged.

"Dyed Sasha—my mother's father—said this saved his life during the Revolution and he could never part with it. Neither could my mother because it reminded her of him." She unwrapped two bullets and handed them to Boris. "That's all there are. Mama threw all of them into the river except these two. She was going to have them converted into cuff links for Papa but she never did." She looked up at Boris like a puppy begging for affection. "Even if this gun doesn't work, you have to take it—for luck. It saved my grandfather's life and it might save yours."

Stunned, he looked at her, then back at the pistol.

144

He'd never seen a weapon in anyone's home before, couldn't believe she owned one. If the authorities ever learned this, she could be imprisoned. . . .

Still kneeling before him, she said, "Boris, take it."

He rewrapped the gun and took the package in his hands. He'd held a gun in the army, but never since.

"I'll take it for good luck. All I want is to return to you." He kissed Lara on the head. "I love you."

She wrapped her arms around his waist, buried her head in his stomach. "Be careful."

He clutched her tightly, wanting part of her spirit to meld into him. Then he wouldn't be alone when he left.

"I'll be back as soon as I can."

He kissed the top of her head, rose, and carefully placed the gun in the plastic bag that had held the *jeanzi*. With a sigh, he made his way to the door. His hand touched the knob. There was no choice but to go, no other method of clearing the way to the future.

"I'll never forgive myself if they hurt Musya."

Behind him, Lara's voice was faint. "I understand, Boris. I want you to go. Really, I do. It's the only way you and I will ever be happy."

Gun in hand, he opened the door and headed off to Revolution Square.

Musya's pudgy fist slammed down the phone. It couldn't be true. This was impossible. Please, she thought, let me wake up. This nightmare must end. After all their work, she and Kyril deserved a reward. Not punishment. Now what was going to become of the caviar, the cutlets Pojarsky, and the silky sour cream she'd bought for tonight?

Kyril's voice hummed over the flow of the kitchen faucet. He was never, never this happy. She'd never even heard him sing before. Against the background of pouring water, she heard his melody rise and fall as he scrubbed up. Musya waited until the water was choked off, and Kyril, rubbing a towel between his hands, stepped into the living room. She hadn't seen that big white face so elated in months, years.

"What's the matter?" he asked blithely.

His sleeves pushed up, Kyril dried the moisture from his hands and wrists. He hummed a few more bars and glanced back over at his lover. "Ready for some champagne? I'll go—"

"*Nyet.*"

"Musya?"

"I . . . I . . ."

Kyril forced a smile. "You look like you've seen a ghost."

"No . . . but I've just spoken with one!"

The smile shrank from his face and the darkness boiled back into his eyes.

"What?" He cocked his head sideways.

Not able to bear looking at him, she stared out the window. "We can forget about our feast—our champagne and the cutlets Pojarsky. We can forget about our first night in our new bed, too." She tapped the phone. "That was Boris."

"*Nyet!*"

"*Da-a-a*. He's alive."

"That's impossible—there were bullets flying everywhere!" He threw the towel to the floor, then started pacing behind the sofa. "With my very own eyes I saw him fall to the ground! Musya, I left him for dead!"

She screwed up her fiery eyes and shouted, "I tell you that was him! I swear it!"

"Tfoo—that pig! How did he come out of the water dry? I can't believe it. I almost got killed myself. He was hit, wasn't he? Tell me that's true at least, please!"

"I . . . I don't know. He didn't say." Sniffling, she mumbled, "He said something about Sergei, but—"

"That friend of his? He's dead, for sure. He just stood there, the flashlights trained on him. He was hit a half-dozen times. But how did that slime of a man escape? Musya, I swear it! I saw Boris fall to the ground."

"Well, apparently he wasn't dead when he fell!"

Tears pushed at her eyes and her lower lip trembled and swelled out even more. They'd had it all worked out, their night to celebrate. A feast. Hour after hour of lovemaking. Then, in the early hours of the morning, they would take the trunk that held Lila Nikolaevna out to the forest and bury it. Such a perfect evening. Ruined. Overcome with self-pity, she turned away from Kyril and wiped her eyes.

"Just how do you think you're going to get a residency permit to stay in Leningrad if that worthless fish is swimming around alive? What do you want to do, go back to the village?" A loud wail bubbled from her lungs and she buried her face in her hands.

"Well, what did he say?" he taunted. "Come on, out with it."

She lifted up a piece of paper on which she'd managed to scrawl the message. "Revolution Square. He . . . he said to leave the apartment because it might be dangerous. He wants to meet there in a half-hour." She dropped onto the sofa.

"Meet? You? He still doesn't think you . . . ?"

She turned to Kyril, shook her head, and smiled through her tears.

"Musya, how did you ever marry someone so dumb?"

"I . . . I don't know. How could *I* have been so

148

dumb to marry someone so dumb?'' She pressed her hands to her face, blotted away the tears. ''I guess that was a blessing, though. I mean, Kyril, he doesn't suspect a thing. We could still kill him, couldn't we?''

''I should hope so!''

''Good, and I want to help this time. She slammed the cushion with her fist. ''Damn him! How typical! He's so despicable. He does nothing with his life. He has no ambition, you know? He never takes the initiative, never sets out to accomplish things. He just reacts. And how is this person rewarded, this person who watches the world go by? He always comes out ahead, that's how! He makes me so mad I . . . I could just strangle him with my bare hands! Oi, why didn't I just chop him in two myself this morning! Then we'd have only bones and flesh to be rid of instead of a slimy worm that won't die!'' She squinched up her nose, caught a whiff of death in the air, waved her hand at the trunk. ''Ach, and we still have Lila Nikolaevna to dispose of!''

''Now, now, my love.'' He leaned over, wrapped his thick fingers around her shoulders, pressed. ''Just relax. We'll figure out something.''

She whined, ''But how could one person be so hard to kill?''

''He has the luck of the passive.''

''But luck is *made*. That's what we're trying to do, you and I. Make our own luck.''

''*Da, da*, you're right. In the end those who try to make order out of chaos receive their just rewards. And we will succeed. We will. Trust me, my love. It's just that the most simple people—like Boris—are often the most difficult to deal with.''

She shook her head. "You don't understand. He's spent all his life trying not to rock the boat. And what does this person—this creature who's not even worth an empty egg shell—get for that? A car, a dacha, the finest apartment in Leningrad—everything! He's incredible. Everything that we want, that we've been so patient about and worked so hard for, has always just been dropped in Boris' lap! That's what I really hate about him. It's not fair!''

"So what did he say?" Kyril asked impatiently. "Tell me everything."

"He spoke of some kind of gang war or some such nonsense. Can you believe it? He went to the head of this gang—this leader in the leather jacket—to promise that he'd be a good little boy and wouldn't spill the beans about the black market. And now he thinks he's caught between the hammer and the anvil in some sort of rivalry.''

"It's a miracle he survived and wasn't caught by the *militsiya*.''

"A miracle? No. it's *kashmar*!'' A nightmare. "He isn't the least suspicious. Can you believe I'm married to such a fool?''

"Not for long. I promise, Musinka, my love. I'd let myself be caught and executed just to be able to kill him for you.''

"*Nyet*! Kyril you mustn't talk like that. We mustn't let anything—especially Boris—separate us.''

150

He moved to her, then took her hand and kissed it. "I already have an idea. Revolution Square, is it?" He kissed each of her knuckles with his rough lips. "And you want to help?"

Her head bobbed quickly up and down. *"Da, da, da!"*

"Then you can be the luscious bait, all right?"

"Oi, *da*!"

He bit at her fingers. She laughed and wrinkled up her pointy nose.

"Oi," she sighed. *"Shto delat?"* What is to be done? "Such is our life, eh, Kyryozhinka? Both of us born in a little stinking village and the only person worth a kopeck is your cousin." She laughed, thought back over the years. Always they were together, in childhood as friends, then since their mid-teens as eager lovers in a barn. "Look at what we've been given and no matter what we try to do, fate is fate."

"That's why we have each other, my love."

"Boris, too, unfortunately." She pulled one of his hands to her mouth and kissed it. "Come on. Boris wanted me to hurry."

She ran into the bedroom for her car keys. Then she dug into a dresser drawer for one of her latest acquisitions: a large T-shirt with English writing on it. She pulled it out and slipped it over her blouse. With a glance in the mirror, she primped herself and rushed out.

"Well, what do you think?" she asked, modeling the shirt.

R. D. ZIMMERMAN

Kyril stared at it but couldn't make out the English phrase. "What's it say?"

Using her finger as a guide, with a thick accent Musya read, *"I shot J. R."* She translated it for him. "Don't you love it? It has something to do with a cowboy who was killed in America."

"Ah, murder on the streets," he smiled as he admired it. "Only the Americans would make a game of it."

"But it's perfect for tonight. I traded Nina a pair of gold earrings for it." She slipped on her rain coat. "Do you have your gun?"

Kyril nodded, and they were out the door like two mischievous students. Musya locked the door, then paused at the top of the stairs.

"We won't have any problem this time, will we?" she asked.

Kyril kissed her on the check. "Don't worry, my love. After all, what could be an easier target than an unarmed man in a deserted park?"

CHAPTER 18

For fear of being stopped by the *militsiya* for driving a damaged car, Boris left Sergei's Zhiguli in an alley and walked from Lara's. He was certain he'd be able to catch a taxi either on Sredny Prospekt or on Makarova Embankment. He was wrong, and after a few blocks he was reconciled to arriving as fast as possible on foot. Cutting behind the Peter and Paul Fortress—where there was no road—might even, he thought, be faster than a taxi.

As he walked, the wind whipped up the Malaya Neva in cold damp swirls, chilling the Finnish granite embankment and everything else it could embrace. Even in the dark Boris could see the river water bent back in tiny waves against its flow. With a touch more rain and wind, the entire river could back up to flood stage. The dark waters would spill over all, pavement and stone houses alike. The city of forcefully tamed rivers and islands would be defeated by nature.

The air blasted through the woolen threads of his sweater, seeming to push right through his pores and chill his bones. His head bent, the plastic bag with the gun clutched to his stomach, he crossed the Malaya Neva. He bent over further as he neared the university's Dormitory No. 6, the residence of the foreign students; he had to avoid them and any black marketeers that lingered nearby. He had caused enough trouble tonight and he didn't want his new *jeanzi* attracting attention. Then he passed the moored sailboat, the *Kronverk*, that had been converted into a bar, and trotted his way across a wooden bridge and onto Zayachi Island, which was occupied entirely by the Peter and Paul Fortress. Just before the towering defense walls, he cut left and followed a dirt path along the canal. The air was still here, and he saw no one along his way until he reached the wooden bridge at the other end of the island, crossed it, and emerged at the tip of Lenin Park. Revolution Square, dense with tall trees, lay to his right, directly across Kirovsky Prospekt. He slapped his forehead.

"Musya . . ." he muttered in frustration.

There, too, was his Moskvich, parked right out on Kirovsky. He'd told her to go to the north side, wait for him there in a less trafficked place. Here she was, though, on the west edge, the car as obvious as the sun in the sky and, parked directly beneath a street lamp, shining almost as brightly.

He leaned against a tree. Oi, Musya, he thought,

154

rubbing the tense ridges of his brow. It's a miracle we lasted this long. You've never listened to anything I've said.

As he pushed on, the plastic bag crinkled in his hands. The gun. Oi yoi yoi. He'd forgotten about it. *Slava bogu*—thank god—he wasn't going to need the thing. Its metal burned cold right through the plastic, seared its meaning into his soul: death. That was the gun's aroma. Blood and violence. He'd endured enough of that in the past day to last a lifetime. So just get rid of it, he told himself.

He turned back toward the embankment. He could hurl the gun like a dead fish out into the Neva, where it would sink to the dark bottom. Lara would understand if he didn't return with her grandfather's gun; all that mattered was that the slow return to sanity got underway. Within seconds he could be rid of the pistol, within minutes he could be rid of his wife.

He stopped. Subtle groans—passionate ones—wafted his way. His blue eyes followed the curved lines of the embankment's iron railing, passed over the double-headed tsarist eagles so finely crafted. There. Two figures. A couple embraced, lips touching, and their dark figures stood outlined as one against the distant golden dome of St. Isaac's. Cool love on a damp night.

He spun on his soles. Just be done with this, he told himself, as he marched back toward Kirovsky. Don't worry about the gun. Just don't take it out of the bag. Tell Musya you no longer love her, send her to a friend's for a few days, then rush back to

155

Lara. She and your baby are waiting for you. They're the ones who really want you, really need you. Without stopping, he ran through the park, across the empty Kirovsky Prospekt and toward Revolution Square. . . .

As he drew closer to the Moskvich, he realized something was wrong. Panic rose in his throat. Musya wasn't in the car. His long legs carried him right up to the tiny vehicle; he smashed against the window.

"Musya! Musya!"

He bent over and peered through the windows. Nothing but empty vinyl seats. She wasn't there, not even curled up sleeping in the back. *Gospodi*! He ripped open the door. Her black plastic purse was on the floor beneath the steering wheel, its contents strewn everywhere. Something was very wrong. Musya would never leave her money and passport and cosmetics behind.

He slammed the door. Hunched behind the car he felt the outlines of the gun's handle through the wrinkled plastic. She had to be here unless . . . unless those thugs picked her up. Perhaps they caught her at the apartment, forced her to tell her where they could find him. Scanning the streets, though, he saw only a distant tram and sparks from its overhead wires. All decent people were at home with their families.

He peered over the roof of the car. Tall and thin trees, planted after the war's destruction, reached to the sky like wooden cornstalks. Off to his left, through the fizzled fall leaves, the double minarets of the pre-Revolutionary mosque poked into the night; outlines that appeared like enormous robots.

Into the little forest of Revolution Square, he called, "Musya!"

Nothing but silence. No cars. No busses. No trucks. No pedestrians. Only the quiet hum of a sleeping city. A strong city, secure in itself that—

"Boris!"

He lunged out over the car roof. "Musya!"

No response came. Only silence as penetrating as the dampness. Shuffle. Shuffle. Step. Step. Step. Someone was running.

"Ai!"

"Musya!" he shouted.

It was her. Yes, he was positive. That shrill voice had almost broken his eardrums any number of times, railing at him, going on and on, how she wanted this pair of shoes or that jacket with the writing in English on the back. The pitch was different this time, though. A tight, new cry he'd not heard before but that could only mean one thing: danger.

He dropped behind the car and pulled open the plastic bag. A bullet. That's all he needed. A bullet or two from the bottom of the bag, an arrow of death that might ensure him life. His chilled hands fumbled with the tiny pieces of metal, then as awkward as a drunk, he loaded the bullets into the pistol. But would the antique even work? Could a gun from the era of the tsars come awake and actually fire? It had to. Life and death are before you, he told himself; they are waiting in Revolution Square. Concentrate on nothing but here, now.

He gripped the pistol, but kept it hidden in the bag. Just in case. He wanted to protect himself, yet he didn't wish to be caught by the militsiya with a firearm. So with the bag aimed in front of him, he started into the small forest. Under the street lamp, where artificial light melted into natural darkness, he waited for his eyes to adjust. Sturdy tree trunks appeared all around. A few bushes. And all the while the robot-like towers of the mosque stared down upon him.

Step. Swish. Step. Step. Step. There on the right he saw a figure scurry down a path. The hushed noise disappeared. The person faded, indistinguishable from the trunks. Boris edged off the path, continued along the grass, continued aiming the bottom of the bag out in front of him. The unseen danger was there, somewhere.

Suddenly someone ran crosswise through the center of the forested square. Short and round, the figure was easily identifiable.

"Musya!"

"Ai!" she screamed.

She didn't stop, didn't seem to recognize his voice. Just escaping. In some sort of panic, that's all she apparently wanted. But escape from what? From whom?

He darted forward. He came to a crosspath, jumped over a low bush, and came down a half-step ahead of himself. One leg started to buckle as he stumbled. His hands flew forward to catch his falling body, and the gun and the bag tumbled out of his hand. He landed on his knees on the far side of the path. He raised his head. No Musya. Instead, only some twenty meters away, he saw a person just as familiar: the man in the leather jacket. In the shadows of night, Boris saw yet a darker object, a black extension of the man's arm. A gun aimed at him.

Boris dove to the side and a split-second later heard a crack of gunfire. Almost instantaneously he heard a splattering of lead and damp wood behind him. Then someone running. No—*two* people running. One toward him. Another away. Musya?

"Run, Musya!" he shouted.

Frantic, he lunged across the grass for his bag. Moisture seeped through one knee of his *jeanzi*. What was it? Water, he told himself. It's cold water. Not blood. Just get the bag. The bag with the grandfatherly gun and the bullets that were meant to be cuff links. If only . . . if only . . .

He looked up. His assailaint was magnified tenfold with each of his lunging steps and a gun like a bayonet stuck out from the shadowy figure. Precious seconds ticked by. Boris feared there was no time to pull his own pistol from the bag.

From the outside, his fingers groped through folds of plastic, hit hard metal inside. But was that the trigger or the barrel or . . . ? *Gospodi.* No time! The man in the leather jacket skidded on the wet walk, then steadied his aim. Boris lifted the clumsy bag, then swung the deep end of it toward the heart beneath the leather jacket. He squeezed. That wasn't

the trigger. His finger dug deeper through the outside of the bag, clenched onto something. The trigger clicked, slamming metal against metal, but the
antique gun didn't fire.

Boris squeezed the lever again and again and
again . . .

Then finally the two guns—one clutched by Boris
and one held by the stranger in the leather jacket—
blasted together in deathly harmony.

CHAPTER
19

Long before Kyril's first shot was fired, Musya had reached the north end of the park. She slowed and looked back over her shoulder as she continued walking. There! A big hulk of a man walked. Such a nice figure, her Kyril's. Such a masculine figure. So sexy back there in the dark, scouting out Boris. The final kill. At last. At long last. Kyril, she knew, would easily dispatch Boris. Finally she'd be a widow. How exciting, she thought. She'd never have to share a bed again with that peasant of a husband. Ach. How she hated the feel of that body, that clean smell that forever emanated from its pores. There was no excitement.

Her arms pinning down her large breasts, Musya trotted down a path. Now that she had lured Boris into the depths of the park, her job was to circle around to the car on Kirovsky Prospekt. Then she'd

drive back to the north side of the park, pick up
Kyril, and they'd take off, following Prospekt
Maxim Gorky. She just had to be quick about it.
This was a safe city and its citizens were militant
about keeping it so. A shot at night would be re-
ported by almost everyone who heard it; the *militsiya* would be here within minutes.

She turned the corner, saw her car—*da*, she
thought, scratching her pointy nose, it would be
hers within minutes—sitting beneath the street light.
She had to keep low here, not attract Boris's attention before Kyril had a chance to fire. She crouched
down, touched some bushes, peered into the trees.
Wait for a shot before rushing to the car. That way
Boris wouldn't see her, run to her, perhaps making
it more difficult for Kyril to kill him. Soon . . .

Soon her new life would begin, the one she'd been
longing for. She and Kyril. Full-time lovers. Mates.
Husband and wife. There'd be no more of this
sneaking around as if she were a prostitute. Actually, that's what she'd been to Boris. A prostitute.
Legal perhaps, but all the same, someone who
spread her legs for something besides love. How
she hated all that she'd been forced to tolerate. She
thought of Boris' smily face, that curly hair matted
on his chest. Oi! How had she ever done it?

Da, *da*, she mumbled and pulled a clump of
mousy brown hair back over her shoulder. For love.
Her and Kyril's love was a special one that had fed
her courage every time she doubted her actions.
How wonderful it would all be now . . .

The first shot cracked through the night. Deep

and loud, it echoed in the stillness like a sonic boom. Sharp and distinct. Perhaps, thought Musya, other citizens might think it was a jet or just a truck—a high-powered foreign truck—backfiring in the night.

She rose, headed for the Moskvich, a glow of relief seeping through her body. The cruiser *Aurora*, that during the Revolution had fired "the shot heard around the world," was moored just down the embankment. For her this shot just fired was an equal symbol of liberation. She was free of her oppressor. A jubilant widow who could . . .

Suddenly a small explosion rocked the night. Musya froze as still as a deer. *Gospodi.* Was that another shot? Or . . . two guns fired at once, just a millisecond off? What had happened? Had Kyril needed a second and a third bullet to kill Boris? No, her husband couldn't be that difficult to murder. But . . .

"Oi!" she cried, her hand to her mouth when the echo of the gunshots rumbled back off a distant building.

That couldn't be Kyril firing alone. Two guns meant there were two people. Either Boris had a gun—but where would that oaf get one?—or there was someone else. Perhaps the *militsiya*. *Nyet*, not that.

She ran for the car. Please, she begged, let Boris be dead. Let Kyril be alive and well.

She fumbled for the keys in her coat pocket and hurled the car door open. She revved the engine, stabbed the transmission into gear, and set the tires spinning.

Hurry, she told herself. Hurry! The *militsiya* will be here any minute, and Kyril might be hurt, Kyril might be dying!

CHAPTER
20

By some miracle, the plastic bag blew apart in Boris' hands. With a burst of light, a bullet tore out of the gun's barrel, shredded the plastic, raced toward the man in the leather jacket. The antique's explosion was so noisy that Boris didn't even hear his opponent's gun.

The moment his gun fired, Boris rolled to the ground, hurling the plastic bag out in front of him. As he ducked, he saw a flash of fire explode from the other gun, and again the bullet streaked past. The leader of the gang, however, was not so fortunate. Smug and overconfident, ready to enjoy a clean kill, he hadn't foreseen any danger in the crumpled bag that Boris had clutched before him.

Boris heard a grunt, knew he'd hit the man in the leather jacket. He saw the dark figure cringe in a pained spasm, heard a shocked groan. Then he, the gang leader, raised the gun again in Boris' direction.

Boris hugged the earth, ripped at the shredded bag like a drowning man clawing for air. He had to find the pistol in the shreds of material, free it. One bullet left and he couldn't waste it on a chance shot. Hurry, he screamed at himself, before your brains are splattered like kasha all over the bushes. He was a living target, pinned here to the ground. A man all but tied to a post for execution. He heard steps. *Bozhe*. I'm dead, he thought. He tore the bag away and grabbed the butt. Then he swung around, tensing to fire at the gang leader and blast him into the sky.

The man in the jacket wasn't there. To Boris' surprise, there was no gun aimed down his throat, no one ready to kill him. Perplexed, he moved forward on his knees. Craning his head, he heard scratchy steps hustling down the walk. There, some thirty meters away, he saw a hunched figure hobbling deeper into the park.

Boris grabbed the remains of the bag and, gun in hand, scrambled to his feet. He ran to the path, where he spotted the leather-jacketed figure diving into the woods. He charged on, saw no sign of the man, then heard a noise behind him and skidded to a stop. At the far end of the walk, at the western most edge of the park, he saw his car, the Moskvich. A figure was in it, charging the engine as if it were a race car. Just barely could he make out the driver's profile.

"Musya!" he screamed.

She couldn't hear him over the roar of the motor. His feet spitting bits of gravel behind him, he charged in that direction. She didn't see him, though, and popped the car in gear and took off in a flash.

"Tfoo!" he cursed.

Musya must have realized her mistake, must now be heading to the north side of the park where he'd told her to meet him. Of all the stupid things. Of all the stupid times for her to follow his precise directions. He had to catch her, leap in the car. They both had to flee. The *militsiya* would soon flood this area with their yellow jeeps and their flashing lights. If the gang didn't do them in first, then both he and Musya were likely to end up in a cell.

Though he ran with all his might, he felt as if he were running through mud. No matter how hard he tried, he couldn't work his legs fast enough. Sweat-saturated, he reached the western edge of the park, then cut north. Through the trees he saw the glowing of a car's taillights.

"Musya!" he gasped.

But he was too late. As he rounded the corner, he glimpsed his car in the distance. And then it was gone from sight.

He clopped to a halt. Bending over, he grasped his waist, trying to replenish his oxygen supply. His insides stabbed with pain. He needed to rest.

But he couldn't. He glanced up the empty road. Musya. He had to find her, find the wife he so desperately wanted to divorce and abandon for the rest of his life. She had vanished, however, as cleanly as if a cow had licked her away with its tongue.

Then, like a great owl raising its voice, he heard the gently arching squeal of tires rise in the night. First one set, then another and another. The *militsiya. Gospodi.* He spun around and saw dozens of headlights oozing forward. Forward to him. They were coming from all over now. He was caught, caught in a web of lights and noise that was certain to wrap itself around him, imprison him forever.

CHAPTER

21

$\mathcal{T}$he tears in Musya's eyes were so thick that she swerved all over the street like the drunkest of drivers. In her work at the hospital she had seen plenty of blood and death, but neither had ever been so close to her own heart. Kyril was bent over in the passenger seat right next to her, his head on his knees, groaning with pain and clutching his arm. She felt horrified, helpless.

He sat up and shouted, "Stop looking at me! Watch the road!"

"Oi, I can't!"

She sped through a red light.

"Look out!" he screamed.

A yellow bus, long and empty and flying at full speed, raced into the intersection. She jerked the wheel to the right, pressed the gas, then swerved back to the left. As the bus sounded its angry horn, the little Moskvich skirted the front of the huge vehicle like a mouse escaping the claws of a cat. Musya sighed with relief until she saw a *militsiya* jeep speeding directly toward them, its headlights illuminating her face. She froze—unable to turn the wheel, unable to take her foot off the accelerator—until it sped past them and continued on its way to Revolution Square.

"Be careful, so they don't stop us," he ordered. "Circle around north and head back that way. Get off this main street."

She stared at him. "Oi, Kyryozha!"

"Watch the road!"

She wiped her nose with the back of her hand, unable to stop her tears. Her loved one was in pain. And the blackish blood—it was everywhere.

"He had a gun!" shouted Kyril, holding his wounded arm.

"I'm so sorry, my little pet."

"Where did that idiot get a gun?"

"I . . . I don't know! He's never owned one. I don't know what's happened to Boris, what he thinks he was doing! How could someone do this to you? Oi, I hate that man. I hate him!"

Sniffling, she steered through a series of back streets until she circled around and came to Prospekt Maxim Gorky. She glanced to her left, saw the distant lights of jeeps four or five blocks down toward Revolution Square. Turning right, she followed the arching avenue around Lenin Park, past the metro stop, past the zoo.

"Does it hurt, my love?"

"Of course it hurts!"

They passed beneath a street light and the right shoulder of his leather jacket glowed a sticky red. A bullet had pierced the upper half of Kyril's left arm, and blood was gushing from the wound. He'd dropped the pistol on the floor before him and now clutched his torn leather jacket and arm with his right hand.

"Just keep pressure on it," said Musya, beginning to calm herself.

"What do you think I'm doing, trying to suck the blood out?"

"*Nyet*, I . . . I . . ."

"If only I'd known that bastard had a gun. It was supposed to be an easy kill."

"Tss-tss. Of course it was. Just relax, *dusha maya*." My soul. "Don't upset yourself. I have my medical kit back at home. I'll take care of you. Everything will be fine."

"I might have hit him, too." He blinked, his dark eyes heavy, his mind sluggish. "I . . . I don't know."

She passed the Exchange on the tip of Vasilevsky Island, then continued onto the Palace Bridge and over the Neva. The Winter Palace loomed to her left, and she raced between that and the Admiralty, swerved right, then turned left at the beginning of Nevsky Prospekt. Not too fast, she told herself. The street was empty and a speeding car would be an easy target for the *militsiya*. It wasn't too far now. They'd be home in minutes.

"Why didn't I divorce him years ago? Why didn't I just forget about that stupid apartment?" She slammed her palm against the steering wheel, then wiped her nose again. "If Boris comes back, I'll kill him with my own hands."

There were only several busses and a few scattered pedestrians as they sped down Nevsky. Just before the Anichkov Bridge, Musya turned left along the Fontanka Canal. She drove a few meters before pulling to the curb in front of her apartment building.

"You just get me bandaged up and . . ." His mouth was moving as if it were wired shut. ". . . and I'll take care of your husband. This time for sure."

"Not without my help," she snapped. "Just the thought of it calms me down. Better yet, let me kill him myself. Let me squish the life right out of him."

That would be her salvation. That was the way she would avenge what Boris had done to Kyril. The excitement glowing across her high cheeks, she turned to her lover.

"Well, what do you think? That's a great idea, eh? I'll kill Boris myself and—"

The body in the seat next to her was slumped against the door. She touched him, felt no life.

"Kyril!" she screamed. "Kyril!"

CHAPTER

22

Boris spotted his only chance to escape the *militsiya*. The triangular strip of land, a separate island of Lenin Park, right across the street from Revolution Square. He dashed across Kirovsky Prospekt, leaping over two sets of streetcar rails. Reaching the sidewalk, the gun in the plastic bag cradled against his side, he dove into a stand of bushes. A yellow jeep screamed around the corner, two men in uniforms in the front seat. They saw him, Boris was certain. Get rid of the gun, he told himself. Hurl it as far away as possible. If they find you with that gun, it'll be Siberia.

Still as a leaf, he peered out from the bush as the first, second, and third jeep raced toward the square. He was positive one of the men looked right at him, but none of the jeeps stopped. Blue lights flashing, the three vehicles continued to the far end of Revolution Square.

Boris headed north. The *militsiya* would split up, circle around, search the entire area. To his right loomed the October Revolution Museum and the stark minarets of the closed mosque. Two more jeeps were coming down another street. *Gospodi.* He was caught between two fires. Hunkered over, he tore from tree to bush to tree to bench. Lonely paths and withering autumn plants fell behind. Avoiding the glowing lamp posts, he reached the north end of the park and hid behind a bush. Glancing back, he saw headlights bounce upward and jag into the sky as a jeep drove over a curb and into the park. Like a hungry shark, the *militsiya* vehicle passed down a slowly curving path, stalking its prey.

Across the street he spotted his salvation: the Gorkovskaya metro station, there in the main part of Lenin Park, its lights a beacon of safety. He looked back. The headlight-eyes of the *militsiya* jeep wove back and forth even closer along the winding path. Ahead of him lay the empty, well-lit Kirovsky Prospekt. Dashing across it would be just as dangerous as leaping a canyon. But he had no choice. He had to make the move.

Behind him the sweeping headlights followed a path in another direction. This was his chance. He edged forward—at a slow pace. There was no way to do this but be completely obvious. He mustn't arouse suspicion. It took every bit of his energy, though, to move his feet in a normal rhythm and not to cower. It seemed a miracle when he reached the other side, where he hurried on to the metro station.

He dug in his pockets and came up with a two-kopeck piece, only enough for a phone call. His heart nearly froze. Of all the times to be without proper change. Frantic, he dug in every pocket, front and back, searching in vain for a five-kopeck coin.

He glanced to the top of the escalator, where a blonde woman in a black uniform and red cap was dozing in a chair. His muscles tensed as he charged the turnstile, then glided over it effortlessly. But when he landed at the top of the escalator, his foot struck the slotted metal step just before it split in two; he lunged for the handrail. He caught himself and hung on. The train platform, buried four or five stories beneath the swamps of Leningrad, was just a dot at the bottom. With his balance regained, he rushed two steps at a time down the moving stairs, his eyes all the while focused on that tiny bit of landing below.

A rumbling rose from beneath like a great mechanical dragon coming to life. A train was pulling in. He cursed the subway for its incredible depth and started leaping down three and four steps at a time. By the time he reached the platform, two passengers had exited the train, and he heard the fateful recording.

"Astarozhna, dveri zakryvayutsya, sleduyuchaya stantsiya . . ." Caution the doors are closing, the next station will be . . .

He dove for the car, landed inside on his stomach just as the double doors slammed mercilessly shut behind him. As the subway carried him beneath the waters of Leningrad, he raised his head and grinned up at the scowling face of a woman.

A scarf wrapped tightly over her head and around her wrinkled face, she shouted, "Young man, decent people just don't act like that. You should be ashamed of yourself!"

CHAPTER
23

"It's just shock," sobbed Musya. "A terrible shock to your system. Everyone would feel faint. You're all right, *golubchik moi*." My little pigeon. "Trust me. I'm a nurse. When you're on the mend, I'll find Boris and I'll murder him. I'll twist that little head of his until it snaps off!"

Her cries had roused Kyril from his deathly state. The stress of the bullet wound and the blood loss caused him to faint, and Musya only quieted herself when she saw his eyes blink and his body stir. She rushed around the car to the passenger door and with a little coaxing was able to stand him on his feet.

Now, her coat on his shoulders to hide his bloodied arm, they were climbing the marble steps to her apartment.

"You've . . . always been good to me, Musya," Kyril managed to say.

"And I always will be, *golubchik*."

She pecked her lips on his forehead. What had begun as an innocent escape into a ravine by two children, then progressed into youthful lust, was now, she knew, locked in the dependency of adulthood.

Musya paused at the first floor, allowed Kyril to catch his breath, then led the way around to the next flight. At least, she noted, the rest of the tenants seem to have settled in for the night. The last thing she needed was a snoopy neighbor.

That, however, was exactly what happened on the next floor. She was leading Kyril around to the last flight of stairs to her apartment when a door cracked open. Immediately she loosened her grip on Kyril and tried to put distance between them. She was, after all, still a married woman and she mustn't provoke gossip.

"Who goes about there this time of night?" snapped a scratchy voice.

She froze, then pushed Kyril upward. Turning, she saw a pale face, drawn with wrinkles and age, poking out of a door. It was Yuri Gennadiovich, the old man who lived beneath her, now emerging like a sleepy badger. He squinted. Without his glasses, though, he couldn't recognize her even as she walked over to him. Not sure who was approaching, he flinched and retreated a bit.

"It's me, *tovarisch*." Comrade. "Musya Aleksandrovna." Her mind raced for the right words as she stopped outside his door. "What an evening I've had! My rogue of a husband and some friends of his got so drunk that I had to go pick him up and bring him home! Can you imagine? I had to get dressed and go out at this time of night. It's shameful, don't you think, that a husband acts that way?''

The old eyes pinched together into little slits. He studied her, then stared at the stumbling figure on the stairs. "Drunk, you say? I suppose he has friends coming over to drink more and make a racket. Well, let me tell you, Musya Aleksandrovna, this hooliganism must stop right now!''

She glanced behind her. Kyril struggled on, pulling himself up by the railing. If only he doesn't fall, she thought, then perhaps I'll be able to pull off this charade.

"Nyet. There'll be no noise. Look,'' she said waving her hand toward Kyril. "Boris, my poor inebriated husband . . .'' She hesitated until she was convinced the old man couldn't identify Kyril. '' . . . can hardly walk. You think he'll make any noise when he can't even stand? Don't worry, I won't let him make any—''

Yuri Gennadiovich leaned toward her. "No drunkards? No loud party tonight?''

Her hand to her bosom, Musya pulled away in shock. "For the lord's sake, Yuri Gennadiovich, what are you saying? Of course not. We have no hooligans in our circle. You should be ashamed of suggesting such a thing!''

"Well, go to bed. All decent folk should be asleep by now.''

"Da, da,'' agreed Musya. "And don't you

worry. You won't hear a chirp from our apartment. Good night!''

Yuri Gennadiovich grunted as he sealed his door. When he secured his latch, Musya clasped her chest and sighed. Then she bounded up the steps as fast as her heavy legs could carry her. She found Kyril leaning against her apartment door.

"I'm here, my love." As she pulled the key from her purse, she heard ringing from inside the apartment. "And everything's going to be fine."

"Hurry," he gasped. "The telephone."

"What?"

"The phone—it's ringing."

"*Gospodi*, who could be calling at this time of . . .'' She jabbed the key in the lock. "That's Boris! That son of a . . .''

It had to be him.

Kyril coughed. "Hurry," he rasped. "Before he hangs up. It has rung many times already."

CHAPTER
24

Boris stood in the phone booth, the two-kopeck piece in his fingers. If only Musya were there, if only she answered, then he'd drop in the money, complete the connection, and try to make sense of this chaos. He'd ridden the metro to Nevsky, then caught the very last train to Vasileovstrovskaya station. Emerging from underground, he'd found the very first phone. He had to call home, test his theory, but Musya wasn't there. The phone in his apartment continued to ring. Just a few more times. Hang on. Perhaps any second she'll come rushing in.

With the immediate danger over, Boris had begun to put the pieces together. He was certain the gang hadn't followed Musya to Revolution Square or even caught her and forced her to lead them. Otherwise, she would not have been running around so hysterically. They would have held her, used her as bait

181

to draw Boris to his death. That left only one other explanation, and at that hideous realization he shivered.

He couldn't believe it. Never in his life had he imagined anything so horrific. He'd heard of cases like this, but never thought it possible that he'd be the intended victim of such a calculated murder. That the man in the leather jacket had been there, waiting to kill him at Revolution Square, only confirmed his suspicions. Now everything made sense. If only he'd understood sooner. How else could that man have known exactly when and where Boris would show up? How else could Sergei and he have been such easy targets at the monastery? Terror and shock overwhelmed his body like a sudden fever. How had he fallen into this nightmare? When would it end?

Boris slammed down the phone. No answer. He stuffed the coin back in his pocket and moved on. There was someone more important to consider—Lara. His whole world would come to an end if anything happened to her. With a fresh charge of fear-driven energy, he tore out of the phone booth and across Vasilevsky Island. He had suddenly decided that he and Lara had to leave the city. Fortunately, he knew exactly where they could hide.

Minutes later, he entered her courtyard and made his way up the steep, dark steps. At the top, her door was pulled open even before he had time to knock. She'd been watching from the window and seen him run down the empty street and slip into the building. In anticipation, she'd placed a kettle of water on the hot plate.

"Come in. Hurry."

When he was inside, she poked her head outside and looked down the stairs. Satisfied that no neighbors had spied them, she eased shut her door. Her large green eyes froze when she spotted the shredded plastic bag.

"*Bozhe*, what happened? You weren't hurt again, were you?"

Wounded? Again? He touched his arm. That's right. A bullet at the monastery had grazed his arm. He'd forgotten. He was just so afraid for Lara that he couldn't take his eyes off her.

"*Nyet, nyet.*"

The steaming kettle of water began to moan. As if it were some bratty child, Lara tried to wave it away with the back of her hand.

"Boris, what happened?" Her fingers reached into his tangled hair. "Are you sure you're not hurt?"

He caught her hand and kissed it. "I'm fine. But we have to get out of here right away. Tonight."

Lara pulled out a chair and pressed down on his shoulder. "Sit. Now, tell me . . ." Her mind reeled through the possibilities and she guessed. "Were you followed?"

"Oi!" He hadn't checked. Could he possibly have been so stupid as to lead someone right here? "No. No, I'm sure of it." No one could have jumped on the subway train after him.

Even as he spoke, though, Lara slipped like a

secret agent over to the edge of the window. Satisfied that no suspicious men lingered in the doorways and alleys of the surrounding buildings, she crossed to the hot plate. She diluted a glass of tea concentrate with boiling water, placed in two spoonfuls of sugar, then upon reflection, added a third. She set the glass in front of Boris just as he unwrapped the gun and laid it out like a dead fish. As if the weapon were a smelly, evil catch, Lara shrunk back.

Boris spilled a bit of the steaming tea into a saucer, swirled it around to cool it.

"If I hadn't had that, I'd be dead," he said, nodding at the gun. "As soon as I reached the park I knew something was wrong." He slurped the tea in the saucer.

The whole sequence of events flashed through his mind, and he recounted everything to Lara.

Her eyes wide in fear, she said, "Oi, Boris. We have to go to the authorities at once."

"*Nyet!* You don't understand."

That was the least safe place they could go. He couldn't believe what a shambles their lives had become. Everything was supposed to have been straightened out by now. Instead, he and Lara and their unborn child were in more jeopardy than before. It could mean the end of all his dreams.

"Boris, you smuggled some stolen goods. But you can make amends for that. The authorities will be lenient, I'm sure, if you're honest with them. You must go to the *militsiya*. Sergei's been killed, who knows what's happened to Musya, and they're still after you.''

He took her hand and kissed her slender fingers. With eyes sagging from sadness and lack of sleep, he gazed up at her.

''Lara, you don't understand. Someone's trying to kill me, but I can't involve the *militsiya* because . . . because they're *already* involved. Some official knows about the smuggling operation, and that I—''

''What? Boris, that's impossible!'' Anger flashed in her eyes and she turned away, not wanting to accept his words. ''There has to be a mistake.''

''No, it's true, Lara. That's the only logical explanation to this nightmare. I'm sorry for the trouble I've caused, but now you're in danger, too. We have to leave here at once—leave Leningrad and hope things settle down. I know where we can go.''

Her face blanched as she dropped into the chair next to him.

''The *militsiya*? Involved? Oi, Boris, are you sure?''

''I'm positive. It's the only way the man in the leather jacket could have known.''

She stared at him. ''Known what?''

''Where Musya and I were meeting, of course.'' He let go of her hand. ''You see, I called her, gave her exact directions, and told her when to meet me. And when I arrived, that man was already there. Musya wasn't followed. Otherwise they would have caught her and held her. I'm certain she arrived and that man was already there. He knew, Lara. He knew where Musya and I were going to meet. He was just waiting for us.''

Lara still didn't understand.

Boris took a sip of tea. ''My apartment phone is bugged. That's how they knew when and where Musya and I were going to meet. They listened in when I called Musya and gave her instructions. You see, someone in an official capacity is either part of the gang or is being paid off. Without someone high up involved I don't think they could tap my phone. In fact, I'm certain they couldn't.''

Her face went as white as frost. ''Does . . . that mean they could have traced the source of the call?''

''*Da.*''

His head hung in shame and he silently cursed himself. Why hadn't he seen the dark clouds coming? Now they were caught in the middle of a vicious storm. This small room, such a haven before, could be the final trap.

''I don't want anything to happen to you or our child.'' He glanced at a clock. ''If we hurry we can make it off the island before the bridges are raised. We can be out of the city in no time.''

During the navigable months, the bridges across the Neva were raised every night between two and three in the morning. They had, Boris knew, just enough time to grab a few clothes, slip out of the apartment, take Sergei's car and make it out of town.

There was however, one more mission to accomplish before they left.

''I have to call Musya.''

He had to warn her to flee the apartment. Time was critical, as important as blood and air. As much as he wanted to, though, he couldn't use the phone here. It would be too dangerous. If they hadn't traced the source of his previous call to Musya, then they might this time.

Boris plopped in the chair and rubbed his forehead. At each crossroad in his life he'd sensed which was the best direction; then, for the sake of others, he'd selected the opposite. All his life those decisions had been at his expense. Now, however, he'd begun to trust his heart and his head—and to let the two work as one. But at what cost? Shouldn't he return to his old ways? After all, he'd begun to change and now others—Sergei, Musya, and Lara— were paying for his mistakes.

He pushed his fingertips into his hair. "I was only trying to do the right things. And because of that people are . . ."

Lara took him by the arm. "Boris, time goes only in one direction."

"But—"

"No. Please. I beg you. You made good decisions, Boris. And you'll make others.

The wrinkles on his forehead faded. He gazed at her with a gentle smile, this fragile-looking woman. There was no way he would let the slightest bit of harm come to her.

He pulled her close and kissed her on the lips. "We have to go," he reiterated urgently.

"Just let me throw a few things in a bag." She rose and touched his hair. "I'll bring books for me, writing paper for you. Oi, and my guitar. Boris, this will be wonderful. I'm glad we're going. The countryside's always so soothing.''

"Perhaps it can be our . . . our honeymoon."

"Da, da!"

While Lara—now more excited than scared—threw an extra change of clothes into a worn plastic bag, Boris edged up to the window. There were no lingering men in dark coats, no idling cars. Down the empty street, parked in an alley, was Sergei's red car. If he and Lara could make it that far, they'd be safe. Then they'd cross the bridge and flee Leningrad. The very thought pacified him.

Lara placed cognac, a hunk of cheese, a jar of pickles, and two small loaves of black bread in a string bag. Then she selected five books from a shelf, a couple of blue notebooks for Boris, and a pencil and pen.

"Ready."

He lifted aside the muslin curtain, checked outside again. They started out, Boris taking the food and the guitar, Lara her clothes and books. She reached to turn off the overhead bulb.

"No, don't," said Boris. "As long as that light's on, they'll think we're up here."

They made their way down and passing into the night, hugged the shadows of the cold stone buildings. The closer they came to Sergei's car, the faster they moved along the sidewalk. When they were less than a block away, they broke into a run. Finally, they ducked into the alley, threw their belongings through the broken windows of the

Zhiguli, and jumped in. Boris jammed the keys in the ignition. Moving the stick shift into reverse, he checked the rearview mirror.

Then froze.

Right behind them was a telephone booth. He could attempt reaching Musya right now. He had to. He owed her that at least. A warning before he and Lara slipped out of town. It would only take a few seconds to call and . . .

Lara grabbed the dashboard and spun around. "What's the matter?"

No, thought Boris, catching himself. They had to reach safety first.

"I was just thinking about . . . about Musya," he confessed. "I hope she's all right."

"Me, too. Maybe you should call her now."

He stared in the rearview mirror at the reflection of the booth. Phoning would eat up precious seconds.

He shook his head. "Later."

He backed into the street, then shifted the gears of the battered car into first. Lara turned and studied the road behind as Boris accelerated. Each moment they expected to see a car or two or three pop out of an alley, zoom after them, headlights like lasers seeking to destroy them. Nothing happened, however, as Boris drove down side streets; it was as if they were moving through an evacuated city, the buildings dark, the night streets void of life. As they sped along, the wind poured through the shattered windows. Lara pulled back her billowing hair and settled in her seat.

"There's no one." She laughed. "Not a single car."

He smiled. "What time is it?"

Lara held up her wrist and strained to see. "We have five minutes."

"We'll make it."

Within seconds they emerged from a valley of blackened buildings and onto the University Embankment. Off to the left were the lights of the Palace Bridge and the Winter Palace. Boris thought they'd be too obvious there and turned right. Soon they were speeding over the Bridge of Lieutenant Schmidt, the sea air bathing them like wild water. Off to their right a procession of tugboats—their lights defining them in the night—had already lined up, waiting for the bridges to rise. Seconds after they reached the other side—the Red Fleet Embankment—lights on the bridge started to flash.

"Up go the bridges," said Lara. "Perfect timing."

A few blocks later they crossed the Moika Canal and neared the Kirov Theatre. On an empty street corner Boris spotted the familiar gray callbox with its red lettering. Automatically, he reduced his speed. Now they were safe. Lara saw the booth, too, and dug in her purse for a two-kopeck piece.

"You're right," said Lara. "You have to try contacting her at least one more time."

He pulled over at the corner and kissed her on the cheek. "I love you."

From inside the glass booth, he grinned at Lara

as his home phone rang and rang. Abruptly it was picked up.

Surprised and relieved, Boris dropped in the coin and, with a rattle, the connection was made.

"Musya?"

There was silence on the other end.

"Musya? It's me, Boris. Are . . . are you all right?"

Heavy breathing came over the line.

"Musya? It's me, Boris. Speak—"

"Boris?" she whispered, her voice quivering. "Just a minute. Let me . . . let me lock the door."

She must have placed the receiver on the couch because Boris couldn't hear anything. Finally, she returned.

"Are you okay?" she asked.

"Yes. I'm fine. You got away safely? You're not hurt, are you?"

"I'm scared."

"Yes, but—"

"Boris, I was so frightened I just ran and ran. I heard shots. Gunshots!"

"I know. But I'm okay. I'm worried about you though. Did anyone hurt you?"

"*Nyet*. Oi, Boris, I couldn't remember where you wanted to meet. So I got out of the car. Someone was there, waiting, and he—"

"Waiting?" he asked. "Someone was already there, you mean?"

She hesitated before saying, *"Da, da."*

So it was exactly as he thought. The phones were

bugged; that's how the man in the leather jacket had known where to go.

"Oi," continued Musya, "that man was there, the one in the leather jacket, and he started chasing me. It was awful, Boris! I ran around looking for you. I was so terrified."

"Just keep calm. I phoned you earlier, but you weren't home yet."

"Was that you? I was coming up the stairs, but couldn't open the door in time. I'm okay, though, Borinka. Really. I just want you. I want you so bad."

Boris shook his head as he talked. No. That was impossible. He wanted never to see her again—except in divorce court.

"Listen, Musya," he said. "There's no time for talk. Things are much worse than I expected. I want you to leave. Go over to a friend's. Go anywhere—just stay away from the apartment. You have to leave immediately. It's not safe there."

"What?" The panic began to grow in her voice. "But what about you? Where will you be? Boris, you can't leave me alone!"

"I can't come back. I'll explain later."

"Boris, you can't do this to me!" she shrieked.

He glanced at Lara, who sat in the car. For an instant, he considered blurting the truth out to Musya. What a relief it would be to tell her that he didn't love her, that he wanted a divorce, that everything from the color TV to the apartment was hers. But he restrained himself. Musya's safety came first. He didn't need to complicate the moment.

"Boris, I love you. I love you so much and I want to know where you're going."

"I—" He cut himself off. His destination had been on the edge of his lips. "Musya, I can't tell you. The phones aren't safe."

"What?" Her voice was flat, reflecting her disbelief. "The phones?"

"Yes. Now just do as I say. Get out of there right away."

She cried, "But Boris, where are you going?"

"Away."

"Boris!"

"I can't tell you. I'm . . . I'm just going to a place where I can think."

"Think? But—"

"I have to go. Stay at Raya's or Nina's until I return. I'll let you know when it's safe."

"Boris!" she screamed.

"Bye."

He slammed down the phone and leaned his aching body against the wall of the booth. You're rid of her, he told himself. You never have to pretend again that you love her. He'd refused her demands to return, and that was the first break. He'd been clear in his warnings too.

"That was hard," he sighed as he joined Lara in the car.

She wrapped an arm around him. "Is she all right?"

He nodded. "She's safe and that's all I care about. I told her to go to a friend's and stay there for a few days."

"Does she suspect anything?"

"About us? No. I almost confessed, but there'll be a better time. I just wanted to know she was safe." He reached over and laid a hand on Lara's leg. "She begged me to stay. It was awful. She wanted to know where I was going, but I wouldn't tell her."

Even as he spoke, though, he wondered if he'd divulged too much. Perhaps he'd given her an invaluable clue. He'd admitted he was going to a place where he could think, and that would mean only one thing to her.

No, Boris told himself as he started the car. Even if Musya had an inkling where he'd be, she'd never come out there. She was afraid of hounds and gypsies and Nazi ghosts.

"Let's go," said Lara. "Our new lives are about to begin and I can't wait."

"Neither can I." Boris took a deep breath, then exhaled. "Onward . . . to Zarekino."

CHAPTER
25

Musya laid the receiver in its cradle. She couldn't believe her ears. Love, indeed, was blind. Boris loved her so much that he couldn't see that all she wanted was for him to die. Only his murder, she knew, was going to free her. There was no other alternative. Not even divorce. Boris was so crazy about her that he probably wouldn't notice if she hacked him in two with her own hands.

"What did he say?"

Cleaver in hand, Kyril stood in the kitchen doorway, naked from the waist up. A torn white sheet served as a bandage around his left arm.

"Put that damn thing down," she ordered. "He's not coming here. At least not tonight. And sit back down. You shouldn't be up yet, *dusha maya*." My soul. "You need rest."

"Just tell me where he is!"

"I can't believe it. Boris is crazy. That man's as

crazy as Rasputin. And just as hard to kill. Go on, now, sit back down. You shouldn't be up yet.''

She bustled across the living room, plucked the cleaver from his hand, and took him gently by his good arm. Thick legs planted to the floor, he refused to budge.

''Kyryozhinka, my love,'' she said through gritted teeth. She leaned into him and he started to move. ''That's it.''

She led him back into the kitchen. The chair at the small table was his destination, and she seated him, then poured him more black tea and sweetened it with globs of raspberry jam.

''Drink this. All of it. And after that, another glass. You need to make up for the fluid you lost. I'm making good beet borscht, too, with lots of meat. I have some caviar too. With protein under your belt, you'll soon have your strength back.''

''Tell me what he said,'' insisted Kyril.

''Oi!'' Her large cheeks puffed up, pressing her almond eyes smaller. ''He still thinks you're a member of that gang. Something about that man in the leather coat. Can you believe it? He called to warn me. We're trying to kill him and . . . and . . .''

Kyril fidgeted with the cotton bandage on his arm. Tightly wrapped, the cloth had a deep red stain at its heart that continued to grow.

''How did you manage to marry someone so stupid?''

She leaned against the narrow gas stove. ''I . . .

I don't know. Of all the men in Leningrad . . . it was just my poor luck."

"He called to warn you?"

Her head bobbed slowly up and down. Could it really be? Had she heard him right? Could he be tricking her?

"He . . . he thinks the phone was bugged. He said this affair with the gang is really complicated." It was either laugh or cry. She chose the former. "He said our line was tapped and that's why there was trouble. Someone knew to wait for him at Revolution Square. So he called to tell me to leave the apartment and stay at a friend's."

Kyril stared at the table top in disbelief. "We're trying to kill him—and he calls because he's worried about your safety? What a fool!"

"I told you he was crazy for me." Thoroughly amused, a fresh wave of laughter rolled out of her. "Oi, *mamichka*. When he looks at me with that puppy-dog face, I get sick at heart. His love for me positively radiates from those sappy blue eyes. He loves me as if I were a goddess." She cupped her breasts with both hands, batted her eyes, and, giggling, said, "Me, me, me. I'm all he wants—and I can't stand him!"

"You should have been an actress, Musinka. You're obviously very talented."

"I've convinced him, haven't I? He really thinks I'm mad for him." She sighed. "Well, if it gets us what we want. But, Kyril dear, with my talent I could have been a famous film star—the envy of every Soviet woman. Instead, well . . . I'm a nurse with a crazy husband and a wonderful cousin that I adore. Speaking of whom, let me see that arm. Has the bleeding stopped?''

Upon their return to the apartment, Musya had carried extra lights into the kitchen and thoroughly examined the wound. To her relief, she found that the bullet had pierced his upper left arm at an angle, tearing through the skin as cleanly as a hole punched in paper. Without striking bone, it had skimmed a muscle then passed harmlessly out the side of his arm. Finding little damage—and relieved that they wouldn't have to call a physician—she cleansed Kyril's arm and tore up a brand new Polish sheet to use as a bandage.

''We might want to wrap some copper coins into the bandages to keep the swelling down,'' she said. ''But the bleeding seems to have stopped. Tomorrow I'll steal some medication from the hospital.''

Not interested, Kyril said, ''So what are we supposed to do? Wait for him to expose himself?''

''No. We can't risk him catching on.''

''So we search all of Leningrad? That'd be like looking for the wind in the field! We'd never . . .'' He saw the teasing in her eye. ''Eh? What's this? You know. You know where he is, my little pussy-cat, don't you?''

Her voice rose in a tease. ''Well, do you think they discovered America yesterday? It's old news, I tell you. Of course I know.''

Kyril's fist slammed the table. ''Tell me! I'm going to kill that horse's ass!''

''He didn't say exactly, but he dropped a hint.

I'm almost positive he's gone to the same place he always runs to when he's confused: Zarekino.''

"The dacha, eh?" Kyril pushed himself to his feet. "Good. Let's go. We can leave in fifteen minutes and probably still beat him.''

"No. You can't. You've been shot, Kyril, and you have to regain your strength. You should eat a good meal, sleep some. You're too weak to go now.''

"Musya, I—"

"Besides, it'll be morning in a few hours. We might as well wait. We could go out in the afternoon.''

"That won't do. Boris might see us coming.''

"Yes, but that way we could be out there and back by sunset.''

Kyril shook his head. "If we don't start now, we'll have to wait till dark tomorrow.''

"No, Kyril,'' she said with a quavering voice. "We don't want to go to Zarekino at night. Believe me. It's very strange. That place . . . that place is a breeding ground of ghosts.''

"Musya, you ridiculous cow.''

"I am not!'' she squealed. "Many people died at Zarekino during the war. During the Revolution too. The peasants strung up the Prince from the grand staircase. Hanged him right there. And . . . and there's this gypsy woman—she killed all these Fascists, knifed them to death. And she has all these hounds. Wild hounds. They howl at night.''

Kyril rose again and pulled her against him with his good arm. Knowing how to convince her, he kissed Musya, rubbed his cheek against hers.

"Musya, we have to go when it's dark. Boris would see us otherwise. But in the shadow of night we'll be able to sneak up on him." His thick hand slid down to her breast. "Listen. We won't go now. We'll wait until tomorrow night. That way we'll have the apartment to ourselves all day. And when the sun sets, we'll go out to the dacha, this strange place, and put an end to Boris."

She sighed and leaned into him. Brushing back a whisp of his hair, she kissed him on the forehead.

"Well, all right." Suddenly she shivered. "But I tell you, Zarekino scares me."

CHAPTER
26

Some ten kilometers out of Leningrad, Boris spotted a pair of lights lurking behind them. Panicking he swerved off the highway, steered behind a clump of trees, and waited. Minutes later, a slow truck churned past.

"Relax," said Lara, resting her hand on his knee. "Everything's going to be all right. No one saw us leave."

"But . . ."

With images of Sergei and guns and corrupt officials ricocheting in his exhausted mind, Boris checked the road behind them yet another time. Reticent to believe their good fortune, yet unable to spot anyone, he drove on to Zarekino, which lay to the south, a few kilometers from Pushkin, closer still to Pavlovsk.

Once they were hidden, once he'd had some sleep, he'd be able to sort out matters and choose a course of action. His mind sifted through a list of his father's powerful friends. Since there definitely appeared to be governmental corruption, he would have to be careful whom he contacted. Even now, though, he could think of three or four trustworthy and influential men. The old guard who'd weathered much worse and who would know how to handle this storm. Without realizing it, Boris had already established his priorities: protect Lara, assure Musya's safety, and bring to trial the one who'd killed Sergei. There was also the prospect of getting a divorce from Musya, but that could come later. Whatever the authorities did with him after that really didn't matter. He was enervated by not living the truth.

The route out of the city quickly melted from a highway to a narrow road to a grassy lane until it was choked off by the dense birch forest of Zarekino. A mass of white-barked trees—all once part of the princely estate—extended for kilometers in every direction.

"There wasn't much left of the forest after the war." As he followed the ruts of the lane, he kept one eye on the rearview mirror. "Tanks plowed over most of the trees—too bad the old palace can't grow back as well."

With only one or two exceptions, all of the country palaces around Leningrad had been captured by the Fascists then sacked and burned. Petrodvorets, Peter the Great's version of Versailles, had been reduced to a pile of ashes and a few standing walls. The royal palaces of Pushkin had also licked the sky with flames, and Zarekino was no exception. The ballrooms and galleries in one wing had been used as a stables, the rooms in the other wing as a barracks. Just before their retreat—just after the murder of Tyotya's family and her bloody revenge—the Hitlerites soaked the hay in the ballrooms and ignited it. Deathly black spires of smoke, seen for miles, slithered into the sky for days.

Boris swung the car to the side, brought it to a stop between two birches, and shut off the engine. Twisting in his seat, he stared out the smashed windows of the car and down the lane. No lights, no sounds of car engines greeted him. He looked at Lara with a flat, exhausted smile.

"We have to walk in from here. It's not far. We don't have a flashlight. Will you be able to see?"

"Sure," said Lara, gathering their belongings. "The moon's terrifically bright."

A misty mushroom rain had ended and the moon, a large white saucer, rolled in and out of the rocky clouds. The birches pulsed light and dark around Boris and Lara, and their skin alternately glowed and faded into shadow.

Standing behind the car, Boris took one look at the back of the smashed Zhiguli and was filled with dread.

"The car—it's so obvious, what if . . . what if . . ."

"Boris, you're getting more nervous, not less. Relax. We're here. If someone were really after us they wouldn't have let us get out of town. They would have—"

Behind him dry leaves rattled. He jumped as if jabbed with a knife, then held two fingers to his lips.

"Ts-s-s!"

"What? Stop being silly." With care and concern, she touched him on the arm. "You're just exhausted."

"Didn't you hear that?" he whispered. "Steps. Someone's out there."

She was quiet for but a moment. "Boris, you're imagining things."

"Ts-s-s!"

There it was again, the crackling of coarse fall leaves. Boris heard it for certain this time. Something was in the forest, a living creature. *Bozhe.* How had they been followed? He'd kept checking, hadn't seen anyone. Could it be, he hoped, the wind? *Nyet.* He glanced up, only to see the semi-naked branches hanging with perfect stillness. He heard a whoosh again, looked to his right, and this time saw it. A huge shape moving swiftly through the birch jungle. He grabbed Lara's arm.

"Get down!"

"Boris, wha—"

"Ts-s-s!"

Huddled behind the car, Boris heard something from the other side. He spun around and saw a figure racing in and out of the trees. His heart began to pound. He hadn't figured on this, wasn't quite sure what to do.

Suddenly, from far away an animal cried out, long

204

and thin. An immediate answer split the night just a few meters from Boris and Lara.

"Ai!" cried Lara.

Boris twisted to the side, spotted a tall white and sable creature that had nearly blended in with the birches. It stopped howling and stared at them like a regal tsar. Elegant and of great height, the animal focused on them with dark, intense, confident eyes. One thick, curly-haired paw rose, then another, as the animal slowly stalked them. Boris pushed himself up, took a step forward. Remembering how Tyotya had dealt with the animals, he leapt out, shouted and swung his arms. The hound bolted, the padding of its paws fading in the distance.

"*Bozhe*," said Lara, clasping her hand to her chest. "What was that? A dog?"

"Half of one, anyway." He scanned the trees which were as thick as the white hairs on a babushka's head. "They're part wolfhound and part wolf."

"What? You recognized it?"

He nodded. During the Revolution, the Prince and every symbol of aristocracy had been attacked by the peasants. That included his kennel, which was superior even to the tsar's in its quantity and quality of Russian wolfhounds, the borzoi. Almost three hundred precious dogs were slaughtered, but a few escaped along with their caged quarry: Siberian wolves.

"Zarekino was as famous for its borzoi as it was for its hunts," said Boris still searching the woods. "All the nobility came here, the tsar and all the grand dukes. Only the most enormous wolves from

Siberia were used. They were released during the hunts and there was great sport to see whose dogs could capture them.''

In the years following the Revolution, what few borzoi and wolves had escaped eventually found each other in the wilds of the birches, and mated. The result was an enormous creature of great strength, part hunter and part hunted, with the tall, sleek body of a coursing hound and the thick skull and powerful jaws of a wolf.

''Oi!'' gasped Lara at the sound of another distant howl. ''They're not dangerous, are they?''

Purposely avoiding her question, he said, ''Come on. They're running loose tonight and we shouldn't be out.''

Years ago Tyotya had tamed a handful of the hounds with great clumps of raw meat. She now bred them and they lived with her in the palace ruins and were her sole means of support. In all his years of coming to the dacha, however, Boris had never seen them run free.

Within a few meters the forest broke, a line of trees that stopped and formed a sheer wall bordering on an open meadow. Before stepping into the clearing, Boris searched the knee-high grass, saw no sign of the hounds. His steps hesitant, he led the way along the uneven path worn through the earth's skin. When the moon appeared again and illuminated the swells of the countryside, he stopped.

''There, that's the palace of Zarekino.''

Across the damp grasses and beyond another strand of birches rose the ruins of the palace. Placed majestically at the top of a hill, its shattered mass broke the natural flow of the land and trees, a black hulk that continued to die even after its death. At one end, iron skeletons of onion domes—their copper skins peeled away revealing their empty innards—poked into the sky. In the center, where a vast dome had once risen over the grand staircase— and where the angry peasants had hung the Prince— a crater now lay. Crippled brick walls, with no roof to shield them and no rooms behind them, stood like images of a nuclear holocaust.

"I knew it was in ruins, but I didn't expect . . ." She spotted the faint outline of a narrow river between them and the hill on which sat the structure. *"Za reka."* Beyond the river. "Zarekino."

"What's left of the place, anyway. It's hard to imagine it was once a glittering palace of over two hundred rooms."

He motioned further to the right, down at a curve in the river. Against a mass of white birches sat a cluster of small dark buildings.

"The dacha's over there—see? We cross the river up ahead."

He started off again, leading Lara across the meadow and into another grove. Just as soon as they reached the birches, another cry—deep and mean at the start, thin and high at the end—split the night. The howl came from somewhere within the palace, followed by a trio, a quartet and more.

Boris said, "Hurry, we—"

A single howl, then two, rose from the meadow right behind them. Boris grabbed Lara by the hand

and they ran to the safety of the trees. Pressed against a birch, Boris studied the moonlit meadow as the crying, flute-like voices of the animals filled his ears. At first he couldn't see anything, then gradually he saw a huddled mass out from which arose a long, lean, arching head. Not ten meters away and also crouched in the grass, the second creature's voice rose, a half-note lower than the first. As the animals howled, their heads continued to rise until their noses pointed almost straight up.

Lara held the bags close to her. "I don't like those things."

"And they don't like us."

The wails of the hounds continued from the palace and from the meadows behind. He glanced through the strand of birches. The bridge across the river wasn't far at all.

"Come on, hurry."

To the cry of the hounds, Boris and Lara ran. Hand in hand, they bolted down the narrow path, struggling to see the way. Boris tripped on a branch and nearly toppled over, pulling Lara down with him. She yanked back, steadying them both. Not slowing, Boris charged on, all the time wondering why the hounds were roaming free. Through the birches he saw the faint outlines of the way across the river. The dacha was still a good distance from that.

Lara glanced back in the dark. "Boris, I—"

The crying had stopped, both at the palace and in the meadow behind. Boris could only make out the sounds of their own running, their own panting.

Then, rising above that, the rhythmic padding of fleeting paws. Boris glanced to the left and saw an all-white creature flitting through the birches like a swift cloud. He heard the same noise to his right and saw the white and sable creature bounding in and out of the trees. *Bozhe*, thought Boris. They're playing with us. But how long would the amusement last?

The gray shape of the bridge emerged right before them, a narrow passage of old wood with a railing on one side. Boris glanced to his right, heard a series of powerful legs skimming over the fallen leaves. He couldn't see either one of the animals, but did see a large branch lying on the floor of the grove.

''Help me!''

Together the two of them jumped off the path and grasped the limb. Working as one, they dragged it toward the bridge. They backed themselves into the wooden crossing, pulling the mass of branches behind them until it blocked the bridge completely. They hurried across the rippling water but were not even a quarter of the way across when they heard a rush of noise behind them. Taking shape out of the strands of birches were the two enormous borzoi-wolves. Boris, shuddering, held onto the single railing, and didn't stop until he and Lara reached the other side. They kept moving toward the dacha, Boris' eyes fixed on the creatures across the waters. As if made of stone, the hounds stood perfectly still, staring at Boris and Lara.

"I'm sorry," said Boris. "Tomorrow I'll have Tyotya pen them up at the palace."

"Oi," gasped Lara, the fear ebbing. "I've never seen anything like them before."

He kissed her cheek, wrapped his arm around her as they made their way along the river's edge. The old palace loomed up on their left, a black mass at the top of the hill. Squinting, Boris stared up but could not see a lamp burning from Tyotya's side window.

The log cabin, its butterfly roof—a v-like peak pitched out over each end—slowly emerged in the night. Carefully set along a curve in the river, the small structure sat low to the ground, its face to the water, its back to still more hectares of birches.

"Oi, a real *izba*. A real Russian cabin," she said, charmed.

"Da, da. All built without a single nail," said Boris, pleased with her enthusiasm. He checked behind them again, but saw no sign of man or creature. "We're almost there. At last."

The dacha's heavy log walls, the little bench of dirt built around the base, and the lace-like carved wood around the deep windows took shape in the dark. It appeared as if from a book of fairy tales, not the cabin on chicken legs that belonged to the wicked witch Baba-yaga, but a safe place for a good, hard-working peasant and his family.

Lara said, "We'll be happy here, I—"

From the darkness alongside the dacha emerged a white shadow. A huge hound, lips curled back over its teeth, stepped furtively around the edge of the cabin. A master of its domain, it stopped directly in front of the dacha's door.

"Don't move," Boris said.

Lara, with no intention of even flinching, did not speak. For a full minute, she and Boris stood frozen, staring at the hound. Then, one small movement at a time, Boris slipped his hand into the string bag. He felt a jar, the hunk of cheese, and dug deeper.

A grave churning emerging from its throat, the borzoi-wolf began to growl. Boris ceased his movements. The animal hunkered as if preparing to spring.

"Oi," gasped Lara, her voice barely audible.

Quickly, Boris jabbed his hand to the bottom of the bag and felt the black bread. He yanked out one of the loaves and in the same movement flung it to the side of the hound. The animal flinched but held firm. Then its nose began to quiver and it raised its snout. With quick whiffs, it caught wind of the food, though it never took its eyes off Boris and Lara. Finally, it ducked to the side, bit into the black bread, and disappeared into the birches behind the cabin.

Boris relaxed at once and turned to Lara. "They won't be a problem tomorrow, I promise."

Lara glanced into the woods, then shook away the memory. "Let's go inside."

With a large iron key, Boris opened the door, led the way into the single-room structure, and carefully shut the door behind them. Like a blind man who knew perfectly his house, he crossed through the dark room to a table. He felt a drawer, opened it, then reached for a box of matches in the upper right corner. He lit a kerosene lantern and placed it on a table in the middle of the room. Just as he had always done, just as his father and mother had always done before him, he crossed to the side window, opened the shutter, and cracked the window.

"A little musty, but nice, eh?"

She set her clothes, books, and the guitar on the bed and spun around with big eyes.

"It's beautiful and, look, it even has an old stove." It was a big mass of clay for both cooking and heating. She stepped on its bench. "I haven't seen one of these since my great-aunt died. When it's cold out, we'll even be able to sleep up top here."

Pushing away thoughts of Leningrad and the hounds outside, he reached out for her. He loved that stove too. Loved napping up on top on a cold fall day. *Da, da.*

Suddenly, as he gazed into her eyes, all expression drained from her face.

"Lara?"

"Boris, I . . ." She pointed past him and out the window. "I . . . I saw someone. . . ."

He spun around to the glass. "What?"

"Someone's out there. I saw a face. In the window. . . ."

"You sure it wasn't a dog?"

"Someone's out there, I tell you! A person!"

He rushed to the window, peered out, and saw only white trees poking into a black night. Lara stood by the table. Then, breaking the tranquility of the dacha, the door was kicked open, and a dark figure stood there, shiny knife in hand.

"What—?" began Boris.

But before he could do anything, the arm cocked itself back, then hurled forward. Like a tumbling bolt of lightning, the knife cut through the air toward Lara.

CHAPTER
27

Musya's eyes opened as quickly as tightly sprung shades. *Bozhe.* Were those footsteps she just heard? Was someone in the apartment? She lay still, stopped her own breathing, and concentrated everything on her ears. All she could hear, though, was her own pounding heart and the heavy breathing next to her.

Carefully she touched the sleeping mass at her side, a body that filled and swelled out of the dent Boris had left in the mattress. At once she felt strange and wonderful. It was odd not to have her husband lying beside her, a pleasant shock to have her lover there instead. She was tempted to reach over and kiss him, crawl atop his massive body, but then she retracted her hand. Kyril needed his sleep. He needed rest to heal his wound.

There! Again! Footsteps! Or could someone be trying to break open the door? Silently, she lifted aside the covers and slid out of bed. Pulling on a robe, she edged on the pads of her feet to the bedroom door. Tap. Tap. Tap-tap. Was that someone moving or someone breaking the lock open? *Gospodi*, could it be Boris himself?

How wonderful that would be. Let him come, she thought. Give me my chance. Let him crawl or charge. It didn't make any difference. She'd get Kyril's cleaver, then whack him in half. Now. Tonight. This very moment.

She spied through the cracked door but saw nothing. Pressing in her breasts, she slipped through the opening without moving the door, then stood motionless. Her eyes cut into the kitchen, swung back into the living room. A patch of light sliced through the window. Nothing. She stepped next to the armoire, her eyes scanning the room.

Her head emerged from around the corner of the armoire. The front door was closed, sealed tight. Whoever was there—unless of course it was Boris with a key—was a professional housebreaker.

There it was again. Tap-tap. Swish. And suddenly, as unexpected as a thunderclap in a blue sky, something leapt out at her.

"Oi!" she tried to scream as someone grabbed for her.

But she could only make a muffled squeal as the broad hands locked over her mouth. In the dark she saw a tall man. He hurled her head back against the wall, stapled her neck against the plaster. Her eyes bulging, she then saw the second one, a shorter man with a dark mustache who cradled his right arm.

215

Her heart caved in on itself when she noticed his jacket. It was just like Kyril's, a dark brown leather one, a jacket almost impossible to obtain. So this was the one, the gang leader Boris had mistaken Kyril for. And it all became so horribly clear. Now she understood why Boris was confused. They must have obtained Boris' address from Sergei some time ago and now . . . now they'd come to . . .

The tall one's eyes pierced hers, and in a whisper he demanded, "Where is he?"

Boris was gone, out of town. Lying in the bedroom, though, was Kyril, her wounded lover who wouldn't be able to protect himself. Would they mistake him for Boris and kill him instead?

She started to mumble something, and the hand was pulled away.

"He's gone," she cried. "Gone out of town. To . . . to Zarekino, I think. He's—"

The hand clasped back over her mouth, fingers digging into her cheeks. Her head was yanked forward, then smashed back against the wall. Inside her skull the night shattered with light, and tears dribbled down her cheeks.

The shorter one, the one with the mustache who favored his right shoulder, stepped to her side. Obviously in pain—wounded at the cemetery, assumed Musya—he pulled a gun from his leather jacket and lifted it to Musya's temple.

"One word and your brains will be splattered like kasha over the entire room," he said, his voice deep and scratchy, his accent throaty like a Georgian's.

He turned to the tall one and whispered, ''He's got to be in the bedroom. I'll hold her.''

''*Nyet!*'' began Musya.

''Quiet!'' demanded the man in the leather coat, cocking the gun.

The tall man's hand slipped from her mouth, and a second, coarser one slapped over it. Pushed back against the wall, a gun to her head, her mouth covered, Musya's horrified eyes watched as the tall man held up a long knife. Then as if he were stalking an animal, he slipped closer and closer to the room where Kyril lay so helplessly. *Gospodi*, dear lord, *nyet*, she cried over and over in her mind. That man was about to murder Kyril. Boris was the guilty one. She wanted Boris dead and buried, too. They were allies of a sort and all this was a mistake and—

She'd never be able to explain. These two thugs would never spare Kyril, never spare her, either. She had to warn her lover, and she stared at the man immediately in front of her. With his good arm pressed over her lips, he held the gun with his wounded one.

Without a second's more thought, she twisted, jabbed her left fist into his wounded shoulder. The man with the mustache cried out and dropped the gun, which by some miracle didn't discharge. Then she plowed her heavy body into him, bowled him down on the floor. Her eyes darted to the side. The tall one was after her, the knife raised high. But there was something more. A shape big and dark emerging from the black doorway. It was Kyril with something glinting in his hand. The cleaver. That wonderful cleaver, poised high and ready to save them both!

And just as the tall man with the knife was ready to slash into her, Kyril attacked from behind. He heaved his weight forward, buried the sharp instrument in the man's spine. Without even a cry, he dropped to the floor.

Musya fell, too. She threw herself forward and landed with her full weight on the gang leader's chest, jabbed a leg into his wounded shoulder. His mustached lip rose high as he cried out like a pained infant.

"Ai!"

The next instant Kyril jumped in, pushed Musya aside, and bloodied the cleaver once again. Its sharp edge sliced through the leather jacket, ripping through bone and muscle of heart.

And then it was over.

Musya felt her stomach twist and rise as she saw the blood bubbling from the two fresh corpses. But she forced control upon herself.

"Quick, Kyril. The blood's going to drip through to the apartment below. We have to drain them in the kitchen."

Musya did most of the work, dragging the two men into the kitchen. There, the lovers propped their victims over the sink so that the inky red blood would flow from the lifeless bodies and down the drain.

"Oi," she said, propping up the mustached man with a chair, "now we have two more companions for Elizaveta Nikolaevna."

"Don't worry." He reached into the sink and smeared blood over his thumb. "We'll take care of them."

Musya's face went sour with wrinkles as she watched him paint the tall man's eyelids with blood.

"Ach, is that necessary?"

"Trust me."

"But it's so—"

"Do you want this thug to seep into your dreams?"

"No."

"Then shut up."

She shrugged as Kyril finished with the second man. "How's your arm?"

He withdrew his hand and blotted his thumb on a towel. "It hurts."

"Oi, *golubchik moi.*"

She wanted to smother him with kisses, tuck him in bed like a little boy. But, with her hands holding the stacked bodies over the sink, she couldn't. First she had to drain the blood, wash it down the sink. Then she'd have to wrap them in a tarp or blanket until Kyril and she could dispose of them.

"If only we could have killed Boris yesterday or . . . or even today," she said. "This is just taking so long and it's making me nervous."

"Ts-s-s. Moscow wasn't built in one day."

"I know, I know. But how long have we waited already? Haven't we been patient enough?" She nudged him toward the door. "Now go on, you need to get back in bed. I'll finish up with these two."

He paused in the doorway, saying, "You mustn't

worry, Musinka. Boris will look like a side of beef by tomorrow night.''

"I'll only be happy, you know, when that premature piglet of a husband of mine is finally dead.''

"Tomorrow night. I promise.''

elpless, Boris saw the knife fly across the room like an eagle diveboming a hare. He saw Lara extend her hands, palms out, as if to block the blade. Flesh, though, could never stop steel. That, he knew.

"*Nyet!*" he screamed.

Within the same instant, the dark figure in the door hurled another knife. flinging it this time toward him. The blade cut through the air like a huge spinning bullet, blade over handle over blade. Then, in the flash of a second, the knives expertly hit their targets in the log wall, one right after the other. With a deep, solid thud the blades struck and all was still.

"*Gospodi . . .*" muttered Boris.

The short figure at the door held two more knives. "*Noo-noo.*" Well, well. "A girl and a boy . . . from the village, I suppose. Come to loot something perhaps? Tell me what brings you to Zareki-no—and don't move or I'll cut you down!''

An old woman, her dark, leathery skin a mass of deep wrinkles, stepped into the faint light of the lantern. Her eyes were as black as the scarf wrapped around her head. Equally black was her skirt, which hung thick and bulky from her stubby body.

''Who are you?'' she screeched, raising two more knives in her fist. ''What do you want?''

Boris cleared his throat. Many years ago when he had doubted her stories, she had marched him to a log wall, then stepped back twenty paces. One after the other, she had hurled her knives, forming a clear outline of the curly-haired youngster. Boris hadn't been afraid then—even though his father almost had her shipped off to Siberia when he found out—but that was twenty years ago. He had been a child, she older than his father. Now he was a man, his father was dead, and she—her eyes not as clear, her arm not as steady—still lived. But were her talents just as fresh as they once were?

''Tyotya, it's me. Boris Ankadievich.''

She squinted, cocked her arm, and prepared to fling another knife. Boris quickly raised his arms.

''Really, it's me. The son of Arkady Yakovich.''

The mass of dried skin rose upward in a smile. ''Little Boris. It is you.'' Her face sank in anger. ''What are you doing here? Why are you coming so late at night? You should be ashamed of yourself—it's almost morning! See what happens when you wake me in the middle of the night? I heard the hounds. The hounds cried out and I knew someone was here so I came to see for myself.''

"Forgive us, Tyotya. It was an emergency.'' Still shaking, he edged over to Lara, put his arms around her. "My friend and I have come to stay here at the dacha for a few days.''

The old head tilted to the side, stared at Lara, then shook back and forth. "*Nyet*. All dachas are closed for the winter.''

"Yes, but . . .''

Shaking her head, she made her way around the table, past Boris and Lara, who dared not move. With one strong pull, she freed the first knife from the log wall, then went after the other. She turned and inspected Lara as if she were a piece of meat at the market.

"I've met your wife before, Boris Ankadievich,'' began Tyotya. "But there's something different about her. My memory's not as clear as it once was but . . . but she wasn't as pretty, I think, as she is tonight.''

Boris cleared his throat, struggling not to be intimidated by this woman who had been as much a grandmother to him as he'd ever known.

"That's because she is not my wife.''

"*Noo-Noo*. You're getting old, too, aren't you? No longer the innocent little boy with curly hair, eh?'' She laughed, slipped her knives into the belt of her dress, then froze Boris with her eyes. "But tell me, why do you arrive so late? It's not morning, not day. you creep into Zarekino like foreign spies.''

223

Lara ventured, "We're in trouble."

Full of distrust, Tyotya's eyes pulsed on Lara, and she snapped, "So why come to Zarekino? There's been enough trouble here to last for centuries!"

"Tyotya, this was the only safe place," said Boris. "Someone was looking for me. Not the *militsiya*, I swear. I just had to leave Leningrad. We won't cause any problems."

The shriveled face turned on him. "Do you think an old woman like me doesn't have enough troubles? A few young hooligans came from the neighboring village last week—to search for old treasures, perhaps. But they don't frighten me. They come because they've heard of the palace, of the hounds, of Tyotya." She pounded her chest. "Is it not because of this that I let my creatures run free at night? You two—you're lucky. I train my hounds for hunting, you know. Just like the Prince did. Mine are the best in all the Motherland. Meat is meat to them, and they can run down anything. Ach! You can't stay here. Besides, it's too cold. You won't get a fire going until tomorrow."

"We'll be fine," ventured Lara. "We've brought warm clothes. And believe us, we seek peace."

The old woman, her mouth puckering into a tight mass, shot her eyes at Lara.

"No others? No hooligans?"

"*Nyet*," said Boris. "We are alone."

"And no one followed you?"

"No one."

The black shape of Tyotya shuffled to the door.

Poking out from the folds of her black garments were her silvery knives.

"There is to be no trouble from you two. You may stay. But beware the hounds. These two you saw tonight, they are my pets and are not so dangerous, just curious. They live with me in my rooms and I will bring them in tonight. But the others are penned up at the palace, stay away from them." She started off. "I warn you, beware the hounds at the palace. They know no other human besides me and I'm readying them for a hunt. They're quite . . . ravenous now."

Tyotya's figure became one with the night, melting quickly into the folds of darkness. Boris slowly walked over, peered out. Squinting, he saw the last of her small figure as she headed up to the shattered walls of the palace. His eyes stared after the point where she had vanished, then he closed the door, leaned against it.

"Bozhe," said Lara from behind.

"I'm sorry." He went over to her and opened his arms. "I didn't expect any of this. Are you all right?"

"I . . . I suppose."

"She's strange, I know, but she meant us no harm. She was only trying to protect the place from intruders. She's been the caretaker, after all, ever since the war."

"Hold me, Boris. Tighter."

"Don't worry. I'll never let you go."

He sighed as he held her, the tension gradually easing from his mind, his muscles. Leningrad, the

R. D. ZIMMERMAN

gang, Musya. Everything began to slip away. All that mattered was this slim waist he held so tightly, this soft back he rubbed. He buried his nose in her hair and inhaled.

"Everyone has his own fragrance, you know—skin, hair."

He could identify by scent all the lovers he'd had in his life. That was both good and bad. The smell of Musya, for instance.

"You're the best." He held his nose to her neck, inhaled, and sensed her richness fill him. "You make me calm and excited at the same time."

He peeled back her blouse and kissed her at that bridge of skin between neck and shoulder. Strands of her hair tickled the side of his face, and she turned into him, her lips nibbling butterfly kisses up his neck, over his ear. Chills shot down his back and he gasped. Then she pushed away.

"Let's get into bed."

He strode to the table and watched as she took the bedroll and unfolded it on the wooden bed. Her fingers pressed smooth the bottom blanket, peeled back the top. She turned to him, and he smothered the flame of the kerosene lamp. In the dark, right where he stood, he began to drop his clothing. His shirt landed on the floor, and he heard the swish of her blouse as it too fell. Then his pants, the buttons striking the wooden floor. The whish of her skirt.

Finally, they came together, their bare hands, hot pokers in the chilly cabin, touching first. Then their lips, soft, moist, found each other. Without speaking, she climbed into the little bed. He pressed in

226

after, half on his side, half on top of her, their legs entangled.

Breaking the silence that had settled upon them was not his voice, not hers. From outside came a human cry that began low and rose to a high, thin note as if from some wild gypsy gathering. Tyotya, thought Boris. That was her, calling her dogs. Answering her came a lonely cry. Seconds later another hound—this one at the palace—joined the chorus. Boris and Lara knotted their hands together and their ears strained to understand what they could not. Then, with the exception of one animal's brief baying, all was silent.

"Oi . . ." muttered Lara.

"Ts-s-s," he hushed, nuzzling her. "Everything's fine. We just need some sleep. It's been a long day."

"But . . . but I'm scared. Aren't you?"

He lied for the first time to her. *"Nyet."*

And before either of them could say another word, they both fell asleep.

CHAPTER
29

Нer joints ground with pain and stiff muscles pulled old bones as she made her way back up to the palace. The damp night, the incline of the hill, and the time of morning all increased her aches. Tyotya raised her craggy face skyward. Soon the night would surrender, black to black-blue to gray. Perhaps today there'd be sunshine. The clouds had cracked earlier. They did again now. She stopped. Her short body turned westward. In a gap she saw the moon. Big and round. A disk of light. She wrinkled up her nose. A full moon like this was not good. It made the hounds nervous.

She cupped her hands to her mouth, and called, "Ah-ew! Ah-ew!"

The bitch Milka was the first to answer, her cry fine and pure, just like her silky fur. Off in the woods behind the cabin came the harsher answer of her mate, Toozik, taller still and equally smart.

Tyotya smiled proudly. Those two were her pride and joy. In these parts their tall, greyhound-like bodies, powerful jaws, and fine, rich coats were legendary. They lived with her in her rooms. They kept her company. The other hounds, many of which were the offspring of Milka and Toozik, she kept penned in the large yard around the palace.

As the other animals at the palace joined in, Tyotya stared at the woods and waited. Suddenly the birch trees seemed to shift, the white bark undulating with life. Then two heads, long yet large, with tongues draped out. And legs. Swift long legs dancing with infinite grace and ease in the trees. Floating in full stride across the forest floor, a pair of hounds—part aristocratic borzoi, part totally natural Siberian wolf—emerged with extraordinary speed.

Creatures of beauty, thought Tyotya as she saw the hounds, Milka and Toozik, erupt from the forest. Like great waves, they rolled in, swept around her. So rapid yet so effortless, a combination of the tsar's best and nature's best. A force of life so powerful they could not help but explode. Curious they were tonight, too. She could tell by the romp in their gate, their big open eyes, so frolicking.

Tyotya chuckled and started up the hill. So the dogs had bothered Boris and his friend. A little. A lot. She didn't know, though she was thankful little Boris hadn't been hurt. She imagined the dogs circling the two people, bounding around like a game. That was the wolf in them, that stalking instinct. They would have circled their prey, perhaps nipped

a bit at the ankles. Sampled the flesh. Then, if pro-
voked, they would have gone in for the kill, Milka
on one side of the neck, Toozik on the other. That
was the borzoi in them, the part that had been bred
in over hundreds of years in an attempt to rid the
Russian steppes of its scourge, the wolf. In this way,
too, developed the sport of the wolf hunt, two *bor-
zois* outrunning a single wolf, a dog biting into
either side of the neck, then jointly flipping it over
and pinning it down until the master came to slit
the wolf's neck. That's the way Milka and Toozik
operated too. Always had, which was why Tyotya's
hunts were always successful.

Suddenly two pointy fists shoved into her back
and she was hurled forward, almost knocked to the
ground. It was Milka and Toozik stabbing their long
snouts—which almost reached her shoulder blades—
into her. Oi, thought Tyotya, where do they get all
this energy? From the wild, yes, of course.

"Stop it!"

She swatted at them and they ducked away as if
this, too, were a game. Unfazed, the dogs slow-
galloped up the hill past her. Their tongues bounced
and flapped, as if they were laughing at her, playing
with her. Tyotya shook a fist with a knife at them.
Bad children these were.

"Onward, home now!"

Her breath heavy, she reached the large wooden
fence surrounding the palace and was greeted by an
army of clamoring white paws. The fence, which
she'd built after the war to hold in the first hounds
she'd lured from the woods, creaked and tilted, just

like the palace itself. It was a tall structure, taller than she, built that way to keep the hounds from leaping out. And like the palace, if it weren't soon repaired, it would all come tumbling down.

But the palace of Zarekino would be restored, returned to its glory—a monument to the defense of the hero-city, Leningrad. Any day now, she thought to herself. First the imperial palaces that had belonged to the tsars, then Zarekino. How could the authorities not? It was here that her family—her parents and six brothers and sisters—had been brought by the Fascists to perform their little circus acts. And it was here, after performing one night for the troops and just before their retreat, that the Nazis killed her family. All except her. But she, part of a knife act with her father, had taken her revenge. Eleven officers and seventeen soldiers.

A paw struck the top of the fence and snapped a board.

''Back! Get down!''

Barking and scratching more hounds hurled themselves against the fence. Paws clambered over the top; noses poked skyward. Food. Meat. That's all they wanted, all they cried for. Their stomachs were empty. She'd kept them that way for days. That would shrink their stomachs, sharpen their noses, their eyes. Already, they had become lean, aggressive. Soon they'd become stalkers of the night and under the lead of Milka and Toozik they would hone their instincts. *Da, da*, she thought. She'd waited all summer until the dachas were closed and now she'd have to wait a bit longer, until Boris and his mistress left. After that, though, she'd begin her hunting. Combined with what she'd earned from her hounds over the summer, there'd be enough to live on for another year.

At the edge of the fence, she turned then ducked through a remnant of a wall. A dirt path led through piles of shattered stone and up to a small wooden door. Milka and Toozik were already there, pacing back and forth in anticipation.

She pulled the door, passed through the troll-like opening. This was her place, what served as a home carved out of the palace ruins. The first of the two rooms was large, with a low arched ceiling, and Milka and Toozik charged in ahead of her.

"What, are you hungry, my children? No catch out there?"

In complete comprehension, Milka and Toozik chomped at the air and pranced around her.

"Well, all right. A bit tonight, but that's it."

She led the dogs into the back room and from a wooden tub sunk in the earth took a chunk of cow's udder, which she had earned from a sale to a neighboring peasant. She placed it on a stump, grabbed an axe, and in four strokes quartered the white mass.

Tyotya tossed the meat to her two hounds, and said, "Remember, that's it. You must stay hungry so that once the people at the dacha are gone, you can lead the other hounds. This hunt must be very successful. I want many killed."

𝒯his had been the longest day of her life. Musya had risen early, watched the late sun slowly make its way skyward. All morning and into early afternoon she had stood at the large windows overlooking the Fontanka and stared at the sun as it passed through the sky. It didn't matter that this was one of the brightest days in several weeks. She didn't even notice the people out strolling—the old men, the young lovers, the babushkas with grandchildren—along the canal, soaking up the sunlight. Musya simply wanted this day to be over, the light extinguished.

Especially thankful that the days were growing shorter, she now stood on the balcony and watched as the sun fell to its death. She stood on the far right of the balcony, the late afternoon rush of Nevsky Prospekt right beneath her. Yet, she didn't even see the busses, the masses of people that had swollen the sidewalks for hours. All she saw was the yellow ball, quite swollen across the street and above the Anichkov Palace. Actually, it seemed bigger than ever, seemed to grow in size, as it burned from yellow to deep red.

"Let's go," said a deep voice from within the apartment.

At last, she thought, and the frown on her face exploded into a grin. She dashed inside, closing the French doors behind her. Seeing Kyril, however, her enthusiasm crashed like a dropped vase. His skin was pale and his lack of energy visible. The left sleeve of his leather coat—a small hole where the bullet had pierced—hung limp; his wounded arm was pressed carefully to his stomach. How could she, a good med-sister, lead him away from his bed of rest and recovery?

"Are you sure you're strong enough? Are you in pain? Perhaps you should stay in bed awhile longer. *Da*, *da*, I think that's what you must—"

"*Nyet.*"

"But, dearest, you—"

"Boris isn't a pot of borscht that will improve with age. We must go now, tonight."

Her head bobbed up and down. She wanted desperately to put an end to Boris, but she simply wasn't certain tonight was the best time. Could Kyril hold up? He'd lost so much blood.

"Kyryozhinka, my love, I think it best that you stay and I go."

"*Nyet.* With or without you, I'm going."

"Well, I'm not staying here with those two fresh

bodies in the kitchen and Elizaveta Nikolaevna crammed in the trunk. Besides, you need someone to look after you.''

''No, I don't.''

''Yes, you do.'' A puffy frown covered her face. ''I've taken good care of you, haven't I?''

When he hadn't been sleeping, she'd been feeding him. Borscht, thick with beef, pink with sour cream. Tea and jam. Cheese. Fresh black bread. And caviar for extra strength.

''Well,'' she admitted. ''I suppose you do look good. I can see it now, the color's even back in your cheeks. But are you sure you feel like going?''

''I assure you, my love, that I won't rest peacefully until this is over.''

She kissed him on each cheek, and they started for the door. Musya took her purse from the sofa and swung her trench coat over her shoulders.

''Do we have everything?'' she asked.

Kyril opened his coat, exposed his cleaver that hung from the cotton noose. She checked for the gun and bullets inside her purse, then went to the trunk by the front door and scooped up the car keys. She pinched her nose and turned to Kyril.

''Foo-foo. The two in the kitchen aren't too bad yet, but I can take only another day or so of Lila Nikolaevna. If we get back early enough, we must do something about her,'' she said, waving the back of her hand at the trunk.

''She has become rather offensive, hasn't she?'' He took Musya by the arm. ''You're certain about this, aren't you? Where he is, I mean.''

235

"Kyril, darling, you can't sleep next to someone for so many years without knowing something about him—no matter how much you dislike him. I feel it. I know it in my bones."

His small dark eyes burned away her last doubt.

"*Golubchik*, I'm positive," said Musya. "Boris is at Zarekino. It's as if his love for me beckons us."

CHAPTER
31

In his sleep, Boris felt the smooth skin spread next to his. He touched it, was drawn to it. More. He just wanted more of it to rub all over his naked body. He cupped one of her breasts in his palm and stroked the nipple. He felt her body shift like a warm sea.

Now half-awake, he rolled on his side and was met by her beckoning hands. She pulled him on top of her. Their mouths met, kissed deeply. His fingers clasped her, pulling her tighter.

She opened her legs and lifted her knees, pushing away the wool blanket. She was ready for him, and he felt himself slide into her easily, warmly. Like a passionate nightmare, their movement quickened, raced, as if this were the end of hours of work. Boris felt his skin spread with sweat. Was this a dream or reality? Faster and faster. He heard her moans in his ear, felt her fingers on his back pushing him deeper into her. Then abruptly, they both stiffened and cried out.

Boris' body went soft and his weight sank on her. Her arms wrapped around him. She wouldn't let loose.

He rubbed his cheek on her shoulder. "What a wonderful way to wake up."

Lara opened hers eyes for the first time. "Who's awake? Let's go back to sleep and do it again."

"What time is it?"

To answer his own question, Boris slid off her and sauntered to the wooden shutter. Outside, the light was low and pale on the birches.

"It's early. The sun's just coming up."

"We've only slept a few hours?"

Boris stuck his hand in his curly hair and followed the beams of light to their source. Wait, he thought. Something's not right. If it were morning, the sun should be over there, across from the palace. Not behind it.

"Oi yoi yoi. It must be afternoon. We slept right through the day." His mouth big and wide, his teeth bright, he laughed. "The sun's already going down. It will be night soon."

Half an hour later, Boris stood by the woodpile near the dacha. He leaned against a tree and stared at the sun that was disappearing behind the palace, and thought of his father. No wonder Arkady Yakovich had loved Zarekino. This was where everything came to a slow stop, where the world rested itself. Out here, there were no politics, there was no Party.

That was why, Boris knew, he still liked coming here. More than simply a safe place, the dacha at Zarekino was where conflict did not exist, where father and son continued to come in closest touch with one another. That was why he wanted to keep the dacha and give Musya the apartment. The flat in town, after all, came into the family simply because of his father's political standing.

Stacking birch logs in his arms, he realized what his father had wanted of him. Actually, he had always understood. That was the problem.

Suddenly the logs came tumbling out of his arms, crashing to the ground. Boris rubbed an eye, felt how dry it was and would remain, and for a moment wished he could be a boy again so he could cry. Slumping on the ground, he sat with his head in his hand, and soon the cool evening air filled him, calmed him like the purest vodka. It had been a beautiful day, a day of women's summer, that special time when fall relapses for a while.

Lara stepped around the front of the dacha, where she'd been tending a samovar. "Boris, are you all right?"

He stared at her, thought a second, and shouted, "It's not my fault he was mad at me!"

"What?"

"I understood him," he yelled. "But he never understood me. He never even tried. He made me feel like I was the one who failed." The truth came blurting out of him, clear and painful, and to the ground he said, "But really he was the one who failed. He failed me, his son!"

He turned back toward the palace, gazed at its broken outline hideously highlighted by the last of the sun. One could stay defeated or one could move on. With a deep sigh, he pushed himself to his feet, picked up the logs, and started for the dacha.

Inside, he found Lara setting a dented samovar by an open window. She blew on the fire of twigs and grass that was growing in its heart, then attached a small chimney that carried the smoke out the window. He followed her movements, then without speaking, crossed the room, knelt, and lay the logs in the large clay stove one at a time. With the strike of a match, the fire began to burn yellow and red, bright and warm. In it Boris saw images of Arkady Yakovich.

Her hands landed on his shoulders, and she said, "Boris . . . is everything okay?"

He nodded and stared at the flames. "I miss him, the old Bolshevik. Especially here. This was the one place we could come and not be at odds."

"Your father?"

"*Da, da*. Papa."

She reached around, felt the ridges, and pressed away the wrinkles in his forehead. "Is it that sad?"

"*M-m-da*, I suppose it is." He shrugged. "It's odd how you find a single key and it opens more than just one door."

As if mourning the loss of the day, the hounds at the palace suddenly started to cry. A whole choir of them raised their heads and emptied their lungs, a requiem for all that was gone. Boris listened, their cries more soothing than threatening and almost as purifying as the ripple of the river's water.

He wasn't sure what key it was that he'd found. Perhaps it was one to his father—and that helped him see the truth about Musya. No. Musya was the first door he'd opened. Realizing the desire to be honest with her made him long for honesty about his father too.

"Sometimes the truth is too powerful," he said. "It can drown you. That's what I was afraid of. Opening something and not being able to survive it. But you . . . you gave me a reason to keep my head above the surface."

"*Nyet*. You kept your own head above the water. You would have done it sooner or later. With or without me."

He kissed her, and all those long-fought battles seemed to fade, neither won nor lost, simply concluded. He knew he was right. He forgave himself and he forgave his father. Actually, there'd been nothing to forgive. All of it—everything—had been a series of stepping stones that had led him up to this very moment. Without the trials, would there be Lara? Would he ever have found her?

"Hungry?" she asked.

"Uh-huh."

"The water in the samovar should be hot soon. We can have some tea. Actually, let's have breakfast, lunch and dinner all at once."

Boris hugged her. Everything, he felt, was almost complete, the puzzle almost solved. Finally, rubbing his forehead, he broke away and went to the window.

"You know, I want to turn my back on my past. I want my new life—our new life—to begin."

"Boris, it's already begun," Lara assured him.

"It has and it hasn't. Something lingers." His father was dead, nothing to do but make peace in his mind. There was, however, someone else. "And that's Musya. I'm determined to tell her the truth even if it kills me."

A s night settled on the palace, Tyotya could stand it no more. She'd kept Milka and Toozik with her all day, never out of eyesight, because Boris Ankadievich and that woman were down at the dacha. But the hounds were going to drive her crazy. Rather than being exhausted from their run last night, they were energized and they wanted more. Run. Outside. Hunt. That's what they seemed to be begging with their big eyes. That's what they wanted each time they nudged Tyotya with their long snouts. Now, inside, the dogs followed her every movement and were never more than a half-step behind her.

Finally, Tyotya threw up her hands. "Oi, we can't start hunting until our visitors at the dacha leave!"

She stomped into the back room and reached into the wooden tub for the last of the udder. Food, she hoped, would calm them. Her anger causing her old muscles to ache, she spread the raw meat on the

243

stump, then with the skill of a knife thrower, divided it perfectly. Almost knocking her over, the tall dogs swarmed around her as she tossed the meat into two dishes.

"Calm yourself!" she snapped, smacking Milka on her nose. "Special food only because you have to stay in again. No running free tonight. You must stay with me."

As the hounds swallowed their food, she went to the other wall and washed her hands in a pail of water. Drying herself on her black skirt, she crossed the large room with its arched ceiling and looked out the window. Down the hill she could see a window in a cabin glow with light. A curl of smoke rose from the chimney too. So they were still there, Boris Ankadievich and the other one. They'd been quiet all day, so quiet that Tyotya wondered if they'd somehow left unnoticed. She didn't like having others around, but at least these two young people wouldn't be a bother.

She wouldn't tolerate any disruption. Zarekino had to be kept safe, guarded from hooligans. That was her job, the reason the authorities let her remain all these years. She had to look after the place until it was restored.

She made her way to a bench along the far wall and sat down. At her feet lay a knife that she used for cutting the finished yarn and a mounting pile of the finest hair—white and sable and silver—that she'd collected over the past month. She didn't need much money, only enough to buy salt and kerosene and a few other things; she grew her own potatoes and cabbage. What money she did need, though, she earned from the sale of the yarn she spun and from the meat she collected from her hunts. Her hounds, after all, were the swiftest creatures in the area, and when the dachas were empty for the winter she would take her animals out, two or three at a time. She almost always returned with a deer or wild dog or other woodland creature, which the meat-poor villagers eagerly bought up.

The hair that lay before her was already washed and combed, and all that was left was to spin it into yarn. Yarn that shimmered and felt like silk yet had the durability of leather. Next week in the village she would find another eager buyer. Or a quick trade, perhaps for more udder. She was always well rewarded. The villagers prized the wool of Tyotya's hounds because it combined the beauty of the borzoi's fur with the warmth and toughness of the Siberian wolf's coat.

From the floor Tyotya took the distaff, a large L-shaped piece of wood, its once decorative paint long ago rubbed off. She slid the bottom of the device under her thigh, attached a clump of hair to the top portion. With the pencil-like spindle in her left hand to hold the yarn, she began to spin. Under her skilled fingers, the wooly hair grew into a tight yarn of rich brown, flecked with silver.

She heard a slight scratching noise across the room. Her eyes rose upward and in the faint light of her lantern, she saw a thick gray body with a long tail. A rat. Pressed against the base of the log wall, the rodent froze.

245

Another one, thought Tyotya. How many can there be? How many mice and rats can the cool weather drive into her home? Still holding the spindle in her left hand, with her right Tyotya carefully reached down and wrapped her fingers around the knife. As slow as a rising moon, she raised her hand, her eyes all the while on the motionless rat. Then she cocked her arm. The rodent shot forward, and Tyotya hurled the knife. In an instant, it was over, the rat speared to the wooden wall.

"Ach . . ." muttered Tyotya, rising.

She hated these things creeping about, stealing her food. Parasites on her existence. Her weathered face expressing a storm of displeasure, she went to the wall, freed her knife with one tug, and lifted the plump rat by its long tail. Holding the bloody pest out in front of her, she moved to the front door and unlatched it. She took one glance behind her, heard the dogs licking their bowls, and went out.

She passed the rear of the palace, a three-story annex—now windowless—that had once contained the kitchens and the servants' quarters. Some thirty meters farther, Tyotya stood on the edge of a small ravine. With one heave she tossed the rat into the darkness, then turned, a scowl on her face. It was hopeless, she knew, but she still hoped the dogs wouldn't find the dead creature.

Her face twisted with disgust, she headed back to her rooms. Passing her window, though, she stopped in her tracks, unable to believe what she saw through the wavy panes of glass. There, on the other side of the thick stone wall and scurrying beneath the table, was a second rat, its nose vibrating in quest of food.

Furious, Tyotya ran to the open door, then stopped herself. If she made noise, she'd scare the thing away. Be calm, she told herself. That was the only way she'd kill this creature too. So without pushing on the door, she slipped in, and spotted the knife just inside where she'd left it.

Concentrating totally on her stealth, though, Tyotya failed to realize that, other than the rodent and herself, her rooms were quite free of life. Milka and Toozik had bounded off into the night.

CHAPTER
33

"**T**omorrow I begin my novel," said Boris as Lara placed the cheese and pickles on the table before him. "I'm going to start living my dream. I can't keep driving a truck and wishing I were doing something else."

"You can do it, Boris. I know you can. And I'll be your editor, read the book as you work on it. All the fresh air here will be good for your imagination too. Not to mention being away from the city."

"*Da, da.*"

He forced himself to push away all the memories of Leningrad. The book—think about the book. War and invasion. Yes, the Hitlerites had come this far. Not even forty-five years ago the Germans had come and taken over Zarekino during the siege of Leningrad. Fascists had covered this entire area. Soldiers camped here by the river; officers were billeted at the palace. For all 900 days of the siege Zarekino

248

had been theirs to use and abuse and to ruin. Horses and trucks in one wing of the palace, a mess hall and hundreds of soldiers in another. Tyotya and her family, her gypsy father and her Russian mother, had been forced to set up their little circus in the grand ballroom. Every night for a month they were forced to perform. Then all except Tyotya were destroyed.

Yes, all this was excellent material for a book. A character such as Tyotya would be the spine of the story and like her, after a bloody revenge, she would survive the war. Perhaps Boris's fictional character, as Tyotya, would live far beyond her tragedy, at first left alone as a war hero, later forgotten.

Boris sketched the face of a woman whose mission in life—the restoration of a palace where her entire family had been murdered—was not even talked about officially, let alone planned. He drew the eyes, small and pained, the face narrow, the hair—

Boris stopped. Emerging on the paper was not the face of Tyotya, but of Sergei, his face caught just as it was before he was shot. Horrified, Boris threw down the pencil, and flipped over the paper.

Lara set two chipped glasses on the table. "Boris?" She placed a bottle of cognac in front of him and sat down on the opposite bench.

He raised his head. At the sight of her gentle face and those green eyes that read his soul, he began to relax. For him she was the only star in the dark sky.

"It's going to be all right," she said.

Wordlessly, they lifted their glasses and, Georgian style, bent close and linked arms. Boris leaned over and kissed her on the tip of her nose.

"To us, to our love, to our baby," he said, his voice low.

Tilting back their heads, they threw the cognac down open throats. A burning sensation shot through Boris and he felt his head swell with emotion. He grabbed a hunk of bread, held it to his nose, and let its rich, earthy smell bring him back to reality.

"We'll come out here every weekend," he said.

"The fresh air will be good for the baby." With her eyes closed, she held her stomach. A silly grin emerged on her face. "I can read and you can write. Can you imagine such a wonderful life?"

"So you like it?" he asked. "Zarekino and the dacha? I—"

Suddenly, his face whitening, he turned in his chair. "What was that?"

With no alarm on her face, Lara said, "What? Boris, come now, you must relax."

"No, I heard something. I swear!"

Boris rose from the bench, certain that something or someone had cried out from across the river.

CHAPTER
34

*T*hey stepped out of the birches and into the edge of the meadow. Musya knew where to look and was the first to spot it. A yellow square of light below and, above, a gray slick curling into the moonlit sky.

Entirely pleased with herself, she whispered, "I told you Boris was here."

Kyril spotted the little window and the smoke rising skyward then studied the other nearby cabins. Everything else was dark.

"Let's hope he's alone."

"Of course he is, Kyril. Down at the dacha, I mean." Musya motioned to the broken palace and a thin strip of smoke off to one side. "Don't forget Tyotya, the caretaker. Look, she has a fire up at her place too." Musya thought about the stories she'd heard. "We have to be especially careful of her."

"I thought you said she was an old woman? he said, his voice hushed.

"She is, but—"

"Don't worry. We'll just be quiet and quick. Slip in and slip out." He opened his coat and pulled out the cleaver. "This shouldn't be difficult."

Fortunately, the bleeding in his left arm had stopped in the early afternoon. Musya was certain there'd be no complications, but she could see discomfort in his eyes, how he strained not to move his arm.

"Oi, I think it must hurt terribly, eh, *golubchik*? she said, reaching her lips to his cheek. "Just let me—"

"Stop it, would you?" He pushed her away. "Of course it hurts, but I can manage. Let's finish here and get back to town."

The two of them had left Leningrad less than an hour ago, Musya driving Boris's car down the Moscow Highway. As they neared Zarekino, she had pulled off the main road into a clump of birches, then led the way on foot down the long lane.

"How do we get across the river?" he asked.

Her lips pushed out in annoyance. "There's a footbridge in that grove."

Kyril started down the path, through the meadow, and Musya followed in complete silence. As she walked through the grass, her eyes on the palace, a chill of fear ran through her. In and out. Quick and quiet. She prayed the deed would be simple. They had to surprise him, kill him, not rouse the old gypsy woman, and everything would be fine. They'd be back in Leningrad in no time.

By the time they were halfway to the bridge Musya was trembling in fear and anticipation. She wanted to be on the far side of the end, not just before it. Ach! How she hated Boris. A simpleton born into a life of luxury, full of all that she wanted. And he didn't even appreciate it, let alone deserve it!

Something whooshed to her right, crushing dry grass as it moved, and she gasped. She searched the meadow and saw nothing but a plain of grass and, in the distance, another edge of birches. Her nerves? Her imagination? No. There it was again. The clear sound of someone in the distance rushing through the field. Biting her lip, she hurried forward and touched Kyril on the back.

"What?" he snapped in a whisper.

Her voice was but a gasp. "Something's . . . out there." She swung her heavy arm across the meadow, brought it back to her bosom. There was nothing to see in the pale light of the moon except an empty field.

And there it was again! This time clearer. A gentle beat, a rhythm of nature like the pounding of waves.

"Listen!" she hissed.

The noise grew louder. Musya's head shot up and she spotted something charging toward them. Then it swerved and was hurled aside.

"Oi!" she gasped in a hushed voice.

"Ts-s-s!" he said. "Keep quiet!"

"But I saw something! Something big and white."

"Where?"

Kyril looked to the river, but saw nothing. "It must have been a birch stump."

She screwed up her eyes. "What? No, I—"

"Come on, we have to get out of this open area. Keep down."

He nudged her with the tip of his cleaver and started off. She hesitated, then glanced behind. There was something back there, she knew it. Shivering, she hurried after him, at the same time reaching in her purse for the pistol. And then she heard it again. The loping, rhythmic sound. She spun around. This time the flash of white was clear before it disappeared.

"Kyril, there's some sort of animal out there!"

He turned. The creature raced nearer, and this time he saw it too. Long furry legs loping through the grass, a large jaw filled with saw-like teeth.

"Keep moving."

Seeking the safety of the birch grove ahead, Musya and Kyril hurried on. As the animal circled, the lithe steps passed from one side to the other to the other. Musya thought it was charging from behind, and she spun around. An odd, massive figure flew at her like a white sheet fluttering through the night, then vanished. As soon as that one disappeared, another flashed in and out of sight directly before them.

"They're two of them!"

"What are they?" asked Kyril.

"Some sort of dog, I think. The old woman out here had some wild dogs that were part wolf. Huge ones. Oi!"

Kyril grabbed her by the arm. "Come on, we'll be safe in the woods. Just keep quiet. We don't want Boris to hear us."

Musya and Kyril broke into a trot, all the while aware of the creatures galloping around them in circles. The padding of paws raced in front of them, then off to the side. Musya glanced up and saw the birch grove just ahead. If they could make it there, Kyril and she might be able to dodge in and out of the trees. The bridge wasn't too much farther after that.

Then suddenly the silence returned to the night, an absence of sound now more frightening. Fearful that they had entered the heart of a trap, Musya and Kyril slowed to a stiff walk.

"Where are they?" she asked. "Do you think they're gone?"

"Am I a dog? How am I supposed to know?"

They gazed down the path behind them, found it empty. Kyril turned forward and saw it first. There, blocking the path, stood a tall, entirely white hound. Its long pointed teeth glowed phosphorous-like in the dark and a gurgling roar emerged from its throat.

"Don't move," said Kyril.

Slowly, he raised the cleaver, then stood motionless, hoping the hound might lose interest. Musya, wondering where the other one had vanished, began to shift from side to side.

"The second one—where is it?" he asked.

"Tfoo, I don't know! I—"

The dry grass rustled to her right. The other hound swooped past her, reaching out with its mouth. Pointed teeth grazed Musya's leg, tore skin free. Musya stiffled a scream and kicked out at the creature, connecting a foot with its rear hip. The dog yelped into the sky, then disappeared.

Kyril caught Musya, balanced her. "Are you all right?"

"I . . . I guess," she gasped, touching her bloodied leg.

The one in front of them flinched, ready to leap. Kyril took a large step forward swinging his cleaver. The hound raised its head but did not give ground.

Then Musya heard the ominous sound again. The rapid padding of paws. A charge. She gasped, spun from side to side, searching the dark. There it was. A white streak, gracefully hunkered down, fur feathering in the wind. And charging directly at her, jaws open. Musya gasped, fear burning at the base of her throat. What did this monster want of her?

Her legs. Musya bent over and tried to hide her legs, to protect them from those piercing teeth. She felt the blood surge in her body, saw the creature flying like an owl of the night. She wrapped one arm around her knee, but as she cowered, she caught her foot on the edge of the dirt path. Her body swayed. She felt herself tip. She looked up, saw the hound hurling at her and now only meters away. Panicking, Musya swung an arm out. Then, completely off-balance, she toppled forward. With arms outstretched, she fell into the creature, caught it full force. Its long head rammed into her stomach and the air burst from her. Claws slashed her face. Jaws snapped into her flesh. And both bodies— human and animal—tumbled to the ground.

CHAPTER

35

*T*he blade of Tyotya's knife grew warm between her thumb and forefinger. It would be a clean throw, a quick kill. She brought back her arm, steadied her eye. The rat, though, noticed something, twitched, and inched forward beneath a chair.

With one of the chair's legs now blocking the way, the scowl hardened straight across Tyotya's face. Her arm relaxed a bit and she stepped sideways a half-step. Paused. The rat saw her, though, and bolted toward the wall. Tyotya bent slightly back, then hurled the knife forward. The silvery blade shot through the air. But the rat was fast, faster than Tyotya thought, and the knife missed it by centimeters. Terrified, the rodent shot into a crevice in the wall.

"K' chortoo!" To hell with it, cursed Tyotya, loosening her knife from the floor.

She froze. Above her own commotion she heard

something. Leaning on the edge of the table, she listened. What was that, coming from so far away? Could it be one of her dogs? No, the noise was across the river, not from the nearby pen. Unless, of course, one of the hounds had jumped the fence.

The calm of her house suddenly struck her.

"Milka? Toozik? Ah-ew!" she called.

She scurried into the other room, found nothing but their empty dishes. Cursing herself, Tyotya ran to the front door. Of course. She'd left the door open. They'd escaped into the night. But why would they cry out like that? What was wrong?

She rushed outside and over the rubble, dread filling her. Her back to the palace, she stood on the ridge looking down. At the bottom of the hill the single window of Boris Ankadievich's dacha was lit up. But there were no loud voices, no strangers. All seemed normal.

Breaking the tenuous calm came the muffled cry of a person. Tyotya cupped her ear. The sound fell away just as quickly as it had risen, but Tyotya was still shaken. People! But where were they? Where had that cry come from? Her eyes ran from the dacha below to the river to the meadow on the other side. Or perhaps it had come from way over there, on this side of the river and to the south. That's where she'd found those boys from the village last week.

Her anger intensifying, she rushed back into the cabin and grabbed her knives. Then she went to the other room and pulled the hatchet from the stump. Milka and Toozik were out there somewhere, no

259

doubt caught up in this disturbance. And whoever had entered the grounds—village hooligans or ruffians from Leningrad—she would allow no trouble at Zarekino.

CHAPTER

36

Lara pressed down on his shoulder. "Please, relax. Boris, no one followed us out here."

Yes, she's right, he told himself. He was just being overly cautious. Cognac. Perhaps another glass would help.

He started to pour some into Lara's glass, but stopped as the sound assaulted his ears again.

"You heard it this time, didn't you?" he asked.

Lara looked up from her glass with a puzzled expression. "Heard what?"

"A cry, I think."

He rose, swung his legs over the bench, and went to the door. Outside, the waters of the river rippled along; the bright moon shimmered on the surface. On the other side, the meadow grass and the birch trees bent and hissed in the night breeze. Off to the right, behind the silhouette of the palace, charcoal clouds rushed through the air as if puffed from a locomotive.

"It must have been one of Tyotya's dogs."

He stared up at the palace, but saw nothing in the gray light of the moon. He could discern only the rustling of dry fall leaves off in the woods as the birches danced in the night breeze. Shrugging, he returned to the table.

"Gav-gav, av-av." Bow-wow, he said, trying to make light of himself. "Maybe there was a dog fight."

Sitting down opposite, Boris reached across the table for Lara's hand. Then he leaned forward, just as she did, and their lips met. Her soft greeting closed everything else out, pushed all his worries far away.

He jerked away.

"There—did you hear it that time?" he asked, looking toward the door.

She wiped her lips. "No, I didn't. I didn't hear a thing." Lara laughed and tried to pull him back. "Boris, you're being ridiculous. We left all our troubles back in Leningrad. Everything's okay now. It's just you and me."

"Yes, but . . ." He turned back to her and was met by her green eyes sparkling excitedly.

"Boris," she began, "I was thinking . . ." She lifted his hand to her mouth and nibbled at each of his fingers. Embarrassed, she laughed a bit.

"Back home—there's just not that much privacy. My apartment's so small and the walls are so thin."

Still thinking about what could lie in wait outside, he gazed back at the door. "So?"

She sat up. "I was thinking it'd be fun . . . you know, like I talked about, to . . . to make love. Outside."

He spun around and grabbed her hand. "Lara, no. I don't think that'd be such a—"

"Boris, no one followed us here and you know it. We both kept checking all the way out."

"What about the hounds?"

She made a face expressing her concern. "Well, you said yourself Tyotya had penned them up. Besides, we could go right down by the river. Or . . . or just behind the dacha."

"Lara, I . . ."

"Boris, you sound like an old married man."

She beamed red with her own accusation and flashed him a mischievous grin. Then, impulsively, she bolted for the door.

"Lara!"

Right before his eyes she threw open the latch. He sat there stunned. What in the devil's name was she doing? She looked at him one more time, laughed, then charged outside. He raced to the doorway. Her lithe figure stood on the edge of the dark some ten meters away.

"Lara, come back!"

"Come on, Boris! Don't be stodgy. Come on out!

We'll do it like the cossacks!'' she hollered disappearing around the edge of the dacha.

"*Nyet*, Lara!'' he screamed. *"Nyet!''*

But she was already gone, swallowed up by the night.

Helplessly, they rolled to the ground, Musya and the hound, a panicked bundle of arms and legs. She tried to scream as teeth bit into her, claws scratched down her, but she had no air in her lungs. No power to fuel her shriek. She felt the dog's legs tear into her as it scrambled madly to dig away, to push the massive body to the side. Like steel traps, jaws snapped here, there, grabbing into her arms, ripping into clothing. Instinctively, Musya rolled to the side, wrapped her arms around her neck and kicked with her feet. Steamy hot breath spewed into her face, and Musya twisted as if she were being raped. She squirmed for escape, found none, as again and again fangs sunk into her. Dead, she thought. She was going to be killed, chewed to a pulpy mass by a crazed hound.

She opened her mouth to scream for Kyril's help. Pathetically, her mouth opened and formed the

words, save me! save me, my love! But there still
was no air within to animate her vocal cords.
Thrashing, she opened her eyes and was terrified at
what she saw through the meadow's grass. The other
hound was attacking Kyril. It was over, she sobbed
in her mind. They were both dead. Oi. Let this evil
creature rip my throat out and be done with me
right now.

Suddenly, the earth below her vibrated with a
tremor. Musya struck the hound above her on the
side of its head and glanced back. A red and white
carcass lay there, a dead, broken mass. Then she
saw Kyril's dark shoes cutting through the weeds,
and, an instant later, a silvery blade appeared, a
shinning spot of hope like a bright moon in the sky.
She kneed the animal in the stomach, forced it up
just as the cleaver came flying down. The blade
skimmed past her, connected with fur and flesh.
There was a crack of bone, and the paws on Musya's chest flexed as if electrocuted, then went soft.
The hound fell off her.

"Are you all right?" asked Kyril, his voice
hushed.

She managed to nod as she clambered to her feet.
Then she spun into him, and Kyril wrapped his one
good arm around and patted her.

"What about you?" she gasped.

"Okay."

"Oi . . ." Her breath was returning to normal.
"It . . . it bit me but I think . . ."

She stepped back and examined herself. Her legs

were dotted red, her skirt torn. Touching her arm, she felt the aching muscles where jaws had locked.

"*Da*, *da*. My clothing protected me. I'm bruised but just . . . just a few nips. Oi, Kyril."

Again she let him hold her.

"Do you want to turn around, go back?" he whispered.

Shaking her head, she pushed away. "*Nyet*! There's no turning back until Boris is dead. Do you understand? I . . . I think I'll go crazy if we don't dispose of him tonight. Kyril, I can't wait another moment, I . . ."

"Ts-s-s." Kyril glanced toward the distant cabin on the other side of the river. "We don't want him to hear us, do we? So we'll proceed."

The two of them set off down the path, melting into the gathering of birches. The trees grew thick all around, a small dense forest on the edge of the river. Abruptly, Musya stopped. Someone was calling out. There, again, a voice came, the clarity of the words lost among the birches. But even though she couldn't understand what was being said, she recognized the speaker.

She pulled on Kyril's sleeve, and whispered, "That's Boris!"

Trying to get a clear view of the dacha, she dodged, gun in hand, in and out of the trees and toward the river. Finally, she could make out Boris standing there in the front door, the light from inside the dacha casting out his shadow. His head turned from side to side as he stepped onto the ground. And then he rushed off to one side, disappearing into the dark woods.

"What did he say?" whispered Kyril, hurrying up behind her.

"I . . . I don't know. The trees sort of blocked it. I couldn't hear."

"Someone else is with him."

"Well, maybe there is," she said, glaring through the leaves at the dacha. "So I was wrong."

"Didn't he call a woman's name?"

Musya gawked at Kyril and her response, though hushed, was quick. "Don't be ridiculous. Of course he doesn't have a woman out here."

"What about a lover?"

"Boris . . . with another woman?"

Musya shook her head, brushed back a wisp of hair. What Kyril was suggesting was utter nonsense. After all, why did they have to kill Boris and why had he been so hard to kill? For one simple reason: Boris was crazy about her, Musya. He adored her, lusted after her.

"Boris could never cheat on me. He's terrified of hurting people. And he'd never hurt me, in particular."

Kyril grabbed her and pulled her down. "Perhaps it was someone from the gang." He stared over at the dacha.

"Da, da," agreed Musya. "That's the answer." Yes, it had to be someone from that silly gang. "We'll just have to take care of them both."

Kyril, peering through the trees, searched the other side of the river. The dacha's door was still open, spilling light outside. There was, however, no sign of Boris or anyone else from the gang.

"You're right," he said. "Whoever they are and wherever they are, we'll just have to get them both. We might have to split up, you and I. Find them and go at them from opposite sides."

Musya kissed Kyril's rough cheek. She rose and started back toward the path, pistol held ready in front of her.

"At least," she whispered right behind her to Kyril, "we know about them, but they don't know about us."

He nodded and, crouching, the two of them made it to the river and across the narrow bridge.

CHAPTER

38

Boris froze by the side of the dacha and listened as Lara ducked behind the cabin. What was she doing this for? And why now? It wasn't like her to do something foolhardy, especially after their encounter last night with the hounds. Perhaps she was just trying to help him escape into pleasure, make him forget all that had happened back in town. Instead, her actions served as a bracing reminder of all the dangers.

When he heard her steps continue past the end of the dacha and into the dense grove of birches, he could stand it no more.

"Lara!"

Nothing came back, not even an echo. Shaking his head, he rushed to the back of the little building. This wasn't a game he liked.

His eyes searched the white birches. No, he wouldn't go any farther. She was certain to give up any moment. Confident, he wandered to a tree, leaned against its white bark, and stared at the river. Its soft rippling was so soothing. The music of nature, that's what he was listening to. A gentle procession of sounds that had always been in harmony, from the time of the tsars, through the occupation, to today. Now how could he write something like—

The crushing of leaves filled his ears, and he spun around. Ah-ha! So he had won. She was coming back. *Slava bogu.* Thank god.

But the woods before him fell silent again and still there was no sign of Lara. He stared in the direction that he thought the noise had come from, but heard nothing. He opened his mouth to call to her when he heard rustling off to his right. Then more noise back to the left. Dread pumping through his body, he realized that Lara was not alone out there.

Liking this situation less and less, he realized he couldn't afford to outwait Lara. Taking a deep breath, he started for the woods. He stopped at the first birch, the very edge, and took hold of its papery bark. Those were definitely running steps he heard, and they were coming from up there on his right. He took off.

There was just enough moonlight for Boris to realize how poorly he could see. A blend of darkness and shadows, of faint light and white birches danced before him. He tripped on a fallen branch, caught himself on a tree. Dusting his hands off, he stood perfectly still. Crinkly steps came from over there.

Wait! No, from across there. He turned around and around.

"Nyet," he muttered.

So deep had he already passed into the forest, so repetitive were the trees, that he no longer knew which direction he'd come from. Was the dacha there, beyond that leaning birch? Or back there, toward that grove of straight ones? If he walked in one direction he would surely come to the other edge of the forest—-eventually, anyway. But which edge? The other side of Zarekino or the side along the river? Ach! For the first time he was truly mad at Lara. Why was she doing this?

Something rushed to his left. He tried to locate the source of noise. Was it charging him? It was so close, growing with each moment. He turned to his left, then to the right. There. Something over there flashing in and out of the trees. A person? An animal? But it passed too quickly, then fled out of reach and out of sight, whatever it was gobbled up by the birches.

"Come out!" he shouted.

A noise came from straight ahead and he charged forward. Weaving between the slender trees, he used his hands to deflect the branches, to propel himself. With each running step, his feet pounded the fall leaves, cracking the dark silence. He was going to find Lara, take her up in his arms, and carry her back to the dacha. He ran like either a hunted animal or the hunter, just which he couldn't say.

Then he stopped. This was hopeless. He was becoming ever more lost and farther, he sensed, from finding Lara. He leaned back against a tree, his heart pounding, his breath spewing out. Suddenly, he heard more footsteps. They were coming from right behind him. He opened his mouth to shout when suddenly a pair of hands shot out and grabbed him. One hand clasped over his mouth, the other over his stretched out neck, then pinned him back against the tree.

$\mathcal{T}$yotya relaxed her grip on her axe and her knives. She was all wrong. She'd thought the cry of her dogs had come from down here, to the south of the palace and on this side of the river. Those hooligans from the nearby village had entered from this direction before. Perhaps they had changed their strategy, though. Or perhaps it wasn't the hooligans but acquaintances of Boris Ankadievich. Well, whoever it was, she wouldn't have anyone stirring up trouble here at Zarekino. She'd find Milka and Toozik and together they'd chase the intruders away.

She scanned the field one last time, checking the open area, the smattering of oaks and pines off to the side. With no sign of life, she turned toward the river. *Da, da.* She was certain of it now. They must have invaded Zarekino directly, passing through the old entrance. Milka and Toozik must have caught them in the meadow just the other side of the foot-bridge.

Pausing a moment, Tyotya itched her thigh with the blunt end of her axe. There was a better way to accomplish this patrol. More subtle. If she passed back down this open field to the footbridge, the hooligans might spot her black figure in the moonlight. And what would they do? Attack her? Perhaps. Which only meant she had to be more careful, retain her element of surprise.

The bend in the river. Downstream, that's where she'd cross. At its broadest point there, the river was shallow and filled with stones and also out of view of the footbridge. The best place for catching crayfish, the water was also easily traversed there, some peasant long ago having laid rock after rock from one bank to the other.

Wasting no time, she hurried through the field, down the embankment and across the river. Making her way through the birch grove on the other side, she neared the footbridge, spied no one, then edged along until she came to the meadow. With one hand to an ear, she listened. Certainly she should be able to hear Milka and Toozik. But the beating of their paws, their deep panting, and certainly their howls were oddly absent.

Puzzled, she emerged from the birch grove into the moonlight and started down the path. Axe held ready, she moved along, her eyes scouring the meadow and the edge of the forest beyond. It was then that she glanced across the river and saw the open door of the dacha. Yellow light poured out on the ground, but there was no one about. Not a single person could be seen inside, nor anyone out front. What had happened? What would cause Boris Arkadievich to abandon the dacha and leave the door wide open on such a cool night? Had this trouble of his followed him from Leningrad?

Not sure what to do, Tyotya stopped. She stared across the river at the dacha, then gazed up the path. It was then that she saw the odd shapes, two unfamiliar mounds lying off in the grass.

Immediately, she raised the hatchet and crouched down. The pale light of the moon gradually yielded vague shapes. A leg, but not a human one. A covering, but not cloth.

"Gospodi!" she cried out.

Her short legs carried her quickly down the narrow path, and each second the horror became more distinct. But no, she begged, don't let it be them!

But it was. Yes. *Bozhe.* Those two slaughtered piles of red and white fur were her hounds, her Milka and Toozik. A knot formed in Tyotya's throat. Her knees buckled and she fell to the ground. And for the first time since before the war, tears spilled out of her eyes.

CHAPTER
40

Boris ripped the hands away from his mouth and throat with surprising ease and threw himself forward. Get away, he screamed inside himself. Get away! But the tip of his right shoe caught in the dirt and he tumbled forward, his hands breaking his fall on the ground. He scrambled desperately in the leaves and rolled on his side. If he was caught, he wasn't going to make it easy on his enemies. He'd fight to the death.

''Boris?'' The person paused, then moved closer. ''What . . . what are you doing?''

''What do you mean? Lara—what the hell do you mean what am *I* doing?''

Her thin figure knelt down, and she caressed his face. An apologetic smile crossed her face. Her game had backfired.

''I'm sorry, I only—''

"No, don't! Don't touch me!" He glared at her. "Why did you come all the way out here?"

"I heard you following and I just went a little bit further. And then I got lost. I'm . . . I'm sorry. Really. You're right. It wasn't funny at all."

Fetal-like, he drew his legs up into him, wrapped his arms around himself. The night air burned his lungs. "I thought you were someone from that gang!"

"Borinka, *mili moi.*" My dear. "Really, I'm sorry. I . . ."

She touched him lightly on the knee. He recoiled. Of all the times to pull something like this. . . .

"It's just all so recent," he said. "Sergei's death and—"

"Ts-s-s. Of course. But we're at Zarekino. We're safe from that gang, from everyone."

That was it, he realized. He was edgier than he wanted to admit. The events of the past days—could it be less than two days since he'd delivered those stolen parts?—hadn't sunk in yet. Yesterday he'd missed out on so much sleep that it had numbed him, protected him in a way. Today, however, he was just beginning to experience the shock of what had happened.

"One day in the life of Boris Ankadievich." He tried to force laughter and sputtered instead. "Oi yoi yoi."

Instead of pushing herself on him, Lara crouched down and sat next to him. She, too, brought her knees to her chest and wrapped her arms around her legs. Relieved at her distance, comforted by her proximity, Boris began to relax.

For a long time, the two of them sat staring into the endless birches that had lost most of their leaves for the season. Above, through the naked branches, the white orb of moon provided a heavenly night-light. Like the luminous hands of a watch, the white birch bark reached skyward and pushed back the dark.

Boris gazed at Lara's pale cheeks, her open blouse. Like the birches, her skin, too, seemed full of its own light, and he was drawn to her. His lips met her body at the base of her throat. Lara's chin rose, her knees sank, and she held his head, wrapped her arms around his shoulders, cradled him in her bosom. Nestled in her warmth, Boris never wanted to move again.

"I'm sorry," she finally said. "Coming out into the woods sounded like fun—"

He touched his fingers to her lips. "Ts-s-s."

The tempo of his heart began to rise again this time not from anxiety. Pressed close to Lara and her lavender scent, he began to recall those after-noons spent hidden in her apartment. His eyes flut-tered as he drifted back into wonderful memories of love and lust. . . .

He pulled at her collar, kissed the flat, silky skin above her breasts. Her hair whisked over his cheek. He caught a clump of it and pulled her down until their mouths met. They kissed deeply, like lovers who had fought bitterly and then pledged never to argue again. A cool night air blew up. Fall leaves danced around them, and Boris and Lara swirled around and fell to the ground.

Lying next to her on the forest floor, Boris said, "I'm the one who's sorry. This was a good idea."

She ruffled his hair and he propped himself up on an elbow. He plucked at the buttons of her blouse, then tugged it from her pants. As her blouse fell away, he rubbed the side of his face over her warm stomach. So smooth, so talcum-soft.

The leaves bristled and crinkled as he rolled on top of her, a knee on either side. They stared into each other's eyes as together they worked her blouse off her shoulders, laying it like a smooth carpet beneath her. Then they freed her bra, and Boris gathered it up in a fist and tossed it far away. In what seemed like a long time, but was actually only a few seconds, Boris knelt above her and stared. Gasping, he dove down, burying his face between her breasts, losing himself in the hot swells of her. Then he nibbled her with his lips, all over on either side, and she sunk her fingers into his hard shoulders.

Something thrashed behind. Boris froze, panic surging his heart as if they'd just been walked in upon. He sat back, turned, strained to hear what he thought were steps in the birches.

He gasped. Two fingers pushed at the hardness in his pants. With her other hand, she pulled at his belt. He took one last look behind them and saw, not a person, but Lara's feet pushing at the leaves, digging with her heels into the earth. As she pried at him, pushed and caressed, he pulled open his shirt, loosened the buttons of his pants. He did not shed them, though. Not Yet. Instead he lay down, pressing his furry chest against her breasts.

Boris felt himself sink deeper into her as she spread wider. His lips devoured hers as he reached down between the two of them and slid his hand into her pants. The flat plane of his palm moved along, his fingers prying under, then inside her clothing. Her skin was hot here, smoothness giving away to soft curls. He pressed deeper still and suddenly she shook as if he'd pressed a magic button. She pushed up at him with a strength he'd never known she possessed; but he held firm, kept his lips to hers, his hand inside her clothing. Her head twisted, broke her mouth away from his. It was then that he saw her eyes, big and terrified as if she were seeing her own death.

"Ai!" she cried.

Boris yanked his hand from her pants, threw himself to the side, rolled to the ground. An enormous figure—entirely dark except for the moonlit blade of a cleaver overhead—charged out of the birches. Boris recognized him at once. The man in the leather jacket—with maniacal determination burning in his eyes.

Boris lunged over Lara, spreading himself as wide as he could to protect her. Not her, he screamed inside. Not her and the child!

A single word ripped out of his throat. *"Nyet!"*

His cry only caused the assailant to gather speed. Boris tried to see the face, saw only the outline of a nose and a crop of dark hair. The leather coat was clear, though. Thick and crisp and shiny. In a secondary pause, though, Boris saw how the left sleeve hung limp. Then time raced ahead again, and Boris stared high, saw that thick right arm with its cleaver pull back, load the muscles with full force. Dread flushed through Boris. The stranger would not only strike him first, but he'd strike with enough crude force to slice right through his body and into Lara. Boris looked directly at him, tensed his body in anticipation as he saw the man in the leather jacket hurl his arm and the cleaver forward.

Suddenly something else appeared. Someone. An old woman. And out of her hand flashed a knife so quickly that Boris almost didn't see it. As fast as an arrow, the blade pierced the air, then slammed into the man's left shoulder.

"Ai!" he cried, still charging them.

Boris saw the split-second of a chance as the man in the leather jacket stumbled a half-step. He rolled off Lara, grabbed her. His entire body turned to a single muscle as he tried to pull her out of the way. He looked up. The huge figure of the man sliced down. With all his strength, Boris jerked at Lara, who was scrambling on her own. The man, knife hanging from his shoulder, fell short, his cleaver striking much too low. For an instant, Boris thought Lara and he had escaped. But then he heard it, the slicing of skin, the striking of bone.

"Ai-i-i-i!" curdled Lara's scream.

The man fell to the side, dropped to his knees, and clutched at the knife in his shoulder. Boris bounded to his feet. With all his force, all his weight, he brought back his foot, kicked it into the man's face, and sent him flying backward.

Boris turned back and was faced with Lara's writhing body. Naked from the waist up, her pants open, she thrashed about in pain. Her agony seared her eyes shut. Her open mouth was frozen in a silent cry as she pulled desperately at her right foot. Boris couldn't believe what he saw.

"Gospodi!"

The man in the leather coat had missed Boris. But he'd caught Lara, nailing the tip of her right foot to the earth. Boris grabbed her ankle, pressed down and held it steady. The cleaver had cut through her shoe, sliced all the way to the sole. Blood swelled out of the slash in the leather, and from the amount of it, Boris knew that a toe or two had been hacked off. With a single yank, he pulled the cleaver free.

"Ai!" screamed Lara.

She twisted on her side, sweeping her foot and a spray of blood through the air. Boris dropped the cleaver, lunged forward, and tried to hold her down.

He glanced back at the assailant. In the dark he saw the man use all his force to grab at the knife jabbed through his leather coat. He pulled at it, cried out like a wounded beast, then tugged again. The knife moved, worked its way loose of muscle and bone. It was only a matter of moments before he'd pull it free and be after them again.

Boris snatched up Lara's blouse, threw it over her stomach, and grabbed her. Scooping her up in his arms, he stood. Steadying himself, he took one last look at the man in the leather jacket, then started to run, Lara in his arms. Just get her away from him, he thought. Get Lara out of harm's way, then come back and, once and for all, deal with him, kill him.

"You'll be all right, Lara!"

With arms locked around his neck, her sobs fell into his chest, her screams of pain muffled by his body. As he ran, her hacked foot bobbed, blood trailing from it.

Trees. Birch trees in every direction. Boris ran but didn't know where he was going. Clutching Lara to him, he turned. The man in the leather coat was gone. Not behind him, not before him. Boris started running again. But was he running right to their assailant? He burst out in sweat. And, *bozhe moi*, there was someone, someone different perhaps, up that ridge and by that tree. Another person out to kill?

He ducked to the left, swerved around two trees, charged off in the opposite direction. He looked back as he ran. No one was back there in the night. No one was following them. He turned.

"Ai!"

A knife was raised right before him, only several meters away. He tried to stop, slid on the leaves. Lara's foot smashed into a tree and she wailed in pain. And then Boris recognized the person just before the knife was to come slashing into him.

"Tyotya! Tyotya, don't! It's me! Me, Boris Ankadievich!"

The old woman's hand hurled forward, but she

didn't release the knife. She hesitated a second, then eyes scanned the dark of the forest. Her attention came back to Lara and the foot. Tyotya touched the ankle, shook her head.

"This way."

Without questioning, Boris followed. Tyotya led them down a low hill, in and out of the birches, which stretched into infinity in every direction. At one point she stopped, seemed not quite sure of which path to take. She stared up at the moon, then started off. Then she paused again. She held her fingers to her lips, looking for something. The sound of trod-upon leaves from behind reached their ears, then abruptly halted.

"Hurry," whispered Tyotya. She pushed him to the left, pointed with the knife. "Go straight, always straight. I'll meet you at the palace."

"How many of them are there?" asked Boris.

"Two. At least two. Now go."

He hesitated. "But . . ."

"Go!" she hissed. "Hurry before she bleeds to death!"

Tyotya's words shocked him into action. He kissed Lara on the forehead, then started off at once, holding her like an injured child. Just focus on one tree, he told himself. Run to it. Then focus on one after that. All the other ones you have to pass by, dare not look at. All the other birches you must ignore. Straight. Charge straight. Hurry.

"Lara? Lara?" he whispered into her ear.

She moaned, stirred her head, and her voice came

from a person on the edge. "The . . . the pain's going away, Boris. It's not . . . not so bad."

"Good." But was it? Was it just shock or was she slipping, the loss of blood causing life itself to fade? "I love you. I love you so much."

She kissed his neck. "I don't want to leave you."

"*Nyet*, of course not."

Her head bounced, then fell forward, and Boris ran faster than ever. There seemed to be no end to the white trees, but then like a wall of rain in the queerest storms, the birch forest suddenly ended. Boris flinched and burst out, then stopped immediately.

His dacha lay down to his left, the palace just up a ways to his right. He searched the open area, glanced back another time, and started off. In the full moonlight now, he saw Lara clutching her blouse over her naked breasts, saw the chill rising on her skin. Her foot bobbed as he ran, a soaking pulp of shoe and skin and bone. Her life fluid was emptying through her mangled foot. He had to get her somewhere warm, somewhere safe, then bandage her foot.

Rising from behind, blasting out of the forest, came a scream so piercing that Boris did not know if it belonged to man, woman, or animal. He looked back down into the birches. Except for the ringing of the scream in his ears, all was quiet.

He trotted onward, his movement slowing under the weight of Lara's lifeless body. Climbing the hill, he felt as if he were running in slow motion. All his energy was being exerted, every gram of power he could muster, but his body just couldn't move fast enough. One leg up, then down. One grueling step after the other upward to the palace. His heart swelled under the strain, pounded as if ready to burst. His body, beaded with sweat, soaked him as if he'd thrashed himself with birch twigs in a sauna.

At the crest of the hill, he reached the fence around the palace and turned. The moonlight, bouncing off the silvery river, shed a haze of light over everything. His log dacha sat quiet, the front door still open. Yellowish light still cascaded from the open front door. The birch forest seemed quiet, too, as if Tyotya, the man in the leather jacket, and everyone else had been swallowed up by the trees. What had happened back there, he wondered. Who had cried out?

A figure moved to his left. Someone below was emerging from the woods, charging up the hill. It didn't look like Tyotya, and so Boris cradled Lara deeper, pressed himself back up against the fence, strained to see who was following him. But he couldn't tell. The moonlight only gave a hint of a person, not an explanation.

Boris couldn't move. His mind was blank. Exhaustion had sapped his ability to think.

Something clawed and shrieked behind him and he leapt forward. It was not just one thing, but many, with long nails and sharp noses. *Bozhe*. The hounds. This was the far corner of their pen, and the pack of them sniffed wildly at him and at the scent of blood. One followed by another, followed

287

by another, began to leap hungrily against the fence, pushing the cracked wood outward.

Down the hill and to his left, Boris could no longer see that figure. Whoever it was had already reached the palace. If Boris slipped around to the left toward Tyotya's house, he'd certainly be trapped. He hunkered down, the weight of Lara numbing his arms. He headed to the right, leaving the pen of animals behind.

"Lara," he whispered into his chest. "Lara, can you hear me?"

As if she were in a deep sleep, her head moved slowly up and down.

"Just hang on. Please, just hang on."

He came to a corner of the fence. He glanced back and saw no one. Right in front was a break in the wall of wood. A gate. He didn't know where it led, only that it was a passage from this open territory and into the protected heart of the palace. He checked over the fence, found the space empty, free of both humans and hounds. Without another thought, he lifted up the heavy wooden handle, pulled it open, and entered a wildly overgrown courtyard. They were right in front of the old entrance to the palace, three stone arched doorways that once opened onto the main entry hall and the great staircase. Princes and revolutionaries and Fascists had all passed through here before.

Boris clambered over a mass of broken boards. That's what he'd do. Run inside the old palace, seek shelter at the top where at least he could see anyone coming. The roof was long gone here at the front of the palace and over the left wing—burned away by the Fascists—but further in there was more shelter. He made his way over some shattered stone steps and passed through an arch. Weeds poked through cracks in the marble floor and a young birch had pushed through a wall, past an old fountain. Towering walls, the shell of a once great body, surrounded him, stuck high into the sky, naked and unprotected by ceiling or roof. Filling a huge window was the moon, white and scabby gray.

Boris kissed Lara again and again as he hurried to the staircase. They were passing through the remains of the entry hall when suddenly he heard a charging noise from over on the right.

"Tfoo!"

Like a speeding white cloud, upwards of ten hounds raced through the palace. Having broken through some other part of the fence, they flew over worn marble, through crumbled walls. Following the scent of blood, they charged Boris and Lara. The creatures snapped at the intruders, yelping with joy as if the long-awaited hunt had finally begun.

Boris hurried to the marble stairs and saw only black sky atop the palace. There had to be some sort of protection, though, some defense high up there, and hugging Lara, finding the last of his strength, he jumped the stairs two at a time. When he was only halfway up, though, the hounds scrambled around the base of the staircase and shot upward. Their crying rose in fervor and signaled the moment for the kill. With snapping jaws, they bounded up, twisted their heads sideways, and bit for a chunk of Boris' leg. Lara stirred, the racket rousing her. Glancing down, she saw the creatures swarming around them and she screamed as if she were lost in a living nightmare.

Boris leaned against the stone railing, attempting to keep his balance. He kicked. He swung his foot out, hurled it into the face of one of the animals. The creature, unfazed, snapped back with whole rows of pointed teeth. Boris lost his balance, sensed something giving away behind him. The railing began to waver, to crumble outward. He jerked Lara and himself back from the edge as the stone toppled to the ground below. But he lost his balance, and as he fell sharply forward on a knee, a hound snapped its jaws on his foot.

"Ai!" he cried.

Another hound bit into the meatiest part of the calf and shook its head, fangs ripping at muscle. Yet another followed the smell of blood to its source. Pulling back, it prepared to lunge at Lara's dangling foot. Boris saw this, yanked himself free and upward, and struggled to his feet. In a frenzy, four hounds started in at him, when suddenly a figure charged up the stairs and waded right through the hounds, hurling them aside.

"Away! Away! Back!" cried Tyotya as she kicked and shoved, swung with the blunt end of her axe.

Caught up in the excitement, the creatures continued to fight and did not obey. One snapped at the old woman. She smacked it on the nose with the side of the axe, beat it away, and one by one they recognized their master and backed off.

As she tried to push away the hounds, Tyotya turned to Boris and said, "To the top—hurry!"

The pain burned in his foot and leg as he carried Lara up the marble stairs. He reached the top, stumbled over a pile of stone and wood. War and weather had worn away the baroque walls here, the florid plaster now ghostly and gray. Boris leaned against a column that rose out of nowhere and watched as Tyotya beat back the hounds with chunks of marble. As she climbed up the steps, she yelled curses at them. A few cowered away, slithered down the stairs, and sunk into the skeleton of the palace. Others jumped back, barking and snapping at the air. Finally, Tyotya made it to the top, grabbed up a handful of marble rocks, and began pelting her animals. She drove them to the bottom; then, huffing, she blocked the stairs with boards.

The short figure draped in black hesitated only a moment as she caught her breath. Next she headed off into a room and waved Boris to follow.

"Who . . . are they?" she asked.

"A gang of black marketeers."

She inquired no further. They bypassed an entire wing of the palace that had neither roof nor floor—simply charred walls—and made their way into a less damaged section. Passing over parquet floors now weathered like driftwood, they wove from room to room. From a roofless ballroom, they passed through a series of small chambers, then walked around the edge of a caved-in floor. Boris glanced back, thought he saw a figure dart out of the shadows, then disappear behind some wall.

"Tyotya, there's—"

"I know. Hurry."

They entered a small chamber that had both floor and roof, and had not gone more than a few more meters when a cry from outside twisted into the sky. Boris' ears perked at something familiar about it, but then the human voice was drowned out by a flood of barking and howling. The hounds had someone else cornered. Already charged up and without Tyotya's interference, the animals would certainly kill this time. Their wild cries grew stronger, almost hysterical, as they whipped themselves again into a frenzy. In a gap of their noise, however, the human voice pleaded again into the night. This time Boris was certain he recognized it.

"Nyet," he cursed to himself. It couldn't be.

Boris ducked across the room to a glassless window. He swung Lara to the side, leaned out, and saw a stocky, familiar figure. He shuddered, couldn't believe this could be happening.

"Musya. . . . "

This was the worst. She was here at Zarekino, surrounded by a pack of wild hounds who were set to rip her apart.

Tyotya rushed up behind him. "Who is it?"

"My wife."

The old eyes opened wide. "Those hounds are being readied for a hunt and they're starved. They'll kill her!"

Panicking, Boris scanned the room for some course—any course—of action. What was he to do?

Where was he to go? Desperate, he looked at Tyot-ya, who at once started to grab for Lara.

"Put her down here in this corner," she commanded. "Don't worry, I'll take care of her. There's a small staircase back there. You have to go down!"

Boris scanned the rooms behind for the other figure, but he saw no one. He didn't want to abandon Lara, but he had to. His only choice was to try and save Musya. She'd be chewed to rawhide if he didn't.

"I'll be back," he said, and kissed Lara as he lay her on the floor.

"Go!" the old woman cried.

He saw the knife in one gnarled hand, the axe in the other, and tried to feel reassured. Tyotya, he hoped, would protect her should the man in the leather jacket or someone else from the gang appear.

"Take this," she ordered, shoving the knife at him.

"Nyet."

Tyotya might need that, and he charged off, limping from the bite on his calf. As fast as he could, he shoved aside a fallen board, and rushed into the next room. A dark shape appeared before him. A passage. He went through it and entered a window-less hallway, then heard another shriek outside. Feeling his way down the hall, he pressed his hand against nothing and almost tumbled down a narrow staircase. He caught himself, found the steps, and heard wood creaking as he made his way down.

Again came the human cry. Then a shot. A gunshot followed by a tortured screech of an animal that went on and on, rising even higher until it disintegrated at its highest note. Then a second and a third shot blasted, one almost on top of the other. *Gospodi*, what was happening out there?

Musya. Damn her to hell! As he struggled to find his way down the black staircase, he thought how as always she never listened to him. He'd told her to go to one of her friend's, hide out there until he somehow contacted her. But no, she did as she wanted, did only what was best for her. He'd spoken too freely, undoubtedly, and she'd guessed he was here at Zarekino. She must have been so scared that she'd come looking for him, taken the car and driven all the way out here. Unsuspecting, she must have been followed; he pictured those hoods waiting for her down by the Fontanka. *Da, da.* That's what must have happened. Musya had left Leningrad and been followed by the man in the leather jacket. It was she, in all her self-serving naïveté, who had led the gang members to him, to Lara.

His fury boiling, he kicked open a door, sent its splintery wood crashing to the ground. From the wreckage he grabbed a board in his fists and plunged outside. Musya was there, only some fifteen meters away, backed up against the fence. Snipping at her ankles, trying to pull her to the ground, was a pack of seven or eight hounds. As if they'd cornered the most prized game, they took turns attacking. Boris watched as one creature—its haunches up to Musya's waist—streaked forward, jaws snapping. Musya swung the gun at it, pulled

294

the trigger. With a blast of light, the bullet hit the creature's hindquarters, threw and twisted it to the ground. More vicious than ever, it snapped at dirt and air, rolled to the ground, struggled with a cry to come to its feet.

Boris ran forward. A spooked animal saw him and leapt to the side. That hound was joined by another and they started snapping at Boris. He swung the board, hit one of them on the shoulder, frightened the other one back. He looked up, saw the shadow of his wife beat back another animal, then turn toward him. She raised the gun, steadied it right at him. In the midst of all the leaping hounds, Boris froze. Could she not see who it was? Or was she trying to shoot at one of the animals biting at him?

"Mus—!"

A hound hurled itself at her outstretched arm. White fangs snapped out, sunk into her wrist. The gun fired, the bullet passing high overhead. Musya screamed, the gun flew from her hand, and as she was twisted to the ground, she kicked the creature in its stomach. The air exploded from the hound. Its lock on her arm failed, and it crumpled into a heap next to her.

Swinging the board, Boris ran forward, beat aside two hounds who were leaping on her. Musya had fallen to her knees against the fence, and he grabbed her, helped her to her feet. A row of razor-sharp fangs sunk into his ankle; Boris twisted around and smashed the board on the animal's head.

"What are you doing here?" he screamed at her.

She was backed right up against the fence next to him, the two of them held captive by the mad beasts. Her hair hung over her face in snarled masses, her clothing was torn in strips from her body. Blood trickled down her arms, her fingers, swirled down her ankles. Shocked, she could hardly speak.

"B-Boris . . ."

"I told you to stay at a friend's!" he shouted, and nearly smacked her with his fist. "What are you doing here? See what you've done!"

"Ai!"

A hound cowered down, shot out its long snout, and nipped at her ankles. Boris jabbed the board at it, batted until it backed off.

He noticed something move above and looked up. Burning his eyes into Boris from a second story window was the man in the leather jacket, the gang leader. He clutched his badly wounded left arm, leaned against the window for support. Then he raised the cleaver, held it high in victory, made sure Boris could see it. The man next nodded, and left the window, clearly heading toward the rear of the palace. His destination could only be one place: the room where Lara and Tyotya were.

Boris had never known such loss of hope. Surrounded by the hounds, their cries piercing his ears, he knew nothing would ever matter again. It was over and he had lost. Lara would be taken away, perhaps Tyotya too. And he might very well die here, amidst these wild animals.

He recognized that this was the moment for truth.

The words of honesty blurted out of him and sent chills of relief up his spine.

"Musya! Musya!" he shouted above the hysterical barking. "Another woman—there's another woman, for god's sake!" He swung at a hound. "I . . . I love her and you have to give me a divorce!"

As if she'd been struck, she fell back, hanging onto the fence and feebly kicking at an animal. The surge of blood that had washed her face now fell away. There was no expression there on those puffy cheeks, in those almond eyes, and she seemed unable to move.

"Wh-what?"

He swung the board in an arc, backed the hounds away, and shouted it as bluntly as he could. "I know. I've pretended to love you, but I don't! I swear it! I love someone else and she's pregnant and I'm going to marry her! If . . . if we make it out of here, you can have everything—the furniture, the car, the apartment. I don't care! Everything's yours. I just want you out of my life! Do you understand—I don't ever want to see you again!"

She clutched at her heaving chest as if she were having a heart attack. Then her fingers jabbed out, clawed into his arm, and she struggled to speak. He pulled away. In his triumph, he had no guilt, no pity, no desire to retract the words, soften them. He saw, too, how right he'd been in his judgment. It wasn't his imagination after all. She was taking this every bit as badly as he'd feared. *Da*. Her love for him was deep and sincere.

She gasped, ''Had . . . had I but . . . but . . . known . . .''

Then, as she stood right next to Boris, clutching him for support, she bent her head back and opened her mouth. Her entire body stiffened in a spasm. Finally, not a cry, not a plea, but a pained sob cut its way out of her lungs, shattered the night. The noise echoed until there was nothing left in her and she collapsed to the ground.

''Musya!'' he shouted.

Dragging her hand over her wounded legs, she cupped the scarlet liquid in her palm. Then slowly she raised herself, brought her right hand back, and slapped him on the cheek as hard as she could.

''*Nyet!*'' she screamed. ''*Nyet!*''

The force of her blow hurled Boris back against the fence. He caught himself, held his blood-splattered cheek, and saw the freshly born hate in her eyes. But he was glad he'd told her, only wished he'd done it months ago. He smiled, too, when she spat in his face, but then, to his horror, he followed the direction of her searching eyes: the gun. Thrown a few meters away, it lay just past the hounds. Boris understood at once where her rash fury now led her: she meant to kill him.

''Musya, *nyet!*''

But it was too late.

Before he could stop her, Musya hurled herself forward into the pack of hounds. Waist high, every one of the animals swarmed around her like piranha, snapping at her, sinking teeth into her rolls of flesh. Still, she went on, kicking and shoving, wading through them, determined in her fury to reach the gun and shoot Boris. Then a hound lunged up, sunk its teeth through muscle and fat, right into her shoulder bone.

"Ai!" she screamed.

Another one jumped up, bit for her neck. Musya screamed again, pushed it away, and stumbled. Boris jumped out, tried to reach her, but one of them bit into his arm. Ahead of him, she fell, and he watched as she sank beneath the hounds. One bit a chunk out of her waist, and Musya's screams shattered the night. Horrified, Boris beat the animal loose from his own arm, only to look up and see Musya's head dip beneath the sea of fur and fangs.

"Ai!" emerged her cry. "Ai!"

Boris swung the board wildly and batted at the hounds that were swarming over the body of his wife. Aghast, he beat several of them aside, saw Musya's motionless feet and legs—saw enough to know there was no hope for her. Still, he pressed on, clubbed two animals, then stopped. The parting closed again. The hounds dove and ripped at the body, and Boris backed away. She was silent. The life, he was certain, had been ripped out of her. Musya, his wife, was dead.

With the realization, his stomach exploded. The muscles of his body jerked him forward and in the same instant his vomit cascaded in a coarse torrent. All his insides twisted like a wrung towel. He glanced up, saw a hound chewing off her hand, and he retched all over again.

He began to pull himself away. Somewhere in the

back of his mind, he was yelling at himself to run, to not give up. Not yet. If he hurried, his hope up in the palace might still have a chance. With the hounds ripping at Musya, he could break away.

He wiped his mouth with the back of his hand, reached for the board, and began swirling the piece of wood harder and faster than ever. He circled the hounds and snatched the pistol from the ground. Sniffing, inspecting their kill, the animals did not follow as Boris ran to the smashed door. He vaulted over the broken wood, felt his way up the black steps. Hurry, he commanded himself.

At the top of the stairs he turned and entered a room that had no ceiling. This was wrong. He spun around and raced in the opposite direction. But which way? Right or left? There were so many rooms; the palace was so huge.

"Lara!" he screamed. "Lara!"

No answer came. He stopped in a wide room, his head swelling with dizziness. Behind him something crashed. That door. *Da, da.* Through there. Hurry! Run!

He flung himself into the next room, found it empty, as was the next. He turned right. *Da.* It was familiar, and he passed through another opening.

A hand stabbed out, grabbed at him. Boris tripped, fell to the floor, and struggled not to lose the pistol. Above him, a tangle of two people battled toward him, then fell over his body and rolled to the floor. It was Tyotya and the man in the leather jacket—locked in a deathly embrace, knife against cleaver, the man was above Tyotya. With his one good hand the assailant raised his cleaver above her forehead, tried to bring it down, to split her skull in two. The old woman held his hand with both of hers, bit into his knuckles. He screamed, trying to gather all his power.

Boris twisted away like a gymnast and popped up on his knees. He raised the gun, steadied it on the temple, squeezed the trigger. The pistol exploded with fire and the last bullet. Ahead, he watched as the force of the bullet burrowed into the man's body and heaved the body up and off Tyotya. Like a great felled tree, the man in the leather jacked tumbled dead on the floor.

Gun still pointed ahead, Boris couldn't budge. Then something moved right in front of him. He swung the gun. His finger touched the trigger.

"Eh!" shouted Tyotya, and froze.

Boris recognized the time-worn face. Horrified, he threw the gun aside, sat back, and buried his face in his hands. Sweat poured down his face as if he'd just run a marathon.

Then slowly, he raised his head, caught his breath. He searched the dark corners of the room.

"Lara. . . . " He jumped to his feet. "Lara, where are you!"

A faint voice called, "B-Boris. . . . "

He turned on his heels and saw a shadow move in the corner. He ran to her, dropped to his knees by her side. His shaking hands reached out, but were afraid to touch. She lifted her head. He gently took her into his arms.

301

"B-Boris?" she asked, her voice fainter than ever.

He nodded and said, "*Da*. Are . . . are you . . . ?"

Her head moved slowly up and down.

He looked down at her foot, afraid at what he might see. Instead of a tangled mess of blood, however, he saw a carefully tied tourniquet around her right ankle. Another piece of material—a black piece from Tyotya's skirt—was bandaged around her foot.

A haggard yet urgent voice behind him said, "You must get her to the hospital right away—she's lost far too much blood!"

Lara kissed Boris on the cheek, and in a weak voice whispered, "I . . . I won't ever . . . leave you. Not ever."

Joy choked him. She was alive. He slid both his hands under her and his aching body lifted her up. Cradling her, he snuggled his face against hers. He kissed her once, and felt her lips press back against him.

Behind them, Tyotya ordered, "Hurry!"

He turned to the short figure. In a bit of light, Boris caught a glimpse of the old face and saw it streaked with dirt and tears and blood.

"This way!" said Tyotya, hobbling off.

With Lara held tightly in his arms, Boris followed the old gypsy woman. He paused for a moment, though, at a large window. Below he saw a swarm of elegant and tall hounds—half borzoi, half wolf— tired and, he thought, a bit confused. Off to the side was Musya's body, two of the creatures sniffing at the limbs, pawing at the flesh. Were the hounds aware of what they had done? Perhaps.

Perhaps Musya knew how much she had done, too, he thought as he started after Tyotya. He hoped, at least, that in those moments before death—and maybe even after—his wife had known she had saved not only Boris's life back at the apartment, but other lives, also, here tonight. If Musya had not lead the hounds away from him, Boris was certain he wouldn't have made it back into the palace before the man in the leather coat had killed Tyotya as well as Lara.

Clutching Lara in his arms, he followed the old woman through room after room and finally down the grand staircase. As he walked, he tried also to stem the rising sense of pity and guilt. He couldn't blame himself for Musya's death. Just be grateful to her and leave it at that. Still, he shook his head. If only Musya hadn't followed him out here. If only he'd found the courage to tell her sooner. If only . . . '

"Poor Musya," said Boris out loud. "She loved me so much. If only I had loved her, too."

Lara's hand reached up and stroked his cheek. With a thin but steady voice, she said, "I'm just glad it's me you love."

"Forever," he said, kissing her hand. "For ever and ever."

Boris followed Tyotya beyond the shattered walls of the palace, beyond the old wooden fence. They hurried down the hill, leaving the dark shadow of

Zarekino behind. As they neared the footbridge over the river, Boris kissed Lara again.

"Tyotya and I are taking you straight to the car, then to the hospital," he said. "Don't worry. You'll be all right. I promise. You might have to stay a few days, but then we'll go home. Think of it Lara, you and I going home together and starting a new life. Just the two of us."

He groaned, however, as soon as the words passed his lips. By no means would the apartment on Nevsky Prospekt be theirs alone. Rather, certain to have returned by now with all her mushrooms and clutter was Elizaveta Nikolaevna.

How he'd love to break her neck and simply be rid of her!

ABOUT THE AUTHOR

After completing studies at Leningrad State University, R. D. Zimmerman received his B.A. in Russian language studies. He later returned to the Soviet Union to work as a guide on a touring American exhibition. He then worked with Soviet immigrants in Dallas and Minneapolis. Zimmerman's novels include THE CROSS AND THE SICKLE and THE RED ENCOUNTER. He also writes frequently for bePUZZLED, a jigsaw puzzle thriller series, and has written nine books in the popular juvenile series, CAN YOU SOLVE THE MYSTERY? He is a member of the Mystery Writers of America and resides in Minneapolis, where he is currently drafting his next novel.

Masterfully told stories of mystery, suspense and international intrigue from...

TREVANIAN

Allow at least 4 weeks for delivery.

TA-85